HEALING NOTES

A Sweetwater Canyon Novel

Rachel's Story

Maggie Jaimeson

Tana,
I hope you enjoy
Rachel's journey!

Maggie Jaimeson

This is a work of fiction. Names, characters, places, and incidents either are the product of the author's imagination or are used fictitiously, and any resemblance to actual persons living or dead, business establishments, events, or locales, is entirely coincidental.

HEALING NOTES

Contact Information: info@windtreepress.com

Cover Art by Bosha Struve

Windtree Press

Visit us at http://windtreepress.com

Publishing History
First Edition July 2012

Published in the United States of America
ISBN: 09835943-2-5
ISBN-13: 978-0-9835943-2-1

DEDICATION

This is for my sisters, Kathy, Susan, Theresa, Denise. All of us suffer from wounds in our past, some of them inflicted by others and some of them inflicted by ourselves. Thanks for always being there no matter what. You are the best!

NOTE TO READERS

This book deals with the difficult subject of rape. If you read the first book in the series, you will remember that Rachel was raped while on tour with the band. Though it is a romance, and I guarantee our heroine will get her happily ever after, I wanted to tell you why I decided to write a book with this topic.

Rape is the fear of almost every woman, both in the U.S. and in other countries around the world. In my own extended family, I have siblings, nieces, and cousins who have been raped—some as young children, others as teenagers or adults. In every case, there has been some emotional damage that lasts a lifetime. It was this knowledge, and my own experience that drove me to deal with a topic that is often not covered in romance.

Though society finds it easy to hug the child or the teenager, or the elderly woman who has been raped. Often they find it more difficult to hug – or even to believe -- the prostitute, the young attractive woman who is seen as promiscuous, or the wife of domestic violence. It is our reaction to this that increases the pain and emotional devastation the victim feels.

No matter the circumstances, no matter the woman's sexual past or her relationship to her attacker, rape is an act of violence and should not be tolerated. As women and men in a compassionate society we should embrace and comfort all those who have suffered from this violence, no matter the circumstances of their past.

I hope that in telling Rachel's story, you will root for her and for all victims of this heinous act. And if you find it in your heart to volunteer at a domestic violence shelter, to man phones for a rape hotline, or simply to be there for your friend, your mother, your sister, your cousin when the horrific happens you will be rewarded tenfold.

Finally, I have to say that though it is difficult most victims need professional counseling to begin to heal from this tragic event. If you know someone who has been raped—or it is yourself—please encourage them to get counseling. Even if it was many years ago and never told. Even if it was as a child and you are now an adult. Rape impacts us, our self-esteem, and our ability to form deep, loving relationships.

Counseling helps to navigate the void and to find a way to live with what happened and to move on in life. Sometimes one has to return to counseling again and again as new life circumstances present themselves.

Thank you for reading Rachel's story. I hope deep abiding love finds each of you.

Maggie

ACKNOWLEDGMENTS

Once again I must thank the Misty River Band. All of the books of the Sweetwater Canyon series reflect my experience with the band's music and the wonderful week they allowed me to travel with them. These women are amazing musicians, song writers, and simply wonderful people. I hope one day that all my readers have the opportunity to hear them. Please note, however, that no characters in this book or any of the series are at all like any members of the band.

I also have a special thank you to fellow Windtree Press author, Melissa Yuan Innes, also known as Melissa Yi. She has pushed me to finish and get this book published even when I thought I should give up on it because my readership on the first book was not as strong as I would of liked. Thank you, Melissa.

CHAPTER ONE

Misty, grey clouds drizzled rain onto the blue-grey stucco of the small clinic and dotted the dirty, pock-marked sidewalk in front of Rachel Cullen's car. Even the doors on the nine small offices were grey. The lack of color matched her mood—no contrast, no feeling, just grey. It was her last time meeting with Dr. Patterson. She should be happy. She'd been fighting the counseling every step of the way during the last six months. Now she'd be free of these weekly visits.

Rachel was stronger now. She no longer jumped at shadows and her nightmares had stopped—well, maybe not stopped. Lessened. The dreams that used to haunt her every night now only appeared once every three or four weeks.

She took a deep breath and held it while she applied a gloss and rubbed her lips together. She let out her breath. Stuffing the tube back into her purse, she swore at the snap that wouldn't close. *You can do this! You're not going to let that bastard control your life any longer!* The snap finally caught. Now she just needed to get out of the car.

Her hands shook as she unlocked the door. She swung her legs from beneath the steering wheel and placed both feet on the ground with a splash, her shoes immediately drenched by the puddle she hadn't seen. "*Cach*," she swore again. It must be a sign—a sign that this session was not going to go well.

Rachel stood tall, pressed down the lock, and slammed the car door shut. She stepped up to the building and followed the short path to suite 109, her shoes squishing with each step. Taking a deep breath she flipped her handbag over her right shoulder to bounce on her hip. She was ready to finally put the past behind her.

As she reached for the handle, the door opened and a little girl rushed out, maybe six or seven years old, with beautiful long blond hair caught up in a blue denim bow. She ran to a light blue sedan next to Rachel's and giggled as she skipped through puddles circling the car. Rachel couldn't help but smile at the child's carefree innocence.

After three circles, the girl stopped at the back end of the car, cocked her head and waved two fingers at her. "Hi."

"Um, hi." Rachel raised her hand and waved back. "Did you forget somebody? Your mommy maybe?"

"Claire, I told you to stay close."

At the sound of the tenor voice beside her, Rachel started. A man three to four inches taller than her had stepped out. In one hand he held several colorful ribbons attached to a bright pink, heart-shaped helium balloon that read *Happy Birthday*. He looked toward the car where the child was still giggling.

The little girl raced back. Skidding to a stop in front of Rachel, they bumped and Rachel teetered slightly toward the wall.

"Careful there." A weathered hand reached toward her and wrapped around her elbow. His touch was softer than she expected, but her knees still locked, ready to spring if she needed to move fast. He held her up with one hand. Deep brown eyes, emphasized by his full head of short, wavy blonde hair, looked at her then turned toward the girl."

"Apologize, Claire. You almost knocked her over."

"I'm sorry." A small hand lifted to touch her other arm.

"That's okay. Really. I should have been paying more attention." Rachel smiled and pointed to the balloon. "*Latha breith*."

"Excuse me?"

"Oh, I..." She had lapsed into Gaelic. Something she hadn't done in public since Kavan left her almost three years ago. "I said 'Happy Birthday.'"

The man looked at his daughter and his smile reached his eyes, sending a tingle along Rachel's spine. What she would give for a man to smile like that when he thought of her.

She bent to the little girl dancing in circles near the door. "How old are you?"

"Six. I get to go to first grade this year." The little girl looked up as Rachel straightened again. "You're pretty, like my mommy. But you talk funny."

Rachel laughed. You could always count on children to be straight.

"Scottish or Irish?" the man asked.

"Scottish. Dunoon. It's a little town on the Firth of Clyde." Rachel concentrated on not moving, avoiding the continued squish of her shoes.

"I thought I detected a slight accent, but it's not a full brogue."

"I've worked hard to lose it. To make myself understood."

The little girl pulled on her father's hand. "Can we go now? I'm ready for my cake." She jumped off the curb, making a big splash and then stood next to the passenger door of the car, her eyes wide. The man laughed and waggled a finger in his daughter's direction.

"She's darling." Rachel said to the back of his head. She didn't want them to leave. She'd much rather go celebrate a birthday with this happy family than walk into that office one more time.

"Daddy, hurry. I'm starving." The little girl's tiny hand rubbed at her stomach dramatically.

With another laugh, the man turned to Rachel. "I can't keep a starving child waiting now, can I?" He took a step away then turned back. "Dr. Patterson is really good. Don't be afraid."

"I, uh…" Rachel flushed that a stranger would know the purpose of her visit. Of course, they must have just left Dr. Patterson's office. Was it the child or the man who needed help? Or both?

She watched the man all the way to his car. She liked the way he walked, his stride confident, purposeful. He thumbed the lock on a keychain and opened the car door. The little girl jumped into the seat and said something that made him laugh. He pointed inside and the girl immediately grabbed the seat belt to secure it. He turned his head toward Rachel as he closed the passenger door. "Have a nice day." He threw the words over his shoulder as he rounded the car to the driver's side, the balloon gaily swaying above his head, adding the only bright spot of color to the grey day.

She watched them drive away until their bright happiness had disappeared from view. Her eyes misted. She angrily rubbed the back of her hand across them. For a moment she'd imagined herself as part of that happy family—a woman out to enjoy a birthday celebration with her daughter and the man who loved her. Evidently, even this happy family had problems.

Resolute, she turned back to the door in front of her and entered. After Kavan had divorced her, she had rid herself of loyalty to any man. Now she needed to rid herself of one last nightmare.

* * * * *

Rachel crossed her arms in front of her and looked down. Why was this still so damn hard?

Dr. Patterson waited patiently for an answer.

"I try not to think about it much. I'm tired of this hanging over my head. I'm ready for it to just go away and forget about it."

"Is that why you've seen me every week for six months? Because forgetting is so easy?"

Rachel clenched her teeth and stared, unblinking, at the therapist. "It might have been easy if you hadn't forced me to talk about it every week, relive every moment, talk about how I felt. I wanted to just forget it and get on with my life, but you made me think about it all the time. I'm glad this is the last session."

"You're using anger as a shield."

Her fist hit the arms of her chair. "Well, it's a hell of a lot better than crying all the time."

Dr. Patterson leaned forward. "Every emotion is viable as part of your healing. If you want to be angry on our last day, that's fine with me."

Rachel shifted uncomfortably in her seat. Dr. Patterson always saw through her attempts not to deal with her feelings. But she was scared. Really scared.

Not scared to talk about the rape. She'd done that a million times too many already. No. She was scared that this was the last time she could count on her once a week visits. Though she'd fought the revealed intimacies every week, she had also come to rely on them. Sometimes the only thing that got her through a week of walking on eggshells with her friends, or avoiding every man who looked at her, was knowing that Tuesday would come and Dr. Patterson would be there to debrief. Now she was supposed to have the skills to handle it on her own.

Rachel sighed. Fear never got her anywhere. "I'm fine. It'll be hard, but I'll be fine. When things get bad, I always have my music."

"Speaking of your music, it's interesting that you've let your relationship with Michele lapse, and have withdrawn from the other two adults in your band. Kat is the only one you've let inside your heart."

Rachel shrugged. "I'm just not comfortable with the looks all the time."

"Looks?"

"Yeah, like I have an incurable disease and they have to be careful around me because they might catch it."

"Do you think being a rape victim is a disease?"

"No. Yes. I don't know. I just get tired of being the one everyone feels sorry for. It's like I burst the bubble of a world filled with love, and they still want to hang onto it and I don't. So…"

"And Kat doesn't make you feel this way?"

"She's just a teenager. She truly believes that love will heal everything, and she never looks at me like it won't happen for me."

"Do you believe it will happen for you?"

Rachel remained silent. Dr. Patterson had maneuvered her back to the painful subject—the one she would probably never resolve. Maybe it was that Kat still believed in true love for everyone that made her hang on. She wasn't sure, but she didn't want her last session to dwell on this.

Dr. Patterson continued, "Michele was married at the end of your tour last year, right? Only a couple of months after you were out of the hospital."

"Don't." Rachel curled her fingers into her palms until her nails bit into the flesh. Even a small physical pain helped keep the tears at bay.

Dr. Patterson's gaze remained steady and she leaned forward. "Don't shut down, Rachel. Accepting Michele's marriage is the only way to re-establish the relationship you want with your friends. You can do this."

"No. I don't want to talk about this. I do accept her marriage. I'm happy for her. Really, I am."

"You accept her marriage in your head, Rachel, but not in your heart. Your heart is still hurting."

Rachel flinched and backed into her chair as her breathing accelerated. She raised her chin. How dare Dr. Patterson assume she knew what was in her heart. Did she think just because she'd been talking for six months she could presume…

"My heart is just fine. It's my head that's screwed up. That's what you were supposed to fix." Rachel stood. "And now our time is up and it's still not fixed. What does that say about your counseling abilities, Dr. Patterson?"

Dr. Patterson sat back in her chair and sighed. "Back to anger? Or can you admit to fear?"

Rachel willed her heart to slow as she paced behind her chair. Yes, it was fear. Fear that Kat's belief was based in the naiveté of youth, fear that she'd never regain her strong friendship with her other bandmates, fear that she would always be jealous of Michele and her happy married life, and fear of not having Dr. Patterson to force her to talk about all this stuff.

In the face of all that fear, anger was her only defense. Maybe that wasn't so bad. At least she could function. At least she would be able to walk out of here with her head high. She grasped the back of the chair and leaned on it.

"Look, I'm thirty-four, divorced, probably can't ever have kids. Is it any wonder I don't believe in true love? So what? Not everyone finds somebody to spend the rest of their life with. I'm okay with it. Really. It's time to move on."

Dr. Patterson was noticeably silent. Rachel itched to fill the void.

She gestured with her palms out to the side and facing upward. "Look, I'm fine." She walked to the front of the chair. "You've really helped me. I can see that. I'm good. Really." She held out her hand to Dr. Patterson, ready to shake and say good bye.

Dr. Patterson leaned back in her chair and crossed one leg over the other, relaxed. "We still have ten minutes, Rachel. No need to rush out."

Undecided, Rachel held her breath. She fiddled with the strap of her purse and glanced toward the closed door. She looked back to Dr. Patterson, still undisturbed in her chair, acting as if it didn't matter what Rachel chose at this moment. Was it really up to her to end this?

Rachel held out her hand again, "No. I'm good. Thanks for all your help."

Dr. Patterson smiled and rose. She took her hand and then pulled her in for a hug. "You'll make it, Rachel. There will be some bad times and some good times, but you'll make it. You're strong. Just don't give up on your dreams."

Rachel's eyes misted. That was the problem. She'd already given up.

Dr. Patterson stepped back. "If you find yourself giving up, or something new comes up…like a man in your life…and the fear is overwhelming, you can always come back to see me."

Rachel snorted, but a soft laugh filled with trust followed. "Yeah, like I'd let you into my sex life too."

Dr. Patterson smiled. "Yes, your sex life *and* your love life."

Rachel frowned. Some people just never believed her. Love was not in the cards for her. She'd accepted it even before the rape. That's one thing that hadn't changed.

"Strong women face their fears," Dr. Patterson said. "They accept the choices they've made and use them to gather more strength."

Rachel flinched. "Well, yeah. I'll work on that. Thanks."

She left the office as quickly as possible. It took all her concentration not to run to her car.

Outside, the rain had cleared and it was a gloriously bright and crisp February day. Typical Oregon as spring approached—mostly rain, but then when you least expected it the sun shined clear and bright, bathing the landscape with sparkles of light and shadow. She shielded her eyes as she looked up at the sky and saw a rainbow in the distance. Rachel laughed as she skirted the puddle next to her car and climbed in. So much for believing in the weather signs. It was as if the whole world was trying to change her mind.

CHAPTER TWO

Rachel's bow dragged on the strings of her fiddle, imitating the drone of bagpipes, as she finished the slow Scottish air. The tone reflected her feelings since leaving Dr. Patterson three weeks ago—that combination of heaviness intertwined with hope. It had been a tough three weeks. Every practice session seemed fraught with potential landmines. So far, she'd avoided them by not talking much. She'd decided today she'd try to be her normal herself, whatever that was these days. She'd participate in the discussions, laugh a little with her friends, and just maybe find something nice to say to Michele—though that would be the hardest.

The air in the practice room hung pregnant with the anticipation of the next song. The band remained silent, waiting for her transition. She paused for two counts and then, as she shifted to a jig, pizzed the transition and set her bow to bouncing off the strings in a spicatto, challenging them to keep up with her. The other members of Sweetwater Canyon joined in with guitar, mandolin, *bohdran*, and bass, moving into the final set of their usual play list.

Rachel practiced her between-song patter, a story about growing up in Dunoon when her father and mother were still together, giving Theresa time to switch from her guitar to the banjo. When the dance music started, all the band members tapped their feet and Rachel's heart soared. The tunes easily flowed from Scotland to Appalachia as Rachel's rapid fingers picked up the pace for the next tune, *Leather Britches*, followed by a medley with a southern bluesy slide. The side of her mouth quirked up at the mix—stiff-lipped Scottish reels and jigs met with a little New Breton attitude. Kat had the *bohdra*n, her Celtic drum, kicking up the percussion to sound like feet tapping the floor and Rachel's mood shifted away from the darkness.

Playing with the band again felt like coming home after a long drought. During the Christmas holiday break she'd lost her way for awhile, but now it was almost spring and she was back. Yes, her heart needed this.

Her thoughts narrowed to sharp focus, melding with the *bohdran's* beat, merging to a steady thrum that set her feet rapping a light percussion as she played. Soon her bow picked up the pace and her fingers skipped across the strings—demanding that the others match her in complexity and speed. The music danced along her skin as the band built to the final crescendo and her feet echoed the racing of her fingers on the strings. Sweat beaded on her brow. She dug deep inside herself to let the notes sing from every pore, lifting her on a cloud of joy all the way to the end.

Exhausted, but with a grin that made her cheeks ache, Rachel flopped into a chair, cradling the fiddle on her lap.

"Whew! That was amazing, Rachel." Theresa wiped down her strings and set her banjo in its case. She took two steps to open a window and let more air into the room.

The sound of rushing water from the river behind the house washed over Rachel, helping her unwind from the music. The quaint cabin tucked in the foothills of Mt. Hood had been the practice place for Sweetwater Canyon ever since they began playing together four years ago.

Theresa and her daughter, Kat, had always provided a place in their home for any member of the band. Twice Rachel had taken them up on their hospitality. Once, when she'd only been with the band for a year and Kavan had left her without support or a place to live. And last fall, when they all returned from tour. Everyone's finances were low then and it had been mostly Rachel's fault as they had all pooled their savings and earnings to cover her hospital costs.

She lifted her face and inhaled the smell of the rain-soaked firs wafting in the open window. She would make it up to them. Somehow. She would find a way to repay them all for what they'd lost.

When Rachel's heartbeat settled into its usual steady rhythm, she turned and walked to her fiddle case in the back of the room on a long table with other instrument cases. She wiped down the strings and placed it carefully in the plush velvet, her fingers trailing along the mellowed spruce wood—the same wood she had seen her father shape and polish when he made the instrument for her two decades ago. She loosened the bow strings and put it in its holder. It had a good sound—the sound only love could imbue in an instrument.

Theresa snapped her banjo case shut beside Rachel. "I haven't heard you play with that much passion in a long time." Her voice was soft and invited a confidence.

Rachel smiled. "Yeah… I thought I'd never get that feeling back—where I could let go and the music could overtake me. It feels good to be lost in it again."

"It's good to have you back," Kat added. Her long blonde bob swayed as she turned from closing her accordion case. "Your fingers were smokin'." She mimed an air fiddle with her left hand. "You've really added some hot riffs to your solo piece. Maybe you could show me a few of those moves later."

"Still keepin' up with yer fiddle?"

"Yup. But I don't think I'll ever catch up with you," Kat answered. Her stomach growled and her cheeks reddened.

Rachel laughed. "Hungry?"

Kat nodded. "Starving." Theresa laughed behind her, and Kat turned. "Hey, I've gotta eat ya know. That practice drained me."

Rachel rolled her eyes. "You've *always* gotta eat. I vaguely remember the joy of being sixteen and able to eat constantly without gaining an ounce."

Kat strolled toward the sliding door between the practice room and the hall to the kitchen. "Anyone want anything before I scarf it all up?"

"I'll take one of your famous lemonades with raspberries," Rachel said.

"Me too. Me too," everyone else chimed in.

Kat stepped through the door. "Back in a few."

Rachel watched Kat take several long steps toward the kitchen. This was her chance to talk with her friends, to be normal again. She turned to Theresa. "Has Kat grown in the last two months, or is it my imagination?"

"Oh, I think she stopped growing at fourteen," Theresa said. "But her shape has changed. She seems to have blossomed. Unfortunately. Over the holidays she also suddenly discovered boys in a big way. Her

Christmas list was all clothes. I think those pants she's wearing make her look taller."

"Yeah, all legs," Michele said, giggling. "What I wouldn't give for even half those legs."

Rachel looked at the bass player and smiled. Michele's thick, wavy chocolate brown hair reached to her waist, almost obscuring her gymnast figure. "Being short isn't so bad. You're only a couple inches shorter than me, and we all know short does not mean doormat for you or me."

"You've got that right." Michele's eyes locked with Rachel's, an eyebrow rose in a silent signal. Rachel looked away. This was so hard. She'd stopped confiding in Michele after her wedding. They'd been close once, but now Rachel felt like a third wheel with Michele and David barely able to keep their hands off each other. That envy was the one last thing she still had to conquer before she could begin to trust again.

Rachel tucked her feet beneath her and scooted closer to Theresa. "So, what's with Kat and the crop top. Is that driving you crazy too?"

"You don't know the half of it," Theresa said. "Exposing her naval just doesn't seem right at her age. We fought about that all through the first week of classes in March, then I finally gave up."

"Has she asked for a bellybutton ring yet?" Rachel asked.

Theresa's face turned ashen. "God no!" Her index finger shook in Rachel's face. "And don't you dare suggest it to her."

Rachel lifted her blouse and pointed to her navel. "See, I don't have one either. I'm not *always* a bad influence."

"At least those can easily be removed." They all turned toward Sarah as she spoke in a quiet voice from across the room. "Sometimes you just have to choose your battles. I remember my brother wanting an earring and Dad said no. So, he went and got a tattoo instead."

"Ouch," Theresa said. "I see your point. I'd rather see a bellybutton stud than a tattoo." She winced. "Oh, sorry, Rachel. I didn't mean…"

Rachel laughed as she proudly flexed her bicep with the blue Celtic knot encircling it. "My mother wasn't too thrilled when I got this either. But it was all for love."

"You're kidding," Sarah said. "You got that for a boy?"

"Oh, he was no boy," Rachel's eyes twinkled with mischief. She felt good. Telling an old story was easy. She could laugh, and shock, and maybe even enjoy herself. "He was definitely all man. I was seventeen. He was twenty-one. He was my first."

"You mean you had sex when you were only seventeen?" Sarah's eyes widened.

"Yeah, I was the late bloomer of my crowd."

Sarah's face turned a bright red and Rachel laughed. She got a kick out of picking on Sarah. She was sure that even at twenty-nine, Sarah was still a virgin or practically one. She was really sweet, but it was hard to imagine being such a goody-two-shoes for that long.

"Not everyone waits until they're madly in love, you know. I just waited until I found someone I thought might know what he was doing. And boy, did he know."

Michele snickered. "By now you shouldn't be so shocked, Sarah. We all know Rachel's been around the block plenty of times."

"And proud of it," Rachel leaned into the sofa, and with legs crossed she placed her palms on her knees hands up. "Come to me with all your questions about sex and I will give you counsel."

Everyone laughed and Theresa pushed at Rachel until she fell sideways.

"Just don't offer any counsel to Kat," Theresa said. "I want her to wait a little longer. Somewhere around thirty would be nice."

"Thirty? Ha. Now that's a mother speaking." Rachel uncurled from the sofa and stood. "Kat's a pretty good egg and I don't think she'd go off half-cocked with a boy, but you don't want to put your head in the sand either. My mother never talked to me about sex, but I had plenty of opportunities to learn anyway. If you haven't had that chat about birth control and protection, you'd better get with it."

"Oh, we've had the chat."

"Gosh," Michele interjected. "I can't imagine what it must be like worrying about a daughter that age. I guess I'll find out soon enough though."

All eyes went to Michele.

"Oops. I didn't mean to say anything yet."

"Ohmigod, you're pregnant!" Sarah shouted, embracing Michele in a big bear hug.

Rachel blanched. Her mouth dropped open.

Pregnant? Already? They'd only been married a little over two months. No, it wasn't possible. It couldn't be. The darkness encroached. Rachel fought it. She didn't want to say anything mean. She didn't want to let the jealousy and fear take over. She silently chanted in Gaelic, trying to gain control.

Theresa dabbed tears from her eyes and then hugged Michele. Everyone started babbling at once about babies and congratulations.

"Rachel, isn't it wonderful?" Sarah said.

"Yeah, it's great." Rachel's voice was flat. As she forced her lips to curve into a smile, she gave Michele a brief one-armed hug and stepped away. "Congratulations."

"Well, it wasn't exactly planned to be this soon. But, we weren't careful a couple of times…and…well, the truth is I couldn't be happier."

Rachel counted to herself, *aon…dà dhà…trí…*hoping the pain in her heart would dissipate. She could handle this. She could. The room went silent.

"Oh, Rachel, I'm sorry," Michele blurted. "I forgot. I—"

She took a deep breath. "No need to apologize. I'm happy for you. Really I am."

"But I know how much you wanted—"

Rachel looked around the room at the women who were her best friends, who had stood by her after the rape, who had given all of their savings to pay her hospital bills. She should be happy for Michele, and she was. But she also couldn't stop that feeling that someone was standing on her chest and she couldn't get her breath right. She was suffocating.

Struggling to keep her voice even, she said, "You are all my friends, and I love you, but let's just drop it. Okay?"

No one could understand what it was like to blame yourself for being raped, what it felt like to actually hope you would die, but then be such a coward you had to call for help. No one could ever know what it felt like when the doctor had put so many stitches inside her to stop the bleeding, or had pumped her full of antibiotics to stop the infection that scarred her womb. But she had fought back. She had recovered. Maybe she shouldn't have called them. Maybe she should have somehow managed on her own. Because, now her friends would never again think of her as Rachel, the fiddler in the band. Or, Rachel, the girl who could get any guy she wanted. Now it would always be Rachel the rape victim who happened to play the fiddle.

Eyes filled with pity stared back at her.

"Stop looking at me like that," she snapped at them. "Let's drop it, okay?" She focused on calm. She forced her voice to be softer, happier. "We're all happy for you. So, when are you due?"

Silence.

"The end of September," Michele said, her voice a little too bright.

"Oh, you'll be big in the hottest part of the year," Theresa said.

"I know, but it's okay."

"I guess that nixes a summer and fall tour then." Rachel winced at how much disdain she'd let show. "Sorry, I'm just…" she mumbled.

Michele touched Rachel's arm, but she jerked away. She didn't want anyone to touch her right now. She might fall apart and that wouldn't help anything.

"I'm sorry, Rachel. I know the timing isn't great but David says, with our CD selling so well, we can do a lot of gigs in the northwest in March and April, and then hit the Midwest for May and June."

"Last year we did a four month tour beyond the northwest, and now we're cutting it to only two?" Rachel knew she should be happy for her friend, but she hurt too much. Right now anger was the best way to keep her pain at bay.

"That's true," Michele said, her voice soft, entreating peace. "But last summer our biggest audiences were in Ohio, Missouri, Kentucky, and Tennessee. If we concentrate on a lot of gigs during those two months it may be the same result in total sales as our four months were before covering smaller venues. Then, when I'm in the last trimester and too big to be comfortable in the humidity, we can return to the Pacific Northwest and be in the studio. We could concentrate on cutting a second CD this fall. David said we made more money on our first CD than on all of our tour last year."

"I just don't think it's enough. I want to be happy for you, Michele, but all I have is my career. I don't have a rich husband to take care of me. You don't have to work, but I do."

"We all want to work," Michele said, her voice a whisper.

Rachel paced. "We can't afford time off now. We're just building our fan base."

Michele's hands fluttered in the air. "David said we drew over three thousand new fans in Branson, if we—"

"*Siota!* Branson! Are you kidding? What did you think? You could force me to go back there?"

"Rachel, calm down. No one's forcing you to do anything," Theresa stepped toward her, her hand reaching for Rachel's arm.

Rachel backed away, her hands up, warning. She was shaking, barely holding on to control. She'd tried to be good. She'd tried to be nice. It was too early. Too much. A baby. Branson. No! No!

The silence roared in her ears. Unable to hold on, she ran from the room, tears streaming down her face. She locked herself in the bathroom. Her pulse raced. Her stomach heaved. She bent over the toilet and vomited. Memories flooded back: the tour, meeting the handsome cowboy in Branson, going to his room, only to find that he had someone else there. Drake. The man who took her soul to hell. She retched again.

"Rachel, please let me in. Let me talk to you." Michele was at the door.

"*Fàg*. Go away." She hugged the toilet bowl, swallowing the bile rising again in her throat.

"Rachel, I'm so sorry. I was just going on about my plans. I wasn't thinking. I— "

"*Fàg*."

She heard feet padding away from the door and took a deep breath. Her stomach was finally empty. She stood on shaky legs, put down the toilet lid and sat, hugging her arms to her stomach as she rocked. This must be one of those bad times Dr. Patterson warned her about. She would get through this. Breathe in. Breathe out. Breathe in. Breathe out. Slowly.

She should be thankful for Michele and her husband, David. Michele's husband was their business manager. His publishing and distribution contacts—his financial guarantee—had helped them cut and sell 10,000 copies of their first CD last fall. For the first time in three years of playing music, the band was on decent financial footing—enough to make up for the disaster she'd caused in Branson. Michele deserved to be happy.

"Rache?" Kat said, tapping on the door. "Are you all right? You've been in there a long time."

Rachel reached over and flushed the toilet. "I'm fine. I'll be out in a minute." She ran water in the sink and splashed her face liberally. She cupped her hand and drank, washing away the awful taste in her mouth. She didn't want Kat to worry. Kat was like a little sister to her—someone she wanted to protect from the evils of the world. She took another gulp of water and dried her hands.

Rachel opened the door and managed a tight smile.

"Did you have a fight with someone?" Kat's eyes were wide, her cheeks rosy with anticipation. "Nobody's talking. I know when everyone's trying to make sure I don't know anything that means something bad happened. Geesh, I go to get something to eat and all hell breaks loose. Who did you fight with, Rache?"

"No fights, honey." She wrapped an arm around Kat's shoulder. "I was just a little overwhelmed by Michele's good news."

"You mean the baby thing?" Kat captured Rachel's eyes. Then she hugged her tight. "I understand. Really I do."

Rachel swallowed hard and hugged her back.

"I was there, too. I saw."

"I know." Rachel bit her lip. She wished Kat hadn't seen her naked and broken, knowing what had happened. A young teen shouldn't have to understand such depravity.

"But it's going to be okay. You'll see." Kat squeezed her again and then released her. "I have your lemonade ready. It will perk up your sourness."

"So, ye think I need to be more sour?" She poked Kat in the arm, getting a laugh out of her. She exaggerated her brogue. "Sure, an ye didn' put an extra dose to pay me back for the comments about that cute laddie you were datin'. What was his name? Dillon?"

"Oh, yeah, I forgot about that. Maybe I better take yours back to the kitchen." Kat turned as if to leave.

Rachel snaked an arm around Kat's shoulder and towed her back. "No ye don't. I need that sourness to hold up my reputation."

"Well…being as Dillon's a has-been already, it's your lucky day. Turns out you were right about him."

Rachel let go and stepped back, looking into Kat's eyes. "Sorry about that, kiddo."

"No need to be sorry about a rat. Besides," Kat added, rolling her eyes, "Mom's always saying there are plenty of fish in the sea."

"But who wants to kiss a fish," they said in unison and laughed.

Kat's youthful optimism had Rachel's lips quirking into a small smile. She turned and held Kat's face in her hands. She looked directly into her eyes. "Have I told you lately what an amazing, bright young woman you are?"

"Only about a thousand times."

"Well, here's a thousand and one." She kissed Kat's forehead, then patted her on the back. "We better hurry before everyone drinks all that lemonade."

"Shall we sneak up on them and see if they're talking about us?" Kat's conspiratorial whisper made Rachel laugh.

"Oh, they'll be talking about me all right. I just ran from the room like a drama queen and retched in the toilet stinking up the bathroom."

"Good to know you haven't lost your reputation for giving us good stories to tell." Kat winked at her.

"Is that all I'm good for? A good story?"

"Yup. I'm going to sell it to the tabloids when you become rich and famous and you're touted as the next Natalie McMaster."

Rachel threw back her head and laughed. "You do that, kiddo. Someone's got to make money off my life—'cause it sure as hell isn't going to be me."

CHAPTER THREE

"Daddy! Daddy, look!" Claire pulled at Noel Kershaw's leg and pointed her mustard-stained hand toward the stage at the front of the Lion's Club multi-purpose room. W

Welches was always the first town in Oregon to hold a spring festival, even though most of Mt. Hood was still covered in snow.

He looked in the direction his daughter indicated. An acoustic band played a rendition of *Home Grown Tomatoes* while a small crowd stood nearby singing along. Outside the windows, stately fir trees dotted the landscape, swaying in the breeze as if inviting people outside to brave the cool temperatures and visit the tables filled with the first spring blooms.

"Let's go see, Daddy. Please."

He bent toward her with a napkin and cleaned the excess mustard from her fingers. "All right, but let me carry your lunch for you, okay?"

Claire nodded, handed over her half-eaten hot dog, and ran toward the semi-circle of chairs fronting the stage. Noel did his best to keep up with her, narrowly avoiding a spill as he dodged two other children running at full speed toward the food line in the hall behind him. When he had safely traversed the large room, he found Claire sitting in the front row, her lunch forgotten. She beamed up at the band on stage and clapped in time to the music.

He sat next to her and balanced the paper plate and milk carton on his lap. They had been at the Snow Crocus Festival since ten that morning and he was happy to be sitting instead of wandering the displays in the adjoining room trying to keep up with an inquisitive six year old.

"Look, a violin just like I want." Claire pointed to the left side of the stage.

He glanced up to the black platform set about four feet off the ground. He followed Claire's finger point to the woman step dancing while fiddling a reel. The first thing he noticed was her silky blonde hair and blinked. That was the woman he'd seen at the clinic. He'd dreamed about that hair and the confusion she'd shown when they met. She certainly didn't look lost now.

Layered loose curls framed her oval face, the soft feathered edges accentuating her large almond-shaped eyes. She looked full of energy, as if she could play for several more hours. She finished the reel with a confident last stroke of the bow and her smile beamed brightly to the audience.

"Thank you," the banjo player, a woman of about fifty, said to the audience. "It's so nice to be back here in Welches again enjoying the first crocus blooms with you. Did you see all the colors in the display rooms? Purples, yellows and whites already out the first week of March! And how about the weather outside? I could almost believe spring is around the corner with that sunshine. Even if it's only fifty-five degrees."

The growing crowd of spectators clapped in appreciation.

The woman with the banjo bore a strong resemblance to the young woman playing the accordion on the far left. They even had similar hairstyles. Both were blondes, though it appeared the older woman's hair was frosted. Mother and daughter he guessed. The banjo player switched to a nylon-string guitar as she continued her patter.

A younger woman, at center stage, put down her large guitar and picked up a recorder. Her thick, straight chestnut hair fell forward around the recorder. She was definitely attractive, and tall. She reminded him of Shania Twain. But none of the band members was as striking as the fiddler.

The woman with the recorder stepped to the mike. "Our next song should warm the cockles of any gardener's heart and keep you tapping your toes as well. It's a round called *Rites of Spring*."

The fiddler struck up a quick jig and the recorder trilled in a counterpoint melody. A petite woman, with long brown hair braided down her back, stood slightly to the left plucking the bass fiddle undertones. Soon the three musicians pushed the interweaving dances to a quicker pace as the other two joined the round in song. "The flowers that bloom in the spring dance with a promise of sunshine."

Noel tapped his toes to the music until the music ended amidst a roar of applause and stomping feet. The mother segued into introducing the next song. "Now Rachel is going to slow things down."

The fiddler smiled and stepped to the mike.

So, her name was Rachel. He'd always liked that name. Before Claire was born it was one he and his wife had considered. It meant little lamb or one with purity or innocence. He glanced at Claire and smiled.

The lilting voice and slight Scottish accent drew him to Rachel immediately. "This is a slow air. A Celtic tune originally written for harp in the 18th century. It's very special to me because I can remember me *athair*, my father, playing it when I was growing up. It's called *'O'Carolan's Farewell to Music.'*"

Slowly she lifted the fiddle to her chin, placed the bow on the strings and closed her eyes. Within the first few bars, Noel was spellbound. The fiddle and the player were one. Instead of the breakneck speed and ornamentation she had demonstrated in the previous piece, she now played at a pace where he could hear every detail. Simple and pure, like the sad vibration of a breaking heart.

The noise from the chattering crowds at the back of the hall disappeared as her solo transported him to the Scottish highlands. In his imagination he pictured a heather-strewn hillside. He could almost feel the mist crawling over the crag. The melody caressed his skin, sometimes diving deep below the surface for an intense massage, and then just as easily rising to the top and dancing as if she was playing the breeze, emphasizing breath and freedom.

As Rachel drew out the last unhurried note, Claire applauded with gusto, waving to the fiddle player. "She's beautiful, isn't she, Daddy? She's beautiful, just like Mommy."

Noel flinched at the mention of his ex-wife. Rachel wasn't in any way like her. Why would Claire make such a comparison? They didn't look anything alike, they didn't move the same, and her interaction with the other musicians seemed caring and loyal—not someone who would abandon her family. And that voice. He wondered if the combination of purity and passion in her voice would also translate to her relationships. He smiled. He might just have to find out.

* * * * *

Rachel looked down at the little girl waving as if they were best friends. She looked familiar. Her eyes strayed to the man sitting next to her, smiling and squeezing her shoulder. She startled when she remembered. The clinic. How could she forget the man and the little girl who seemed so happy together, the two-person family she had briefly fantasized about joining?

Suddenly, the father captured her eyes. His seemed to invite her to intimacy. She wanted to go there. She wanted to experience the feeling of being with a man who cared for her. She shook her head to clear her thoughts, and his lips quirked up as if he could read her desire.

"Rachel." Sarah whispered from behind her. "It's your intro."

Her eyes wide, Rachel turned. She swallowed to find her voice, but no sound came out.

Sarah stepped in. "That was beautiful, Rachel. Thank you. As usual, you mesmerized the crowd."

The second round of applause helped Rachel recover her senses, but she still felt stunned as she turned back to the audience, nodded and smiled.

Sarah continued to cover for Rachel. "I see a lot of young people in the audience today. Why don't you all come down here to the front of the stage and we'll do a song just for you. Does anyone know *Froggie Went A-Courtin*?"

A clamor of little voices called out to the band for attention. Twenty or thirty children gathered near the stage, jockeying for position nearest the musicians. The man Rachel had recognized lifted his daughter to his shoulders so she could see over the heads of the parents clustered nearby.

"On this song it's very important that everyone sings along with us," Sarah continued. "I want you to sing as loud as you can. Especially on the 'uh-huh uh-huh' parts. Okay?"

Still in a haze, Rachel picked up her fiddle and began the intro while Sarah played the guitar and sang, carrying the audience with her.

"Froggy went a-courtin' and he did ride, uh-huh uh-huh."

The children took up their parts in earnest and their parents merrily joined in. Soon, heads nodded in exaggerated unison for all of the uh-huhs. The banjo and the guitar worked in brief solos between verses. Then the entire band joined in the finale, repeating the chorus twice.

The enthusiastic audience remained standing and thundered applause as the band joined hands at the end. Rachel took her bows along with the rest of the band, clenching Sarah's and Kat's hands on either side. Thank God there was no time for an encore. The schedule was tight, allowing the next band only fifteen minutes for set up.

She rushed to pack up her fiddle and get off the stage and out of the auditorium before that man and his little girl could find her. She didn't want to see that man again—to ache to be part of him, part of his family. Dr. Patterson would say to confront her fears, but this was one fear she was definitely not ready to confront.

A hand touched her shoulder and Rachel swung around with her fiddle case, almost knocking Sarah off her feet.

"What's wrong, Rachel? Are you feeling ill? What happened up there?"

"Uh, it's nothing. I just…have a headache."

"I have some aspirin in my purse. Just a minute I'll get it."

"No, that's okay. I think I'll just take a lie down in the motor home for a few minutes."

"But we have CDs to autograph at the table. This is a good crowd. It could take up to an hour. Think you can make it? Really, let me get those pills."

Damn! In her haste to get away from the man and his daughter she had forgotten about the customary signings after a set. With the few venues they would be playing this year, they needed to push their live recording at every gig. They needed to build a following so when they released the next CD, they'd have plenty of willing buyers right away.

"That's all right, Sarah. I'll be fine. Maybe just some water will help." She felt a little guilty as Sarah rushed to the back of the hall to get her a bottle of water.

Rachel weaved through empty chairs and food-laden parents and children to the hall outside the main room. At the far end was the makeshift booth for the bands. Folding chairs were arranged behind two large tables. The previous band had already left and two volunteers exchanged the banner. Within minutes, a printed sign ,with a tan image of Mt. Hood and the name Sweetwater Canyon, hung above the table marking the spot.

Kat and Theresa were already seated and a line had formed in front of them. Michele was a few steps ahead of Rachel, lugging the bass on her back.

"Hey, Rache." Kat shouted, waving her over. "You seem to have a young fan who wants only *your* autograph."

She saw the little girl but not the father and breathed a sigh of relief. If she could get the little girl on her way quickly, maybe she wouldn't have to talk to the father again.

Rachel squared her shoulders and smiled as she slipped into her place behind the table. "Hi there. I remember you. We met at Dr. Patterson's office."

The little girl giggled and held out her hand with the Sweetwater Live CD. "You're so pretty. I like you. Your white hair is like an angel."

"Well, thank you. I like you, too," Rachel responded.

"I like Dr. Patterson too. She lets me draw pictures and play with the doll house while I'm there. Did she let you play with the dollhouse too?"

Once more, Rachel was reminded that things weren't all as happy as they seemed with this family. She wished her therapy sessions had included playing with dolls. Maybe it would have made it easier.

"No, we just talk." She poised a special gold tipped marker pen over the CD. "So, what would you like me to write on here?"

"My name's Claire. That's C-L-A-I-R-E."

Rachel nodded as she wrote 'To Claire' with a flourish. "That's a pretty name. And it goes with a very pretty little girl."

"I'm named after Mommy. Her name is Clarissa. But she's been bad. She had to go to jail. I live with my Daddy."

"Oh!" Rachel was unsure what to say to such a revelation. "So, where do you live?"

"We live in Sandy, but we don't have a house right now. We have to live at the River Inn until our house is ready. But it's okay, because I can still go to the same school. We had a house before, but Daddy had to sell it and buy a different house because he was sad about Mommy, only our new house still has people in it. It's a little bit smaller, but it has a nice backyard and a swingset and..."

It had been a long time since Rachel had been around children. She was fascinated with how easily Claire moved back and forth between serious topics and happy memories with no transition, sprinkling questions all along the way.

"I wish those other people would hurry up and move," Claire finished her rambling observations about their new house, "because I'm worried about Missy."

"Who's Missy?" Rachel asked, assuming it was a doll.

"She's my puppy. I couldn't bring her with me cuz Daddy said she wasn't allowed at the motel. She had to go to a special motel just for dogs. I saw it and I wouldn't want to live there. Would you? She cried when we left." Claire's lips formed a pout.

"Well, I don't know. Some of those places are pretty nice and Missy will get to make some new doggie friends. Right?"

"I guess." Claire's voice trembled, as if she might cry.

Rachel searched the crowd. Where was the father? At first she'd feared facing him, but now she was concerned he had abandoned this darling girl. With a mother in jail and the two of them living in a motel, what kind of an environment was he providing for Claire?

Not finding the father, she smiled at Claire and with her best penmanship finished her text on the CD while reading it aloud. "To Claire, the smartest little girl I've met today."

Claire's pout changed to a wide grin. Then she bent close to examine the special flourishes Rachel had included on the greeting.

"You have pretty writing," Claire said. "You made my name look pretty." She leaned forward and cupped her hands around her mouth as if she was going to share a confidence. "Do you live with your mommy or with your daddy?"

Rachel laughed then cupped her hand in the same fashion and whispered. "Don't tell anyone, but I'm too old to live with my parents anymore. I live by myself."

Claire stepped back and cocked her head, her brow furrowed. "Oh! Just like my Daddy. Are you divorced, too?"

"Um…" Rachel looked down and added her signature to the CD then handed it to the little girl. "So, Claire, do you want to be a fiddle player?"

"Nope. I want to be a violin player just like you."

Rachel beamed. It was rare that a child looked up to her. "The violin and the fiddle are the same instrument, just played differently."

"Really?"

"So, why do you like the violin so much?"

"Cuz it's so pretty. I can feel the music all over me. It tickles. Not a hard tickle but a soft tickle."

"I agree." Rachel jumped at the sound of his voice as he stepped up behind his daughter. "For me it's more than a tickle, it's a breeze. No, it's more like a wind as the warm, full sound of your fiddle carries me from beautiful seasides to high mountains almost in one breath."

His eyes twinkled and his smile undid her. He seemed to swallow her whole, as if memorizing every feature.

Rachel felt the flush creep up her neck and onto her face.

When he broke contact, it seemed he'd taken a part of her soul with him.

"So, you're Scottish *and* a fiddle player."

"That's right." She glowed in the warmth of his praise. "And you are?"

"A poet and a teacher. Not necessarily in that order." His dark-brown eyes searched hers again, and she lowered her lashes under his scrutiny. "I teach English at Sandy High School. Just down the road about sixteen miles."

She relaxed her face and smiled, then formally held out her hand. "Rachel Cullen, fiddler. Nice to meet you, Mr. Poet and Teacher."

Claire giggled. "That's not his name. His name is Daddy or Mr. Kershaw."

His laugh was sincere and accepting as he took Rachel's hand and shook it. "Noel. My name is Noel."

A quick jig played up her arm and then stopped when he slowly removed his hand from hers. She rubbed at her shoulder to make sure she hadn't imagined it. She noticed the merest flicker in his eyes. Did he feel it too?

"Noel? As in Coward, the playwright?" she asked.

"That's right," he said. A small dimple on the left side of his chin drew her focus to his lips when he smiled. "My mother loved his plays. When I was born she insisted on naming me after him, even though my father was chagrined at the thought his son would be named after a flamboyant gay man of the theater. In a small town of loggers most boys had names like Rex or Derek."

"I like the name Noel," Rachel said, unable to take her eyes from his. "You must have been razzed a lot though."

Someone jostled Noel from behind. He looked over his shoulder. Three or four people milled about the table next to him waiting to get an autograph.

"I…um…guess we should pay for this and go." He pointed to the CD clutched in Claire's hands. She held it against her chest as if protecting it from any potential thief.

Rachel cleared her throat. Yes, that was a good idea. She needed to move Mr. Kershaw along before she started fantasizing what she would like to do with him. "That will be…uh…fifteen dollars."

He pulled his wallet out of his back pocket and extracted a twenty. "Got change?"

"Sure." She leaned toward the middle of the table to get a five from the cash box. A beefy hand closed around her wrist and yanked, nearly pulling her off her feet.

The odor of stale beer and cigarettes assailed her. Her heart clutched and her lungs burned for air.

"Some nice playin' there, little lady."

She struggled to regulate her breathing. She didn't know the guy, but he was obviously drunk. She tried to extricate her wrist but he wouldn't let go.

"Thank you, sir. Now, please release my wrist." When he didn't immediately free her, she began to tremble. She wasn't sure if he still hung on for balance, or for some darker purpose. She bit her lip to gain some control. "I asked you to let go."

"Oh. Sure." The man lurched backward then abruptly let go. She sprawled across the table, knocking over the cash box. Bills fluttered to the ground on the other side. The man, oblivious to what had just happened, turned and walked off.

Sarah and Kat materialized at her side. "Rachel! Are you hurt?" Sarah asked.

"Who was that?" Kat asked.

"I'll help. I'll help." Claire laid her precious CD on the table and stooped to the ground to gather the money.

"No one I know," Rachel said, her voice a shaky whisper. She couldn't stop shivering. "I…I…" She squeezed her eyes closed to stem the tide of tears. Puddles formed behind her lids, then leaked into small rivulets making their tortured way down her cheeks. She wiped at her face angrily. She should be over this. She'd dealt with drunks before. It was part of the business.

* * * * *

Noel helped Claire gather the money and put it back on the table near the cashbox, his gaze unable to stray long from Rachel. She was putting on a good front, but it had been obvious she was frightened by the drunk. Memories of his ex-wife engulfed him: The times she came home shaky from needing her next fix and scared that a drug dealer she owed money to had followed her. For a moment he'd thought he'd felt a connection with Rachel, something he might want to follow up later; but now he wasn't so sure. She was obviously running from something, and the last thing Claire needs is a woman with excess baggage. She was too fragile to have her heart broken again.

"Thank you," Theresa said to him and Claire as they put the last dollar on the table with a few coins.

"Are you going to be all right?" he asked Rachel. He wasn't sure if he really wanted to know, but he couldn't leave feeling she still needed help. For Claire's sake more than his.

Rachel looked at him, then at his daughter. With obvious effort she smiled. "Oh, it's nothing. I shouldn't have been so jumpy. I was just taken off guard, that's all." He heard a little too much sing-song in her voice to make it ring true. "Sometimes people take you by surprise, that's all. Don't worry, I'll be fine."

She reached beneath the table and produced a colorful pen with the name Sweetwater Canyon emblazoned on it. "Here." She handed it to Claire. "Thanks for your help. You've been super."

Claire took the pen but her eyes were still glued to Rachel.

"Well, now isn't that nice," Noel said to Claire, a little too cheerful himself. "I'm glad Ms. Cullen will be fine. It was a very nice concert, wasn't it Claire?" When she didn't speak, he stepped in front of his daughter blocking any further view of Rachel. "Are you ready to go, Claire?"

She looked up, her eyes wide and misty, and nodded. She lifted her arms, entreating him to carry her. He scooped her up and hugged her close. He nodded to Rachel, and mouthed a thank you, then turned and walked away, trying to put space between his daughter and any problems Rachel might have.

"What's wrong, Daddy?" Claire asked, her voice cracking on a choked hiccup. "Did we do a bad thing? We didn't take any money."

He stopped and looked her in the eye. "No, sweetheart. We didn't do anything wrong. We helped. You were *very* good, Claire. I think Ms. Cullen just got scared when she fell. She was very happy you helped pick up the money and gave it back."

"I hope we helped her Daddy. I saw tears, even though she wiped them away, I saw them. It reminded me of Mommy. I don't want her to end up in jail too."

His heart ached. Even though it had been two years, the legacy of his ex-wife still left a large shadow over his little girl. He would do anything to take that shadow out of her life. He just didn't know how. Somehow, his love alone wasn't enough.

CHAPTER FOUR

Rachel grumbled and pulled the blanket over her head. It had been a rough night. After the concert in Welches, and the fool she'd made of herself over a stupid drunk, she'd chosen to go home for the rest of the day and avoid the world.

Her nerves were shot when she arrived home and the only way she could manage her emotions was to lose herself in her fiddle. It wasn't until four hours later she had finally felt calm enough to eat. Munching nachos in front of the television and watching old reruns of Saturday Night Live had helped to keep her mind off her fears. She'd barely made it through one beer when she fell asleep in the recliner.

She vaguely remembered waking again about two in the morning and catching the end of "Blithe Spirit" with Rex Harrison on the classic movie channel. It was silly, but watching the show helped her feel that perhaps her meeting with Noel hadn't been a complete disaster. When the movie ended, somewhere around three, she'd crawled into her bed emotionally exhausted.

She flipped the blanket away from her face, groaned and rolled toward the radio alarm clock on her bedside table. Nine already? Sighing, she tossed aside the covers, then sat up and padded barefoot to the bathroom.

"Ooooo," she said as the chill of the bathroom floor raced from the bottoms of her feet up her spine. "Wake up call."

She soaked a wash cloth and gently scrubbed her face. The warm water felt good against her skin.

"Ugh," she said to her reflection when she noticed the red blotches that usually appeared when she scrubbed hard. "Who could ever wake up next to that?"

She applied moisturizer and the blotches receded. She drew a comb through her short locks and smiled. "Better. No great beauty, but it will have to do."

Dressed in a tee and underwear, she stuffed her feet into warm slippers and loosely tied a long robe about her. She moved slowly into the kitchen as if each small step reinforced she was still alive. Her wits would return as soon as she injected some caffeine in her veins.

She rooted in the cupboard for coffee and measured it into a filter. This morning she felt like she could drink the entire eight-cup pot. She filled the carafe with water and pressed the button, immediately placing her cup underneath the drip spout. She never waited for the pot to fill first. When her cup was full, she deftly removed it while at the same time slipping the coffee pot under the spout.

"Hmmm." She sipped the hot brew and gloried as it moved down her throat to her stomach and the warmth spread to chase away the chill. Dark, black coffee. Strong. She never did understand why anyone would doctor it with sugar and cream. To her way of thinking, once someone did that it didn't taste like coffee anymore. She leaned on the counter waiting for her brain to kick in.

The one bedroom apartment in Welches, in the foothills of Mt. Hood, was just the right size for her needs: a bedroom and bath for privacy, and a small u-shaped kitchen that opened to a great room on one end. She'd been lucky to find it after the band's summer and fall tour last year.

Finding a rental when ski season was in full swing was no easy task. Fortunately, her previous work as a waitress at The Resort at The Mountain had helped her make several friends in the small hillside community. When another waitress decided to move to Bend and needed out of her lease Rachel was able to step in to this apartment without much problem.

The aroma from the automatic coffee maker urged her forward again. She quickly poured herself a second cup and took a satisfying sip. "Ah, yes."

She held the warm cup between both her hands and took several more sips until she felt her brain clicking in again. Coffee in one hand, she ambled toward the front door to retrieve the morning paper. She stopped in her tracks. Near her purse on the side table was the CD and a yellow post-it note she'd put on top of it. She'd forgotten about it.

In all the confusion yesterday, little Claire had left the autographed CD behind. Rachel brought it home and put the note, River Inn, on top of it so she'd remember where to return it. No matter how embarrassed Rachel might be at her reaction to the drunk, she was determined to go to the River Inn and make sure that little girl was okay. Well, maybe she wanted to see the father again too, but mostly it was the little girl she assured herself.

After taking her time with the newspaper, Rachel found herself staring at the clothes in her closet. She didn't want to appear as if she was trying to impress him. She'd already convinced herself the spark she felt with Noel yesterday was just wishful thinking, nothing to pursue. She scanned the skirts. No, too much leg would send the wrong message. Casual, with just a hint of flirtatiousness was what she sought.

She settled on a coffee-colored pair of jeans that hugged her figure, but not so tight it looked like she was poured into them. Then she slipped on a navy blue, long-sleeved tee and tucked the shirt hem into her pants. She liked how the tee brought out the deep blue color of her eyes. She turned to one side and checked her profile—casual but smart, yet something was still missing. She searched through her small jewelry box and finally came up with the right accessory, a necklace of pastel stones that would contrast with the dark blue and liven up the tee—just right for that little bit of flirtation.

After dressing, she drove down the mountain, exceeding the speed limit by about fifteen miles per hour as was her usual habit. She drove like she played, fast and furious. She could see the reflection of Mt. Hood growing smaller in her rearview mirror as she negotiated the sixteen miles to Sandy. About halfway there, the shiny fender of a police car poked from behind a tree on the next curve. She braked and reigned herself in, resetting the cruise control to exactly fifty-five for the rest of her journey.

The sunshine from the day before had held, though clouds gathered again this Sunday afternoon. She pressed the button on her radio to change the station to Oregon Public Radio and hummed to the opening number for "Prairie Home Companion." Garrison Keillor hailed from Minnesota, but he captured the essence of small town life everywhere. In fact she could picture his characters in the people she knew in Dunoon. Even on her crankiest days the show made her roll with laughter.

When she pulled into the River Inn half an hour later, she was tapping her fingers to a rollicking tune by Keillor's guest band, Old Crow Medicine Show. She sat in the car until the song finished. Her mood positive, she bounded out of the car and headed to the reception desk, CD and purse in hand.

The desk clerk dialed the room and handed her the phone. She balked. She hadn't actually thought about what to say. She swallowed and counted the rings, one, two.

"Hello?"

"Uh, hello Mr. Kershaw. This is Rachel Cullen, from Sweetwater Canyon. Claire forgot her CD at the concert yesterday and I, uh, was in the area and thought I'd return it." She tapped the CD on the desk in front of her. Why was her voice shaking? It wasn't as if she was interested in him. This was just an errand.

"Thank you, Claire's been asking about it and I had no idea how to find you again except to wait for your next concert."

"May I bring it to your room?" She gulped. Asking to come up to his room? Why didn't she just say she'd meet him in the lobby. Surely he wouldn't read anything into that with Claire right there.

"Sure. We're on the third floor in 348. Claire will be happy to see you."

All the way up in the elevator and walking down the hall, Rachel worked to school her breathing into its regular pattern. There was nothing she could do about the racing of her pulse. At least that wouldn't be visible. At the door she took a deep breath and let it out slowly, then knocked.

The door opened and Noel stood in the entry, blocking any view into the room. His eyes were questioning, almost inviting; but his stance was firm, blocking entry.

"Hello, Ms. Cullen. Are you feeling better today?" His words were clipped, as if forced into polite conversation.

Claire yelped, scooted around her father and threw her arms around Rachel's legs, squeezing her tight. "You're all right! You're all right!" Claire's pale face pressed firmly against Rachel's stomach. "I was worried."

Overwhelmed by Claire's greeting, all Rachel could manage was to return the child's hug. She didn't dare look toward Noel for his reaction.

When Claire finally pulled away, Rachel crouched down to look her in the eye. She smoothed a stray hair away from Claire's pale face. "I'm fine, Claire. I'm sorry if I scared you. I was just a little surprised by that man. Sometimes when I get surprised like that I cry. I'm sorry you were worried."

She paused to make sure Claire understood. "You were such a good girl, helping to pick up all the money before it got lost. In fact, you were so busy being good that you left this behind by accident." She held out the CD. "Do you still want it?"

Claire's smile added a little color back to her cheeks and her eyes brightened. "Thank you. I thought it got lost." Her small hand grasped the CD while her finger traced the gold writing as if she wanted to make sure it was the right one. Then she hugged it to her like a favorite toy.

"It was kind of you to come here just to deliver this," Noel said, his voice more natural this time.

Rachel pushed herself up to her full height and faced him. "It was the least I could do after everything that happened."

He smiled and his eyes quickly regained the twinkle she remembered seeing yesterday. He draped an arm across Claire's shoulder and his stance relaxed. "Where are my manners? There is no need to keep you in the hall." He moved to one side to allow her entry. "Please, come in for a moment. Can I offer you a drink? Water? Soda?"

Rachel gulped. "Uh, just water would be fine."

She experienced only a small hesitation before crossing the threshold into the room. She hadn't been in a man's hotel room since Branson. Though this wasn't anything like that experience, she still counted it in the win column for her recovery.

As she glanced around the room, she noticed both beds were neatly made. A Connect Four game grid was set up on a small table at the front of the room with some of the checkers already inserted, as if it were an ongoing game.

"You can sit on my bed," Claire took her hand and led her to the bed closest to the door. "Daddy makes me make the bed every day, even though the maid would come and do it anyway.

"That sounds like a good habit to get into," Rachel said, stroking the comforter cover. She was glad to have Claire filling in the holes in conversation. It helped her focus her concentration away from Noel.

Then he stepped next to her. "Here's your water."

She reached to get it, but he seemed to hold the glass a little longer than usual, the touch of their fingers lingering enough to make her wonder at his intent. Her slight intake of breath indicated her surprise at the candid interest she saw in his eyes. "Thank you," she whispered, lowering the glass to take a sip.

Once again she was arrested by his presence. His hair wasn't as controlled as it was at the concert, it was loose and full, almost grazing his shoulders. It changed his look from the firm-but-kind school teacher she had met previously to a man who exuded a quiet confidence and substantial sensuality. She realized it was more than curiosity that made her want to get to know him better.

Don't be an idiot! She silently told herself focusing on reality. The last thing a nice man like this—with a beautiful daughter and obviously an ugly past with his ex—needs is another woman in his life with a lot of problems of her own.

A small hand grasped hers firmly, drawing her attention back to Claire smiling up at her in anticipation.

"We're going to the zoo. Wanna come?" Claire said.

"I…uh…don't want to interrupt your plans any further." Rachel looked from Claire to Noel. "I really should be going." Even though she loved the idea of spending a day with them, she made a show of standing and adjusting the strap of her purse on her shoulder. Claire refused to let go of her hand, as if by holding tight her father would have no choice. Rachel bent toward the little girl and kissed her on the forehead. "It was nice to see you again, Claire. I hope you'll come to another concert real soon."

"Please, Daddy, can she come with us? Please?" Claire's hand held firm.

Embarrassed, Rachel looked to Noel, hoping he could read the message in her eyes that she didn't mean to put him in a difficult position.

Noel searched Rachel's face. Though she'd seen sexual interest before in his eyes, she wasn't sure if it was more than that. She knew she should make some excuse and leave as quickly as possible. There was no way she should even consider dating this man, but she couldn't find any words to help him say no when she really wanted him to say yes.

"Claire, it appears that Ms. Cullen has other plans today," he said.

Rachel's shoulders dropped in resignation. So the interest she saw earlier wasn't the dating, get-to-know-you kind.

"Do you?" Claire asked, her eyes pleading with Rachel for it to be otherwise. "Do you have other plans?"

Rachel wasn't sure what she should do. It was obvious Claire had bonded with her—though she was at a loss to explain why. Should she lie to the girl and give Noel the out he wanted? Or was she misreading him? She took a deep breath and made a decision.

"Well, I don't have any specific plans for today, but I think your Daddy wants to spend time alone with you, and that is *very* important."

"Do you, Daddy? Do you want to be alone with me and not with Ms. Cullen?"

Noel laughed and stepped toward Claire, ruffling her hair. His eyes twinkled as he looked at Rachel. "She does know how to get to the heart of things." Then he bent to Claire. "You're right, sweetheart, we should all go together. It would be a nice way to thank Ms. Cullen for returning your CD."

Claire let go of Rachel's hand and hugged her father. "Thank you, Daddy. Thank you."

"Well, if you're absolutely sure," Rachel hesitated, looking over Claire's head and into Noel's eyes. She'd gotten her wish, but at what cost?

"I'm sure," he said, his eyes steady on hers as Claire danced toward the back of the room.

"Hurry up. Let's get going." Claire sounded as though she were mimicking an oft heard phrase.

Noel laughed and walked to the back of the room. Her eyes traveled with him, where he bent over a single large suitcase on top of a folding rack. A few items of clothing bumped his head from the open closet above.

"We were going to leave in a few minutes anyway," he said as he stacked several items in front of him. "Claire, I think you might want to put on a sweater over your shirt. Which one would you like to wear?"

"The green one!" Claire fingered through the small stack of clothing and pulled out a neatly folded sweater. It was a hunter green cable-knit pullover with a mock turtle neck and sleeves just a little too long for her small arms. Claire quickly pulled it over her head and Noel adjusted the arm length with two rolls of the sleeve.

"How about you?" he looked at Rachel. "Do you have a jacket in your car or something warmer?"

Rachel glanced at her long-sleeved tee. It wouldn't be warm enough for an entire day outside. "I…uh…hadn't originally planned to be outside very long."

Noel slipped a Pendleton shirt off a hanger to his right. "It may be a bit big, but it'll keep you warm."

"I'm sure it'll be great." She walked toward him and slipped her arms into it as he held the shirt for her. The sleeves dangled about two inches below the tips of her fingers. His spice and musk scent wrapped around her senses, making her feel a little giddy.

He moved toward her and tapped a sleeve. "May I?"

She nodded as sparks of anticipation skipped up her arms.

He deftly rolled each sleeve for her. When he finished, his fingers lingered at her wrist for a moment. She was sure he could feel the racing of her pulse, and she thought she saw a question in his eyes. But then he turned away and shrugged into a lightweight jacket.

"We better hurry and get going," he said, his voice slightly hoarse. "Ready, Claire?"

"I want to see the polar bears first, and then the elephants, and then the monkeys, and then…"

Rachel worked hard to tamp down the expectations that were running rampant through her mind. This wasn't a date, she told herself firmly. It's only because his daughter was so taken with her that she was invited to go with them at all. He obviously doted on Claire, and giving in to Claire's demands was not the same as him asking her out on his own.

In spite of what her head told her, Rachel couldn't help smiling as Noel opened the car door and directed her into the front seat of a basic, black four-door sedan. The Chevy Prizm wasn't that different from her own car, though her Daewoo was a two-door model and metallic blue. She guessed the car's age was similar to hers as well, three to four years old, which wasn't surprising considering he was a single-parent raising a child on a teacher's salary.

Claire clambered into the back and strapped herself into the seatbelt, continuing to expound on all the animals they would see at the zoo.

"Penguins?" Claire asked as they got on the freeway.

"Yes, they have penguins too," Rachel said. She was having fun. Something she hadn't experienced in a long time. As far as Rachel was concerned, no matter how this day had come about it was a great beginning; and in the past few months she had learned to seize any new beginnings she could find. Yes, this was turning out to be a good weekend after all.

"How about creepy things?" Claire asked.

"You mean like snakes and bats and spiders?" Rachel asked.

"Yuck! Do you like spiders?"

"No, but I love bats. Have you ever seen a bat?"

Noel glanced at Rachel as she animatedly discussed the nuances of bat life. He remembered how hard it had been for his ex to keep up with Claire's energy, yet Rachel seemed to have no problem at all. In fact, she was clearly enjoying the conversation.

He still wondered what secrets she held, and if those secrets would hurt him and his daughter down the road. He took in a deep breath and let it out slowly. Maybe he was just jumping to conclusions. The counselor had warned that he might be using Claire as an excuse for not dating. Maybe that's what he was doing—tangling with the ghosts of his marriage, comparing her to his ex-wife.

"Does it have four legs?" Claire asked. He guessed she was playing twenty questions.

"Yes," Rachel answered.

"Is it bigger than me?"

"Definitely yes."

"Is it an elephant?"

"Yes! You guessed it." Rachel turned toward the backseat and he noticed how her grin caused Claire's face to light up. "Now, you think of an animal," she said to Claire.

"Okay, I have one. Ask me a question."

"Is it as big as me?"

"Nope," Claire giggled.

Noel let the conversation fade into the background again. There was no doubt he was attracted to Rachel. She was full of energy, mysterious, and he'd already had fantasies about her since they'd met at the clinic. He rolled his shoulders to release some of the tension. He had to be careful. If it were just him, he'd take a chance and pursue Rachel based on attraction alone. But with Claire, he couldn't afford any mistakes with women. Claire needed stability. The easiest way to give her that stability was not to bring another person into their lives.

He heard another giggle as Rachel guessed wrong again.

On the other hand, Claire had definitely decided Rachel was a good person, and he had to give a lot of consideration to her feelings. It was true that Claire was naturally trusting, but she seemed to have a sixth sense about people—who was safe and who wasn't.

"Do you have a long neck to reach to the trees?" Rachel asked.

"Yes!" Claire leaned forward in anticipation. "Do you know it? Do you know it?"

"A giraffe?"

"Yea!" Claire clapped her hands and looked out the window. "Are we there yet, Daddy?"

Noel rolled his eyes at the familiar question. "Almost, sweetheart. About fifteen more minutes."

"Yippee! Then we can see a real giraffe."

"So, what kind of animal are you?" Rachel asked.

Noel's breath caught as he immediately wondered what kind of animal Rachel would like him to be. He risked a glance in her direction wondering if she'd intended the double entendre.

"Yeah, Daddy, what kind of animal are you?" Claire echoed loudly.

He swallowed and forced the brazen picture of Rachel out of his mind.

"Ask me a question," he said, checking the rearview mirror. Claire's open and cherubic face reflected back.

"Give me a hint," Claire said.

"I'm a very special kind of animal. One that's very difficult to get rid of."

Rachel caught his mischievous grin and laughed hard.

"Would I like you if I saw you?" Claire asked.

"Oh, yes. You would definitely want to take me home," he answered.

CHAPTER FIVE

"We have the wedding for the Governor's daughter in two weeks," Sarah said, her hand poised with a marker at the wall calendar. "This weekend there isn't anything booked, but we've been asked to do a couple of pub dates on Wednesday and Thursday. Both family places, so Kat would fit in."

"I think we should definitely take them all." Theresa said. "With our shortened season, we need to make sure we're pushing our CDs at every opportunity."

"Nothing scheduled this weekend?" Kat's eyes looked wide with hope. "You mean I might actually have a weekend all to myself."

Rachel tapped her lightly in the arm with her fist. "That's right, kiddo. Two whole days to get yourself in a heap of trouble."

"All right!" Kat pumped her fist in the air.

Michele looked up from the small calendar she was marking and smiled. "A whole weekend? Whatever will you do?"

"Walk around, see friends, go to the mall, meet a boy, have sex…"

"Whoa there!" Theresa stood, a finger pointing at Kat.

Kat giggled. "Just seeing if you're listening, Mom."

"Having sex is not to be taken lightly. You know we've had this conversation, and I told you—"

"Chill. I'm just teasing."

Theresa's lips drew tight. "That's not a teasing matter, Kat."

"Geez, Mom. You're so uptight about sex. You need to take some lessons from Rachel."

Rachel caught Kat's eye and shook her head. She really didn't want to be held up as an example. Kat had become obsessed with sex lately. Rachel remembered what it was like to be sixteen. Hormones were out of control and any boy who paid attention was a potential candidate for experimentation. Everyone talked about sex, some of the girls bragged about not being a virgin anymore, and those who were virgins wondered what they were missing.

She looked at Kat's impudent smile and shook her head again. Kat was at a dangerous age. She was aching to prove her independence. She thought she knew everything, but the truth was that she'd led a rather sheltered life. Theresa had always kept her close, and when the band was on the road, Kat had three mothers watching after her.

"You shouldn't take it so lightly. I don't want you to get a reputation for being easy. You're my daughter. I love you. I don't want to see you hurt. I just don't think you're ready."

"Yeah, yeah. Let's drop it, okay?"

"Fine by me."

An uncomfortable silence filled the room.

"So, how's the nursery coming?" Sarah turned to Michele.

Rachel groaned. Great. From Kat and sex to Michele and her baby. Could there be a worse conversation? She'd grown a little more accustomed to hearing about Michele and the baby over the last few weeks, but it still hurt.

"I haven't had much time to go shopping. I think I have a color scheme planned though."

"Do you know what it's going to be yet?" Kat asked.

"I don't have the ultrasound for another month, when they can usually tell. But David and I have decided we don't want to know."

"Geez, I'd definitely want to know. There was this girl at my school, and she had to leave because she was prego, but we all went to a shower, and she already knew it was going to be a girl, which was great, so we knew what to buy. So, you just have to find out or we won't know what to buy."

Michele smiled and rubbed her belly. "We just want to be happy no matter if the baby is a boy or a girl. We just want to concentrate on healthy. Besides, I don't believe in all that pink for girls and blue for boys stuff. We'll just forego the little dresses and if we end up with a girl, we can go shopping for dresses later."

"That's really sweet." Sarah reached for Michele's hand. "So, what is the color scheme?"

"I want the nursery walls to be painted red on three sides and one wall in white. Then the bedding to have yellows and greens and reds in it."

"Red is an unusual choice, particularly if it's a girl." Theresa said.

"David and I have done a lot of reading about using primary colors and providing stimulus. I think red will be perfect."

"I think it will be perfect too." Sarah's eyes seemed to mist. Rachel looked away. She couldn't take much more of this female bonding over baby stuff.

The phone rang and Kat jumped up to answer it. There was a muted exchange and then she said, "Sure, just a minute." She handed the phone to Rachel. "It's for you. He sounds yummy."

Rachel raised an eyebrow. All eyes were on her.

"Hello?"

"Rachel, I'm so glad I tracked you down."

"Noel?" Rachel couldn't keep the pleasure out of her voice. She saw everyone lean forward to listen. She glared at them and made her way to the practice room for privacy. She could hear Kat laughing as she walked away.

"Sorry to call you during practice, but I never got your home number. I looked up Sweetwater Canyon on the Internet and this was the number listed."

Rachel smiled, remembering the trip to the zoo, the nice dinner afterward, how much she wanted him to kiss her. Of course, with Claire nearby that was unlikely to happen. By the time she arrived home, she had already written him off. He'd made it pretty clear that there wouldn't be a second date. Maybe he'd reconsidered? Maybe he was interested after all.

"Well, I'm really calling for Claire." Rachel's heart dropped. He wasn't interested. "Ever since she saw the band and met you, she's insisted on learning to be a fiddler. She's been interested in violin lessons, but now she insists it must be fiddle and it's different. I really don't know who else to call. I know you're probably too busy with gigs and don't do lessons, but I thought...maybe...you could make a recommendation for a teacher."

Rachel's pulse quickened. "I'd love to teach Claire."

"Are you sure? I mean…if this isn't normally what—"

"I do give lessons, and will be doing it even more this year because our bass player is pregnant which means we won't be doing as many gigs." An audible sigh floated through the earpiece. Was that a good sigh or a bad sigh? "I really like Claire. She's bright and sweet. She'd be a pleasure to teach."

"Thank you, Rachel. I really appreciate this. I…"

She waited for something more, but it didn't come.

"I really enjoyed the trip to the zoo with you and Claire."

"Claire hasn't taken to another woman since her mother went to prison. I'm a little concerned at how quickly she's grown to like you."

"I see." Rachel's heart dropped again. She'd hoped maybe he was using the fiddle lessons as a ruse to see her. He did seem a little shy. But it was obvious, just as before, it was only what Claire wanted. She'd never had a problem attracting men before. What was it about Noel that he didn't seem at all interested?

"Not that I think you're a bad influence or anything."

Rachel laughed. "Hmmm. Could I ask you to say that to Theresa? She thinks I'm driving Kat to sex and ruin."

There was a pause and Rachel kicked herself. What was she thinking? Talking about sex and ruin was not the impression she wanted to leave with Noel.

He cleared his throat. "Well, um, I think Claire's too young for sex and ruin." He paused again and his breath hitched. "We spent a nice day together at the zoo. I think I can trust you for an hour each week with Claire. Let's just leave it at that."

"Sure. I'm sorry, I thought…Nevermind. So, do you have a pen and paper? Let me give you directions to my apartment. I teach all my lessons there."

After she hung up, Rachel stared out at the river behind the house. She had goose bumps along her arms. She could listen to his voice for a long, long time. Why did this man intrigue her so much? Was it just because he didn't seem interested? Yes, that must be it. He was safe. He had a kid and he wasn't interested. That meant they wouldn't get involved. She wouldn't have to deal with the usual three to six month affair and then wonder why it ended.

As she walked back to the kitchen, she felt bereft. Maybe six months with Noel wouldn't be so bad. He seemed so caring. Maybe he could help get her back on track. She shook herself. No, it was better not to get anything started. She'd had enough disappointment with men.

All conversation stopped as she entered the room and the women looked at her in anticipation. She had the urge to say nothing just to be difficult.

"Soooooo, who's Noel?" Kat took the receiver from her. "I liked his voice. Sounded real sexy."

Rachel took a deep breath and pasted a nonchalant smile on her face. "Remember the little girl at the last concert who wanted my autograph? Noel is her father."

"I see." Theresa drew out the word as an invitation for more.

"It's not what you think. It turns out the little girl wants fiddle lessons. Since she saw us play, she's gotten it in her mind that she wants to learn. He had no idea who to call, so he thought he'd call the main number for the band to find me. He didn't even think I gave lessons, just that I could make a recommendation."

"Uh huh," Michele said, a note of disbelief in her voice.

"But he *is* cute, right?" Kat insisted. "And you *are* interested, and something *could* be going on, right?"

"Wrong."

"Ah, come on, Rachel. How can you not be interested in that voice?"

"It's just fiddle lessons for the little girl. The girl is sweet. I'm happy to work with her. As for the father, nothing is going to happen. Believe me."

* * * * *

Noel sat in his car, waiting in line with the rest of the parents. He loved picking up Claire from school each day. In first grade, it seemed she was learning at the speed of light. Every day she shared a new amazement and he reveled in her enjoyment of the world of new found knowledge.

It had been a tough day at his school. A full one-third of the students in his grammar class had failed the quiz today, and he blamed himself for not being a better teacher. Most high school kids hated grammar, and he could hardly blame them. He'd been fighting to change the curriculum for years. He wasn't convinced that the ability to diagram sentences actually led to better grammar. In fact, he didn't remember performing well at that task in high school either.

In his creative writing class, students learned grammar by listening and observing. He never noticed a student dissecting a piece of prose by drawing one line under the subject or two under the verb and drawing a circle around the direct object. Why did grammar come so easily to some and not to others?

It was time to change tactics. With only three months left in the year, he needed to do something different. He pulled out his notepad and wrote "grammar guardians." He'd recently heard of this technique but hadn't tried it. He would research more tonight after Claire was in bed.

The bell finally rang, and children of all shapes and sizes ran toward the cars. He stepped to the curb, keeping a watch for Claire among the many blonde heads bouncing from the open doors or skipping hand-in-hand with a friend. Finally, she emerged from the building, her bright blue backpack hanging only on one shoulder. Their eyes connected and she ran full tilt toward him, the backpack slipping from her shoulder and falling to her wrist as she ground to a halt and put her arms up for a big hug.

He grabbed her around the waist and twirled her in a circle as she laughed.

He opened the car door and ushered her in. "So, did you learn anything new today?"

"You'll never believe it, Daddy. I got to be in charge of the globe today."

"The big one at the front of the room?"

"Yup, and then we played a game. The teacher asked a question about a country and then someone had to find it on the globe. And I was in charge, and if the couldn't find it I got to show it to them. I think I should be a teacher."

He waited until she'd buckled her seat belt before running to the driver's seat.

"So, what was the hardest place on the globe you had to find?"

"Madagascar!"

He turned the key and pulled out of the line. "Oh yeah, I know where that is. It's in Canada."

"No, silly. It's part of Africa." She giggled as she poked him in the shoulder. "Not the big part either. It's an island."

"Oh, now I remember, an island by Egypt."

"No." She crossed her arms and rolled her eyes. "By *southern* Africa. You know, the Indian Ocean."

"Oh, right, right." He pulled into the drive to the River Inn and parked. "How did you get so smart, anyway?"

"I don't know. It sure wasn't from you." She giggled and popped out of the car before he could catch her.

She loved her first grade teacher, and he was equally impressed after attending the first parent-teacher conference. She was patient, creative, and had a real knack for making every topic exciting. This was just one example, where she took the opportunity to use the movie Madagascar—a favorite of several young children—to teach a bit about geography. It was brilliant. He'd bet most adults had no idea where that large island was located.

He caught up with Claire in front of the motel room door, her backpack in one hand, the strap lying near her foot. She held out her hand for the keycard. "Hurry, Daddy. I have to write a story tonight and you have to help me. Then I have to have dinner.

Then I have to take a bath, and say my prayers, and go to bed."

He laughed as he handed the card to her and she slipped it in the lock. "Sounds like you're really busy tonight."

She pushed the door open and ran inside, plopping the bag next to her bed and then she sat on the end, her legs crossed. "Yup, because I have a lot to think about." She paused, wrinkled her nose, and placed her chin in one hand as if it was difficult to think so hard. "Tomorrow's my turn for show and tell, and with so much stuff packed away I don't know what to bring."

"Hmmm. That's a hard one. I might have an idea, but you have to close your eyes."

"A surprise?"

"Yup. Now close them. No peeking."

She scrunched her eyes closed and clasped her hands in front of her.

Noel rustled through the closet, making a lot of noise. "I know it's here somewhere."

Claire giggled with anticipation. "My eyes are getting tired. They're going to pop open if you don't hurry up."

"Not yet, not yet. I'm getting closer. It's really heavy. You have to be patient." He drew out the small case and tiptoed back to the two beds. He softly placed it just behind her, being careful not to jiggle the mattress.

He'd picked it up at Rose City Strings soon after Claire mentioned wanting lessons. He was surprised to learn there were actually half-sized violins. It would be perfect for her tiny fingers. Now that he knew Rachel was willing to teach her, this was the perfect opportunity to present his surprise.

"Okay. Open your eyes."

She popped up from the bed and looked at him standing in front of her. She looked to the right, toward the bathroom. Then she turned her head to the left, toward the door. Her lips turned up, and she raised one finger as she slowly turned in a half circle.

Her eyes landed on it immediately. "Ohmigod! Ohmigod!" She danced in place, as if afraid to believe it was true. "Is it really mine, Daddy? Is it really a fiddle?"

"I don't know sweetheart. I think I put a big popsicle in the case. It's probably all melted by now."

She moved closer and unlatched the two locks. "I don't think so." She lifted the case and her breath whooshed out. "It's just like Ms. Cullen's fiddle, only my size."

"That's right, and Ms. Cullen has agreed to give you lessons, starting Saturday."

She reached in and carefully lifted it from its case.

Noel's eyes misted, as she took it out and lifted it to her chin. Her index finger posed above the strings for a moment, hesitating, then she plucked each string in order and smiled.

"It's perfect, Daddy. Just perfect." She held it to the side as she hugged him at the waist with one arm.

It had been so long since he'd known what to give his little girl besides his love. They'd had a rough year together—a year he didn't want to repeat. After the concert in Welches, all Claire would talk about was the fiddle music she'd heard. She'd liked all the instruments, but it was the fiddle that had captured her heart.

Usually when Claire latched onto an idea, it lasted only a couple of days. But not this time. She talked about it constantly. In the restaurant she would point out whenever a violin was playing in the background music. On television, she'd flip channels often finding a PBS station with someone playing fiddle music. It seemed to call to her. Maybe it would help her heal.

Claire carefully put it back in the case. "This will be the best show and tell ever."

CHAPTER SIX

"I'm off with friends." Kat stepped into tennis shoes and tried to sneak out the door before her mom could ask any questions.

"Who?" Theresa appeared in the hall. "And what is that outfit?"

Kat looked down at her low-rider jeans and a cropped top that revealed her stomach. The top said 'Bite me' in bright neon-pink script. She'd hidden a small bottle of Glow perfume by JLo in her pocket to dab on after she left the house. She didn't want her mom to guess any of her plans.

"It's the weekend. It's casual. Come on, Mom, don't get in a fight with me now. I have to get going."

"Who are you going with?"

"Chris."

"I don't know her? Where did you meet."

"It's just someone from school. It'll be fine, Mom. I'll be home by nine."

"Nine? That's the whole day. Are you going to be having dinner at her house?"

"Geez! Why the third degree? It's the weekend! We don't have a gig. I just want to spend the day with a friend. What's the big deal?"

Please, please just let me get out of here, she chanted to herself. She didn't know what she'd do if her mom asked too many questions. She put on a smile and kissed her mom on the cheek. "Gotta run. Really."

"Do you have your cell phone with you? How about a jacket in case it rains?"

Kat pulled the cell from her purse and held it up, then turned and grabbed a lightweight jacket out of the coat closet. "Gotta run, we're meeting at the Brightwood store."

"That's a two mile walk. I'll drive you."

"No need, Mom. I need the exercise. Love ya, bye." She wiggled her fingertips and hurried out the door, not daring to look back for fear she would tell her the whole truth—the truth that Chris was a boy not a girl. Actually, he was a man. At nineteen he already worked in construction, and when she'd met him at Megan's party last week her knees went weak and she could barely think. All the girls thought he was hot, but it was her he'd gravitated to. She couldn't even remember what they'd talked about—just that he paid attention, he had a really cool motorcycle, and he was already grown up and had his own place.

No, she didn't dare tell her mother any of that. With all the gigs and touring last summer, it seemed she never had time to meet guys. Even after school, with the sixteen mile trip from their house to Sandy High School, she had to be on the bus—wasn't allowed to ride with anyone—then directly home for dinner and homework. She didn't want the sheltered life her mother had fashioned for her. This was her first real date and she was determined it would be heaven.

When Chris had asked her out, she was so excited and scared at the same time that she'd wanted to tell her mom all about it, but she didn't. She didn't want the third degree or any lectures about being careful, or, God forbid, an insistence on meeting him. For once, she wanted to do everything for herself without any recriminations.

Kat jogged for about a mile and then slowed to a walk. She didn't want to be totally sweaty when she got to the store. Her heart was already working double-time in anticipation of spending the day with him.

The motorcycle parked in front of the store slowed her further. She'd recognize it anywhere. She ducked behind a tree, dug in her purse for the perfume and dabbed it at her throat, the inside of her elbows and the back of her knees. On tour last year, she'd seen Rachel do that before meeting a guy and she figured Rachel really knew what she was doing.

After all, she'd probably had more sex than everyone in the band put together. Well, except for Michele and David lately, being newlyweds and all.

Kat took a deep breath and sauntered over to the bike. Resting her hand on the seat, she draped herself over it in what she hoped was a sexy look.

It seemed like only moments when Chris appeared. He stopped on the porch, looked her up and down and whistled. She moved a step toward him and stopped as a shiver danced up her spine. He walked over to her without a word, his eyes never leaving hers. She held her breath, confident she would never be able to breathe again. This was just like the movies. Certainly firecrackers would go off at any minute.

He stopped in front of her, his legs in a wide stance. His jet-black hair shined in the sunlight. His eyes were as blue as a cloudless sky. He swung a leg over the bike and nodded to her to climb on behind him. She did, without thinking twice. She'd never been on a motorcycle before, but she knew it was sexy and she wanted him to know how sophisticated she could be.

She slipped her arms around his waist, like she saw in the Harley commercials, and inhaled his scent. No cologne, just all male. For a moment, she thought she might pass out at the feel of him and loosened her grip a little.

"Hold tighter," he said, and he pulled her arms around him until her breasts pressed so firmly against his back she thought sure he could feel her nipples puckering beneath the shirt.

"Watch your left leg. The pipe is hot. I wouldn't want to scar those beautiful gams."

Wow! He'd said she was beautiful, or at least her legs were beautiful.

"Ready?"

"Yes," she whispered into the back of his neck, barely able to get the words out.

They roared around the corner and headed further up the mountain. She kept her eyes closed, enjoying the feeling of the wind whipping her hair back. She leaned her cheek against his neck. She wanted to kiss him, but the time didn't seem quite right yet. He shifted gears and increased the speed once they hit Highway 26. With each long curve up the mountain, the bike leaned dangerously close to the ground and her heart jumped, forcing her to hold even tighter. The combination of motion and fear drove her to a frenzy of excitement she'd never experienced before. *Is this what being in love is all about?*

She pictured herself as Mary Murphy in *The Wild One*—a movie her mother loved to watch. And Chris was Marlon Brando. She laughed, glorying in the thought of saving him from himself. It may have been an old black and white movie, but it was the best motorcycle love story of all time.

They spent the afternoon taking the loop around Mt. Hood, stopping at waterfalls, hiking a few trails, and then back on the cycle. He held her hand when they walked. She held him tight when they rode. He didn't talk much, but he obviously knew what he was doing. Their silence with each other provided further proof of how compatible they were. Kat was in heaven.

As dusk began to set in, Chris turned off the highway at one of the forest roads. She vaguely noted it was road twenty-three, about halfway between Government Camp and her house. They passed by tall firs where people often came to cut Christmas trees. The bike continued climbing up the dirt road higher and higher. The bumpy road pressed her harder into the seat, and soon even more heat generated between her thighs in secret places she'd never paid attention to before.

As the night turned dark and the stars came out, Kat imagined they were all twinkling just for her—a clear romantic night designed for her first real kiss on her first real date. It was perfect.

Chris stopped the bike at the next clearing and gave her his hand to help her off. He placed an arm around her waist and turned them toward the view of snow capped Mt. Hood glowing in the darkened sky. It stood like a sentinel, blessing her and Chris as they stood hand-in-hand in the open. In silence he pulled her to the meadow where he guided her down to sit in front of him as they faced the mountain.

He slid his arms around her shoulders and hugged her to him. She turned her face up to his and smiled. He met her mouth with a light brush of his lips, then turned her to face him and kissed her again. This time it was slow and intense, and she naturally opened her mouth and let in his tongue.

At the first taste of him, she thought she would faint on the spot. She was frenching! Ohmigod, it was kind of weird but also exciting. This was the real thing, the proof he liked her. No one would french a girl he didn't like.

His hands slid under her shirt. His touch was hot, and her skin tingled all over. He held her sides and ran his hand up and down her back. He stopped kissing her as he felt for her bra and easily unclasped it. He pressed against her mouth again as his fingers inched toward her breasts. Her face was on fire, she could barely breathe.

"Oh, Sheila, you're so good."

"Who?"

She pressed her hands against him and stood, wrapping her arms across her chest to cover the fact her bra was unhooked. He didn't even know her name. What was she doing?

"Who's Sheila? I'm Kat. Obviously, I've made a big mistake."

He laughed and stood to embrace her, but she danced away.

He laughed again and grabbed her wrist, reeling her in to him like a fish on the line. When she was at his side, he took her face in both hands and looked directly into her eyes. "I know who you are. Sheila is an Australian name for girl. All girls are called Sheilas. It's like an endearment. Didn't you ever see *Crocodile Dundee*?"

"Oh." Kat looked down. Stupid, stupid, stupid. Of course she remembered the movie. She should feel special then that he had a pet name for her already. But she'd really prefer he use her real name.

He tapped his finger under her chin to bring her eyes back to him. One look and she melted. Of course he knew her name. Maybe he went to Australia once. He must be really worldly to know about Sheilas. She figured that's what happened when a boy became a man, they knew these things.

"Come here, my Sheila." He pulled her closer and kissed her again as his fingers pushed her bra up toward neck and he touched and circled her nipples.

Kat's knees gave way.

He caught her and held her, covering her mouth with his and touching his tongue to hers again as his fingers continued to do their magic. Her entire body ignited in a way she'd never felt before. As they worked their way to second base, she only hoped he didn't know it was her first kiss.

He took her hand and guided her down to the ground. He lay with his back against the grass and sticks and pulled her on top of him, his hands running up her bare sides and back. He pushed her shirt all the way up and buried his head between her breasts with a groan of triumph.

Her breath clutched in fear—fear of going too far, but then she saw the stars and the mountain standing as witnesses, and she felt his kisses raining across the tops of her breasts and she sighed. It was romantic. Wasn't this what it was supposed to be like?

His mouth fell full on her breast as he took her nipple in and sucked greedily, his teeth causing a sharp pain.

"No." She pulled away. No, this was too much. She'd only wanted kisses. Maybe a little caressing was okay, but she wasn't ready for anything more.

He pulled her back.

"Come on, Sheila. I want you."

"No. This is too fast." She pushed away again.

He stopped then and let her up. She tugged her shirt back down, trying to push her breasts back into the bra. She wished she could easily reclasp it, but she didn't know how without taking it off and turning it around toward the front. She settled for just keeping the shirt down, and trying to hide the wad of material threatening to crawl up her neck and shout *I have no bra on.* He sat beside her, his arm around her, his fingers under her shirt caressing her bare back. But he didn't try to feel her breasts anymore.

Oh God, what should she do now? She concentrated on her breathing, on getting her heart back under control. At least he'd stopped. At least he knew she meant it when she said no.

"The mountain is really beautiful," he said. "Just like you."

She couldn't say anything. Her mind was so confused. He hugged her again, more lovingly than before.

"Look." He pointed to the sky. "A shooting star. That's a sign we were meant to be together."

She looked and he was right. It had a long tail. It was a good sign, like God was blessing her. These intense feelings were confusing. If they were in love, maybe it would be okay to go further.

She liked Chris and he thought she was beautiful. Maybe he even loved her. Kissing and a little touching should be okay. Maybe she was just being a prude. Geez, she was seventeen. A lot of girls already had had sex by now. She better at least get back to the kissing part before he figured out she was inexperienced and decided never to ask her out again.

She turned toward him and hesitantly pulled his face to her. She brushed her lips against his and then withdrew. He hugged her tighter and kissed her back, not in the passion he had before—just nice and soft. The way he held her was the most romantic thing in the world. Now it felt just like the *Princess Bride,* sweet and pure.

He tenderly laid her on the ground and kissed her again. This time the kiss was more passionate—as if he found her so enticing all he wanted to do was kiss her all night long. His lips were hot and delicious. She couldn't help returning his kisses. This time when his hands pushed her shirt up again she just sighed and let him kiss and suckle her breasts.

"Kat. You are amazing," he said as he moved from one breast to the other.

"So, I'm not a Sheila anymore?" Secretly she was happy he was using her real name now.

He laughed and pinched her nipple. She let out a little yelp of pain. "Now you're all woman, my catwoman," he answered, his mouth back on her hers.

She giggled and purred like a cat. Yeah, she could be sexy. She liked the way he wanted her, as if he needed to possess her. His woman. She'd never belonged to anybody beside her mother. It felt good. She opened her mouth and let her tongue answer him. French kissing still felt kind of weird but she knew this was the sophisticated thing to do.

Something big and hard inside his pants pressed against her leg. It excited her a little, but mostly it scared her. She'd heard other girls at school say that sometimes when a guy got hard it actually hurt them if they couldn't have sex. She didn't want that to happen to him. She didn't want to feel guilty by saying no again. Even while she was thinking about what to do, it seemed to grow even harder. She was afraid it would rip his jeans right open.

"Oh, Kat." His breathing changed from deep to shallow and he moved that hardness off to one side. She was relieved.

His hands went up under her shirt again and his mouth followed in rapid succession. The heat of his touched overwhelmed her. She arched up to his mouth and crushed his head to her chest. Then she lost control. It was like she was above her body watching. She started moving her hips against him. She didn't even mind that his hardness was rubbing against her. The heat continued to build beneath her jean shorts. Some part of her knew she should slow down, but she didn't want to stop, she couldn't stop.

His hand unzipped her jeans and then his fingers dipped into her panties. He groaned and grabbed her hand, guiding it to caress the huge rock-like thing that was pressing against his pants.

Oh no! He wanted her to let it out. Her hand froze. Her fingers refused to move. She tried to withdraw her hand, but he held tight, pressing her hand against himself, forcing it to stroke.

"Please, Kat. I hurt for you."

Her fingers were pointed toward the zipper. It would be so easy, but then there wouldn't be any returning. She didn't move.

“Just pull,” he said.

A jolt of fear shot through her body. She was afraid of looking stupid. He was hurting. He loved her, didn’t he? Did she love him? She didn’t know. It was a first date. This wasn’t at all what she planned. She’d just wanted to hold hands and kiss. Today had been her first kiss.

His mouth was on hers again and her head was swimming. He wrapped his hands around her fingers and guided the zipper down. She felt his hard thing spring free, and her hand accidentally grabbed it. No! She pressed her fingers against him and wrapped around it, as she tried to push it back into his pants. He gasped and she immediately let go.

Ohmigod, what had she just done? Would he take that as an invitation? She squeezed her eyes closed. She didn’t want to see it; she didn’t want to see it!

Before she knew what was happening she felt flesh and prickly hairs against her stomach. The big hard thing was naked against her stomach and he was groaning as he rubbed against her. She took a peek and almost died. It was ugly and there were two big hard round things scrunched up against it.

It was her debut penis. She’d seen pictures of course. Her and her friends had seen pictures of naked male models on the Internet. But it was all romantically posed and sexy. This, on the other hand was just scary and it looked so big. Way too big to fit inside of her. She tried to push away, but he misunderstood.

He lifted himself off her and in one movement yanked her jeans and panties down to her ankles.

"No. Wait." She reached toward her legs to pull them back up but his full weight was on top of her now and he was separating her legs with his thighs.

"You are so beautiful, Kat. You make me want you so much. I'm going to make you feel so good."

Her eyes filled with tears. She couldn't speak, she couldn't move. What was wrong with her? She was terrified. She went perfectly still, hoping if she didn't move he would just stop.

Isn't this what she'd been fantasizing about ever since she'd met Chris at the party after the basketball game last month? She'd had plenty of dreams about him since then. Only her dreams involved kissing and music in the background, and words of undying love. None of this.

Isn't this what all the girls thought was so cool? What they bragged about? They all said that once you went all the way, you'd be dying to do it all the time. She wanted to be sophisticated and grownup. Maybe she was just being a baby about this.

His fingers were near her private parts. She clamped down, not wanting him to touch her there and tried to squirm away.

"Whoa baby." He rested his palm on her and rubbed in circles. " It's okay, Kat. This is natural. This is beautiful. We are in nature as it should be." His mouth took hers again and her head spun out of control. How could she think when he kept kissing her like that?

He stopped and she gasped for air. His fingers were moving so fast, rubbing her, pinching her and she didn't like his groans. This wasn't romantic at all.

"I don't know," she said. "I don't think this is right. I don't think I can do this." She tried to push against him, but her arms couldn't get between their bodies.

"Is it your first time?"

She nodded, tears in her eyes. He must think she's such a baby.

He smiled and laced her fingers of one hand with his and raised it above her head. "I'm good with first timers. Just look at me and it will be okay."

She looked into his eyes, but she couldn't really see him as her eyes blurred and tears squeezed out and ran down her cheek. He stopped them with his kisses.

That was love wasn't it? Kissing her tears away, just like in the movies?

"You're my special Sheila, aren't you, Kat?"

It was the endearment again. She swallowed and looked up at the stars. If only she could see another shooting star it would be all right. She would know it was okay. She searched the heavens but saw nothing. She felt his hand at her privates again.

"It's just that this is our first date and…well…I just didn't think…this is too fast."

"It's fast because you're special, Kat. I've never wanted someone as badly as I want you. I need you. Right now, right here."

She choked back more tears. She'd been attracted to Chris because he had a little of that bad boy attitude. He was strong and self-assured and knew what he wanted. He was the kind of guy who took without regret and she'd envied that confidence. She knew she should be happy he wanted her so much. A million girls would probably be dying to be here with him.

Then he kissed her again. This time it was as if she was a little baby, a baby that might break and that he loved so much he would be careful and gentle. His hand moved away from her privates and slowly caressed her breast. Instead of being so insistent he barely touched her. His breath felt like a warm, sweet breeze, sending shivers over her entire body. His kiss was warm and slow and it made her heart melt and she felt cherished.

Kat let her arms go around his neck. She kissed him back. It was just like the movies. Their hearts beat together as one. He moved against her leg. The rock hard thing didn't feel quite as alien this time. His hand slaked up and down her side, dipping toward her privates but not forcing anything.

He eased her legs apart again and she could feel his rock nestled against her opening. She couldn't help clamping down. He kissed her more passionately and she could feel it pressing harder and harder. It started out as just a nudge, an uncomfortable fitting, but then he panted and groaned and pushed against her. Her back pressed hard into the ground. Sticks and small rocks pushed indentations into her spine and pocked her bottom.

She felt him inch inside her and it hurt. She clamped down again.

"No. It hurts. Stop! Please stop." This wasn't right. This couldn't be how it was supposed to happen. He pushed his penis further. She felt like she was being torn open. She'd never even worn a tampon before.

"Relax," he said, groaning with obvious frustration. "Don't be a cunt. Just let it happen…"

"No," she whispered, tears hot in her eyes.

"If you don't relax, it will hurt like hell. Come on, now."

He pushed again, this time with force.

She cried out.

He was fully inside her and she felt sure she was going to die. He was panting and he was hard and sweaty and pushing, pushing, pushing in and out. She thought sure he was tearing every part of her. He moved faster and her back and bottom ground the rocks deeper into her tender skin. She wasn't sure if it was minutes or hours, but he finally yelled out "Sheila!" and collapsed on top of her.

She cried in jags, unable to breathe and unable to move. She could taste the salt of her tears. She cried for her mother, for her friends, for wanting to go back to innocence. If this was love she didn't want any part of it. How could anyone think this was fun?

Chris raised himself off her and she took in a deep, choking breath. He gave her a quick brush across the lips then rolled onto his back. "Not bad, girl. Not bad."

Not bad? It was awful! She reached for her pants, tangled around her ankles and pulled them up as fast as she could. When she raised her hips to shimmy into them, a sticky wetness spilled down her leg. Then she just felt sick to her stomach. She didn't want all that stickiness so close to her. It was all so disgusting.

She heard him stand, and she looked up and saw him zipping his jeans. He didn't even offer her a hand up. She tugged her top down and pushed herself off the ground, zipping her own shorts as she stood. She didn't want to look at him and it seemed he didn't want to look at her either.

"It's getting late," he said. "Better get home."

Kat couldn't speak. Was that all he had to say? Where was the sorry I hurt you? The least he could do is acknowledge he had just taken her virginity.

"You ready?" he asked. He stood near the bike as if he expected her to just climb on and everything would be as it was before.

She couldn't speak. She was too frozen to move. She couldn't even imagine getting back on the bike with the soreness now between her legs. She felt like she was rubbed raw.

He shrugged and climbed on by himself. When she still didn't move he started it up and took off down the road. She watched, numb, not knowing exactly where she was or if she could even get home. All she could remember was they'd turned on road twenty-three.

She heard the skid of tires and watched as a light bounced back toward her. He spewed rock as he turned and brought the bike to a stop in front of her, the engine idling.

"Kat?"

She didn't know what to say. Nothing had turned out the way she wanted.

"Come on. Get on and I'll take you home."

"How could you? How could you do that to me?"

"Hey, you wanted it too. You were kissing me back plenty. Now, get on, or I'll leave you here."

She didn't move. She couldn't. She didn't want to touch him ever again or to have him touch her.

"Have it your way." He roared away again.

Her mouth made a word to call out, but she had no voice.

Before long she no longer heard the motorcycle. He'd really left. She was alone. Completely alone. Only the white crown of Mt. Hood and the stars kept her company. A wail snaked up from her chest and burst out full force, reaching all the way to the heavens; and all the stars disappeared from her eyes.

CHAPTER SEVEN

Kat wasn't sure how long she'd been sitting against the tree, her arms wrapped around her knees, crying her heart out. She just wanted to die, right here in this spot—the spot of her unveiling, the violent unveiling. It was nothing like the movies.

Was it possible all those other girls at school were just liars? Or was she so inept that sex would always be horrible for her?

She rolled her head back and gazed up at the sky. What would she do now? She couldn't walk home, could she? She was at least ten miles away. She was so tired, she didn't feel she had the energy to walk even one mile. Surely it was past her curfew by now. Her mom would be worried.

Oh, God. Mom. She couldn't possibly tell her mom how stupid she'd been. It would break her heart. A new crying jag took over.

Rachel. She could call Rachel. She would understand. She'd been in trouble before. She could swear Rachel to secrecy. Wiping a hand across her eyes, she pulled out the cell phone her mother had insisted she take with her. The glow from the screen added a small semblance of warmth to the cool night as she dialed from memory.

Two rings. "Hello?"

"Rache?" She choked back a new sob welling in her chest.

"Hey, Kat. Whatcha doin'? I thought you'd be out with friends on a Saturday night.

"Rache, if I ask you to do something without any questions, would you do it?"

There was silence on the other end and Kat crossed her fingers.

"Are you in trouble, Kat? Did you do something illegal?"

"No, nothing illegal. Could you just come get me? And please, please don't tell my Mom?"

"What's going on, Kat? Where are you?"

She couldn't keep the tears out of her voice. She tried to sound brave and steady but she couldn't. "You have to promise me, Rache. You just have to."

"Okay. I promise. Now, where are you, what's wrong?"

"I'm not completely sure." It burst forth with a sob. "I remember turning on road twenty-three, but that's all. I don't know if there was another road after that. I don't think so, but I'm not sure. I can see Mt. Hood from here. There's kind of a meadow. It's pretty. At least it was pretty."

"Ah *chac,* baby, what's happened?"

Kat could hear the car turning over in the background and she sighed. Rachel was coming. She was going to find her.

"Thanks," she whispered.

* * * * *

Rachel sped up the mountain, talking to Kat all the way. Visions of herself hurt and left to die in a motel room in Branson played in her head. If anyone hurt Kat she was going to kill him with her own hands. Who would leave Kat in the dark, alone, on a mountain. *Chac*!

Her eyes scanned both sides of Highway 26, trying to make-out the small street signs for the forest service roads. Road 10. Road 12. Finally, she found it, Road 23, and made the left turn across traffic.

The headlights speared the trees on either side of the road and dirt spewed from her tires as she negotiated the curves. This was one of many roads that people took for cross-country skiing in the winter, or four-wheeling in the summer. Over 500 miles of back roads and trails surrounded Mt. Hood. How would Rachel ever find Kat if she'd taken other spurs off this one?

She continued to talk to Kat as she drove, trying to keep the conversation light. It was getting cold and she could hear the chatter of Kat's teeth over the phone.

She braked quickly. There Kat stood, like a deer in headlights. Cell phone to her ear. Twigs and pine needles in her hair. Her shorts and top were covered with dirt. Her face filled with rivulets and red-rimmed eyes.

Kat dropped the phone and Rachel rushed from the car to pull her into her arms.

"I didn't think you'd find me." Kat shook violently against Rachel's warmth.

"Of course I'd find you. You can't get away from me that easily." She hugged Kat tight, running her hands up and down her back as she sobbed. After, about twenty minutes, Kat quieted and Rachel bent to retrieve the cell phone and shepherded Kat back to her car.

She sat her in the passenger side and wrapped her in a blanket. When she stood to get back to the driver's seat, Kat grabbed her hand and held tight. Rachel turned back and embraced her again, just letting her rock and cry.

"Oh, baby. What happened? How did you get stranded up here?"

After what seemed like an hour, Kat quieted. "I can't go home, Rache. I just can't. Can I stay with you?"

"Sure, honey. Sure." She hugged her tight again. "Are you ready for me to drive now?"

Kat nodded, her chin firmly implanted in her chest.

Rachel strapped the seatbelt around her and closed the door, trying not to make much of a sound. She moved back to the driver's side of the car, climbed in and took Kat's hand in hers. They drove in silence back to Welches.

"Would you call my mom?" Kat sat curled on the sofa, the blanket still wrapped around her, her legs tucked under.

Rachel handed her a cup of hot chocolate. "What should I say?"

"I don't know, just tell her I'm spending the night. Don't worry her, okay?"

Rachel dialed as she watched Kat out of the corner of her eye. She'd offered no further explanation and Rachel wasn't pressing her to talk. She just hoped she would open up sometime tonight.

"Hi, Theresa." She put a note of cheer in her voice. She saw Kat watching her with fear.

"Rachel? It's kind of late to be calling isn't it?"

"Well, you'll never guess what happened. I was…um…in Sandy and ran into Kat with her friends. We got to talking and before I knew it I'd asked her over for a slumber party."

"What's going on, Rachel? Is she in some kind of trouble?"

"Oh, nothing like that. I'm just feeling a little lonely and I figured you wouldn't mind if she spent the night."

She clenched her teeth in the half lie as the silence drew out. She knew Theresa wasn't buying it.

"I don't know what's going on, but I can tell you're not giving me the whole story. And she's there listening to you, isn't she?"

Rachel glanced toward Kat again. She didn't want to keep Theresa in the dark about her own daughter, on the other hand she didn't want to break the fragile trust Kat had given her.

"Really, it's nothing awful. If you'd rather she came home that's okay with me too."

Kat waved her hands and shook her head no. Rachel held up a finger and winked.

"I guess I'm just being a little paranoid. She was supposed to be home an hour ago and I was just getting ready to ring her cell phone. If you're sure everything is okay."

"I'm sure. It's just a girl's night out. You know I think of Kat like my little sister. We're just going to rent some movies and chat about girl stuff."

"Well, okay. Can I talk to her?"

"Just a minute, she's in the bathroom. Let me see if I can get her." Rachel motioned to the phone and pointed at Kat. Kat shook her head, her eyes wide and pleading not to talk.

Rachel walked down the hall with the cell and made a show of pounding on the door. "Kat, you in there. Your mom wants to say good night." She paused as if she heard Kat talking. "Yeah? Okay."

She made loud footsteps back to the kitchen. "Uh, can she call you back, Theresa? She's in the shower. You know how teenagers are. They have to be perfect even for a sleep over."

"Oh, never mind. Just tell her I love her. By the time she gets out I'll be in bed. Have a good time. Don't let her get on your nerves."

"I'll tell her. See you tomorrow."

Rachel hung up and saw Kat's shoulders drop with relief. Rachel was surprised she'd pulled it off.

"Thanks, Rache." She could barely hear Kat's voice. "I really am going to take a shower now. Okay?"

Rachel held her eyes for a moment, but Kat looked away.

"I can't talk right now. I just can't."

"It's okay. You don't have to."

Like a woman sentenced to the gallows, Kat moved slowly toward the bathroom. Rachel heard the lock engage and then finally the shower.

Rachel pulled into herself as she started to shake. She had a pretty good idea what had happened to Kat. She remembered that hollow feeling—that feeling that the darkness would swallow her whole. Rachel knew that nothing she could say would make Kat talk until she was ready. But whenever that was, Rachel vowed she would be available—day or night.

* * * * *

The next day, two hours after Rachel had dropped Kat at home, a small knock sounded on her front door.

She peered through the drapes and saw Claire holding a violin case in one hand, her face straight toward the door with such serious intent that Rachel almost burst out laughing. She composed her features and opened the door with a smile.

"I know we're a little early," Noel said when she opened the door. "I wasn't completely sure what traffic might be like and we didn't want to be late."

"Lookee!" Claire raised a small violin case up for her inspection.

"Looks like it's just your size. Come in, come in."

Claire stepped over the threshold, but Noel held back.

"I…uh…thought I'd make myself scarce. I don't want to interfere with the music."

"Good idea." Rachel was disappointed he wasn't staying, but she did agree he might make Claire nervous. In her small apartment there wasn't really anywhere he could get out of the way except her bedroom, and that definitely was not a good idea.

"Thought maybe I'd wander over to the ski shop for awhile. How long will you be?"

"About an hour."

He nodded and backed away as she closed the door. Odd, he seemed reluctant to leave too. She shook her head and turned to Claire.

"So, why are you here again?"

"I'm going to be a fiddle player like you." Claire's smile lit up her entire face.

"You are, are you? Let's learn how to take this fiddle out of the case then and get it ready to play."

Claire's fingers fumbled with the clasps but she managed to open it up on her own. She took the half-sized instrument from the case and held it by the neck to show Rachel. Then she tucked it under her chin, her small left hand grasping the neck like a vise.

"I tried to play something for Daddy but it sounded terrible." Her fingers plucked at out of tune strings. "Then I tried the hairy thing Daddy called a bow, and it was even worse."

Rachel held back a laugh. She didn't want Claire to feel stupid. "Hmmm. Can I see your fiddle? I may have to do some fixing first."

Claire handed it to her. "Is it broken?"

"No." Rachel balanced it on her lap and plucked each string then adjusted the tuning pin. "It's just out of tune. This is something you have to learn, but it's kind of hard, so I'm going to do it for you the first couple of times. Okay?"

Claire nodded, her eyes transfixed on Rachel's hands as she continued to adjust the tones.

Satisfied she handed it back to Claire. "Okay. All fixed now." Claire replaced it under her chin. "It looks like you're already pretty good at how to hold it."

"My Daddy showed me."

"He did? He must be pretty smart."

"Yup." Claire plucked the strings again, her left hand still tight around the neck. "It still sounds funny."

Rachel picked up her own fiddle and demonstrated how her hand needed to be open on the neck. "See balance it like this. Don't hold tight. Then we are going to just put one finger down on the string, like this." She plucked the A string open and then placed her index finger to play the B note.

Claire did the same thing. When the note didn't sound right, she automatically moved her finger until it sounded the same.

"Very good, Claire. I can see you have a good ear."

"Of course. My ears aren't broken."

Rachel laughed. "That's right. They are perfect ears." She reached out and wiggled one lightly. "A good ear means you can hear the sound of the music and know when it is right."

"Oh. That's funny."

Rachel spent the next fifteen minutes working with Claire on learning how to finger the D scale. She would demonstrate and Claire would copy. Claire easily picked up the notes and adapted her finger position to the right sound.

Soon, they were talking about a song to learn and the two were playing together, plucking out the notes to *Oh, Susanna.* She followed with instruction on how to tighten the bow, rosin it, and play with the correct hand positions. Again they played *Oh, Susanna* together, this time with bowing. Claire telegraphed her delight with each stroke, matching the emphasis and positioning of Rachel with ease. When she thought Claire had the notes down, they played a duet together with Rachel adding additional notes to fill out the sound.

At the end of the song, Claire beamed up at her. "We play good together, don't we?"

"Yes, we certainly do. Want to learn another one?"

All too soon the lesson was over and she heard a firm knock on the front door.

"Daddy, daddy," Claire raced to open it, her fiddle and bow balanced in one hand. "Did you hear us? Did you hear us making the music?"

"I sure did, sweetheart. It sounded amazing." Noel rustled the curls on Claire's head.

"You did great, Claire. Now I want you to practice *Oh Susanna* and *Wake Up Susan* this week. And I want you to make up a song of your own using the notes you learned from the key of D."

"Make up one? But what if it isn't right?"

"It will be right because it's your very own song. Only you will know if it's right."

"Really? Do you make up songs?"

"I sure do. All professional musicians make up songs."

"Okay." Claire walked to her case with an unsure glance toward Rachel.

"You can do it."

Rachel watched as Claire's brow furrowed in concentration. She carefully laid the fiddle into the case and then loosened the bow, placing it in the holder in the lid. She opened the pocket below the neck and slipped the rosin in its box. Satisfied, she closed the case and latched it again.

"Good job!"

Claire turned, clapped her hands and smiled. "See, Daddy. I know how to do it now."

Noel grabbed her up in an embrace. "You sure do. Before I know it, you'll be playing on the stage and everyone will be clapping just for you."

Rachel tore her eyes from the little display of affection. She felt a pain in her stomach and a lump in her throat. Why was she so intent on family lately? It was all Michele's fault. The whole baby thing was really starting to get to her.

Rachel cleared her throat. "So, same time next Saturday?"

"It'll have to be two weeks from now. We're moving into our house next week."

"Oh? Do you need any help?"

Noel shifted from one foot to the other. "That's okay. We'll get along."

Rachel wasn't sure if he was brushing her off or just shy about accepting help.

"Do you have anyone coming to help?"

"My parents are coming up from Yachats on Friday, and a couple of the teachers from school might show up. I'm not really sure."

"Well, I'll definitely be there, then. Theresa has a truck she uses to haul wood. I can probably borrow it."

"Look, you don't have to."

"Are you purposely trying to keep me away?" Rachel decided she might as well get it over with right up front. She liked Noel and she wanted to spend more time with him. But if there wasn't a chance he was interested, she wanted to know now.

"No…I…just…oh hell."

"Daddy, you aren't supposed to say hell."

He raked his hand through his hair. "You're right, sweetheart. I apologize." He turned to Rachel and smiled. "Thanks. Yeah, we could use the help. Saturday at ten then?"

"Good." Rachel followed him as he and Claire stepped out the door.

He turned and placed a hand on her arm, a question in his eyes. But he said nothing and then dropped his arm and turned back to the door.

He clasped Claire's hand in his and walked toward the car. Claire turned and waved but Noel didn't look back.

CHAPTER EIGHT

At exactly ten o'clock the next Saturday, Noel saw Rachel drive an F-150 pickup through the open security gate near his storage unit. He wiped the sweat from his brow and jumped down from the back of the U-haul. He had to elbow his way through a throng of box-bearing friends and relatives to reach her. Then, when he got to her, all he could do was stare.

A sky blue and white Pendleton hung from her shoulders over a dark grey shirt. The blue emphasized the depth of her eyes, those deep pools of blue that reminded him of Crater Lake. Her white hair seemed to provide an angelic crown of curls as the sun shone behind her. Her jeans were black and followed the curves of her shapely hips and legs so closely that he had to restrain himself not to reach out and touch. She wore workman-type boots, but even those looked sexy on her. *Wow!*

"Hi." She flashed one of those dazzling smiles that showed the single dimple on her left cheek. "I hope I'm not late." She gestured to all the commotion. "You did say ten."

Noel shook his head. Even when not dressed to kill, she was so damned beautiful. It was enough to make a man's tongue stick to the roof of his mouth. Hold on there. You're letting the testosterone take over. Before you know it, you'll be jumpin' her bones and then you'll fall in love, and then you're in big time trouble.

"Umm…nice truck. It should haul plenty," he finally managed to say.

She stared, wide-eyed, at all the people bustling to and fro between the storage unit and the truck. Noel followed her gaze and winced as he heard a stream of swear words from his father as he and his brother wrestled a sofa bed into the truck.

"Sorry 'bout that. He's a logger and used to being out with a bunch of men."

Rachel laughed. "No worries. I've been known to let a few fly myself. Fortunately, there usually in Gaelic."

His brother's kid, now two, threw a tantrum and his sister-in-law hurried over to calm him. Noel pulled Rachel to one side as a large bookcase rolled by on a dolly. More boxes followed in lines of two or three people hustling into the back of the truck, and to the other side he heard his mother yell out, "Who did the packing of these knick-knacks? My word, Noel, did you want to break every last one of them?"

"Sorry, Mom," he yelled back. "Do what you can with them, please."

Two other teachers from the high school moved past with dining room chairs over their heads to avoid smacking anyone, and a young girl of about seven ran up and slid to a stop directly in front of him.

"Uncle Noel, where's Claire? We can't find her."

He pointed to a second opened unit. "She's over there supervising Grandma on how to pack her toys." The girl ran off, alternating skipping and giggling with yelling Claire's name.

Noel turned back to Rachel. "It's a bit chaotic. Let me introduce you." Lifting his voice to a yell, he said, "Hey everybody, this is Rachel. Introduce yourselves and be nice to her. She barely knows me and still volunteered to help."

A knowing laugh tittered around the parking lot.

A tall man, a good four to five inches taller than Noel, emerged from the U-haul and held out is hand. "Hi, I'm Derek. Noel's bigger and smarter brother." A woman with amber hair in a ring of short curls came behind him and smacked him on the butt.

"Don't listen to him. He may be big, but I'm not so sure about the smarter part." Derek pulled her into an embrace and squeezed her bottom in a possessive move.

"Two can play at that game."

The woman giggled and lifted her face to him for a quick kiss, the two-year old trailed behind her, quiet now.

"And this is my wife, Karen," Derek said. "A vixen is what she is."

"And don't you forget it." She beamed up at him, then turned to Rachel. "Welcome to chaos."

Noel smiled. It never ceased to amaze him how much his brother and sister-in-law loved each other. He remembered how much they'd fought before they were married, but the minute they'd said their vows it seemed it was all behind them. He'd envied their relationship, the passion they had. He'd loved Clarissa, but it was never that passionate, in anger or love. It seemed he could never give her enough—enough material things, enough love, enough attention.

"Hey bro, movin' up in the world are you?" A brunette with jet black hair hanging in a ponytail to her waist put her arm around Noel and looked at Rachel with a half smile. "Aren't you the fiddler in that band, Sweetwater Canyon?"

"Yes, have you seen us?"

"Sure have. Love your music. It would be great to have you and the band for the house warming. Add a little culture to this lout's life." She playfully slugged Noel's shoulder.

"This is my nosy sister, Kathie." Noel gave her a peck on the cheek. "She also belongs to Katie, the little girl you saw a few minutes ago looking for Claire. And her husband is that he-man hauling the dryer on his back." He pointed toward a man stepping slowly up the ramp.

"Won't he hurt his back doing that?" Rachel stared at Noel's brother-in-law, her mouth agape.

"Nah, he's strong as an ox. Won the caber toss at the logging games last fall," Kathie said with obvious pride. "He'd be offended if you questioned his strength."

"I'll definitely watch my step then."

Kathie hurried away and disappeared into another open storage unit. Noel watched as Rachel scanned the parking lot.

"So, what can I do to help?" she asked. "Theresa's truck has lots of room."

Noel pointed to the next two doors of units. "Believe it or not, I rented five of these things to be able to store the whole house. While my father and brothers are clearing the big furniture and book boxes, you can help my Mom and Kathie get all the art work, linens, toys and all those things we didn't pack so well."

"Don't think I have enough brawn for the big stuff, eh?"

Noel looked down to his feet. "I…uh…"

"Just teasing. I'm not looking to set any strength records. I'll head over there." She pointed to the third unit where a woman hunched over a box with packing tape in her hand. Claire and Kathie were standing close by.

"That's my Mom with Claire, here I'll introduce you."

"Hey, Noel. Stop jabberin' and give us a hand here." Noel turned to see his two brothers struggling with the armoire. It was at least a four-man job.

"Don't worry, I'll introduce myself. You go help them."

And just like that, Noel lost her as he turned to help his brothers.

Rachel stepped quickly toward the storage unit. She wasn't completely sure why she was here, but she knew she couldn't stay away. The woman Noel had pointed out as his mother crouched over a box of stacked china and glassware. She first set all the pieces off to one side. She then flattened newspaper and began rolling each piece and packing it carefully into a box. She was the prototypical grandmother, slightly rotund, close cropped dark hair with a generous helping of gray streaked throughout, and an easy smile as she worked.

Rachel approached with a little hesitation, but then saw Claire off to the side with her own stack of objects to wrap. "Hi Claire, how are things going?"

Claire's face lit up as she turned and met Rachel halfway, her arms immediately encircling Rachel's hips in a welcoming hug. Then she took her hand and dragged her to where Noel's mother knelt on the concrete rolling glassware for packing.

"Grandma, this is Rachel. She's teaching me how to be a fiddler like her. Did you know it's called fiddling not violin playing, because it's fiddle music. And she's from Scotland, which is why she talks funny. And she likes my Daddy and me too."

"Is that right, now?" The dark-haired woman pushed herself up to stand. She gave Rachel a hug as if she were already part of the family. "I'm LaVerne. I've been hearing plenty about you from Claire. It's so good to see my little doll so happy."

Claire turned to Rachel with a serious face. "I'm not really a doll. Grandma just likes to call me that."

Rachel chuckled and bent to Claire's height, her brow raised in mock puzzlement. "Hmm…are you sure? Let me see here." She turned Claire around with her back toward her and patted around her shoulders. "Where's that string that makes you talk. It seems to me you're a Chatty Cathy doll."

Claire giggled. "Maybe I'm a Chatty Claire doll."

"That's it, Chatty Claire." Rachel turned her back to face her. "I can't find that string though, so maybe you're not a doll after all."

Rachel stood again and faced LaVerne. "I've been relegated to this section of the storage units, so tell me what you need me to do."

For the next two hours, Rachel helped repack boxes that had been thrown together carelessly and loaded fragile or individual items into the back of Sarah's truck. She fell into an easy rhythm of small talk and work with LaVerne and Kathie. Claire dashed in and out depending on if her young cousins were vying for her attention or not. Before Rachel knew it, everything was packed in trucks and cars, and they all followed Noel and the U-haul out of the storage lot and up the road to his new home a few miles away.

The line of cars snaked along the two-lane road toward the back side of the small town of Sandy. They were only a couple miles from the high school, but it felt like it was in the countryside. Eagle Canyon Road dropped off on the north side in a steep hill of evergreens and overlooked the valley. The south side of the road was dotted with homes on one to five acre lots. Half hidden behind cedars and firs, well-tended yards of rhododendron and azalea still waited to bloom. Rachel could only glimpse shapes and colors as the line of cars meandered by.

The lead car signaled and everyone turned into a narrow drive that headed up a gentle grade. She couldn't see the house from the road, but she suspected it would be at the top of this hill. A cute

Cape Cod home nestled among towering trees. As she followed the cars to parking in the back, her mouth fell open. She parked and scrambled from the car to stand and take in the magnificent view.

The back side of the house opened onto a meadow that looked straight into the Sandy River watershed and a crystal clear view of Mt. Hood beyond. She liked the thought of Noel standing on his back porch and looking toward her home in Welches. Would he think about her?

She felt a breath near her ear. “Beautiful isn’t it?” She shivered at Noel’s closeness even though he wasn’t touching her. His arm raised close to her side and pointed toward the mountain. “Your place is right about…there.”

Rachel closed her eyes, afraid if she looked at him she wouldn’t be responsible for her actions. She turned to offer her mouth, and Claire grabbed her around the knees, breaking the mood. Rachel laughed. Just her luck.

“Isn’t it wonderful?” Claire grabbed her hand and pulled her toward what appeared to be a small guest house or office Rachel hadn’t noticed before. Noel chuckled and waved her on her way, as he headed in the opposite direction to guide boxes and furniture into the house.

“Look, look!” Claire stopped at the front door of the guest house and turned the handle. “It’s like a baby house, only bigger. Daddy said Grandma and

Grandpa can sleep here sometimes, and when I'm older maybe I can sleep here. Maybe you can sleep here too Rachel? We could have a slumber party."

Rachel glanced around the small room. A queen-sized bed, a small table and two chairs, and what appeared to be a recliner outfitted the room. A counter ran the length of one wall with a microwave and toaster on top, and a mini-fridge underneath, She assumed there was a bathroom behind the closed door at the end of the counter. Cozy. A nice arrangement for parents or overnight guests without having to accommodate them in the main house.

"So, would you like to come to a slumber party? Huh?" Claire bounced on the bed as she spoke.

"I'm not sure, Claire. I don't live that far away. I think I would like to sleep in my own bed."

Claire's mouth drooped into a pout. "But Daddy said I'm not old enough to sleep here without an adult, and Grandma and Grandpa take up all the space so I can't sleep with them."

Rachel could see the dilemma but she could imagine a much larger problem if she became too attached to Claire. Who was she kidding? She was already attached.

"Well, we'll have to see how things work out in the future." She wrapped her hands around Claire's waist and lifted her from the bed with a big twirl before setting her on her feet. "Let's get some things out of the truck and into a safe place, then you can show me around your new house."

"Okay." Claire raced from the room and was already half way to the back door of the main house before Rachel could cross the threshold and close the door. By the time she reached the living room with her first load of artwork, Claire was nowhere to be seen.

The next couple of hours were a chaotic dance of boxes, people, and furniture, interrupted by pizza and soft drinks at about 2:00. Then Noel's mother commandeered Rachel to help her unpack the kitchen.

"I'm not sure we should do this without Noel." Rachel used the box cutter to slit the tape and start unwrapping dishes.

"He won't mind, dear. Noel may be a poet but he has very few organizational skills. In fact, when he and Clarissa were married he was practically banished from the kitchen."

"I vaguely remember him saying something about enjoying cooking. Maybe he's changed."

LaVerne shook her head. "Mark my words. If we don't unpack now, it will sit in boxes for months and they'll be eating off paper plates."

Still unsure, Rachel stacked stoneware on the counter beneath the honeyed oak cupboards, thinking about what would be the best placement. She liked the layout of this kitchen. It was truly at the center of the house and open to the backyard and a family room, as well as an informal dining area. In fact, the entire house exuded a cozy, relaxed appeal.

"So, how do you know Noel and Claire? He hasn't mentioned you."

"Oh, he wouldn't really mention me. We aren't together or anything. I give Claire fiddle lessons and when I heard about the move I wanted to help."

"Uh huh." LaVerne didn't sound like she believed the explanation. "You know about Clarissa then?"

Oh yes. Rachel knew more than she wanted about the ex. Claire had spilled those beans the first day they'd had a chance to talk. In fact, that was exactly why Rachel was determined not to get involved with Noel. She knew her past would not come up to his standards.

"I think Claire has had a hard time dealing with her mother being in jail," Rachel finally said. "But I think Noel is an excellent father and she will get better as time goes on."

LaVerne stopped her unpacking and looked at Rachel without blinking. Then her cheeks lifted and she winked. "I think you might just be the one to help Noel get over her, too."

"Oh no. I'm not interested. I'm just a musician giving lessons."

"You don't find my son handsome and romantic?"

Rachel stared, her mouth slightly open. Was she being set up or what? Then she let out a laugh that began low in her belly and worked its way up her throat. "I can't win with anything I say to that."

"I have a little bit of psychic powers, you know." LaVerne opened a cupboard to the left of the sink and placed plates and bowls into it. "And I predict you and my son will be seeing a lot of each other."

Rachel wanted to roll her eyes, but she restrained herself. She didn't want to offend. Silence was definitely the best option here. She concentrated on opening and emptying the next box.

LaVerne hummed *Swing Low, Sweet Chariot* as she worked unwrapping cups and saucers and then placing them on the shelf above the plates. On the second verse, Rachel picked up the harmony a third lower. By the third verse, they had made it into a round and both were smiling. Soon they were working in tandem, sometimes singing and sometimes humming a variety of old gospel tunes providing a happy rhythm to their unpacking and shelving. Within about half an hour more they had the kitchen done.

Rachel flattened the two large dish packs and hauled them out the back door to the porch. The view once more arrested her, as the first hints of pink began to fill the sky and the white snowfields glowed golden on the mountain peak.

"It's perfect, isn't it?" Her heart jumped as she felt Noel's closeness behind her. She didn't dare move. "This is the reason I bought this place. This kind of peace and serenity is what Claire and I need."

For a moment, Rachel imagined herself seeing this view every night with Noel's arms around her. She closed her eyes and felt his hands on her shoulders, massaging them. She luxuriated in the feeling.

"Rachel, I really appreciate you coming today…and all you've done for Claire. She…really loves the fiddle."

"She has a natural talent."

He turned her toward him and she saw the passion in his eyes. She lifted her face to him, expecting a kiss—a kiss she now realized she was hungering for.

"Oh, there you are."

Noel stepped back from Rachel. "Hey, Kathie. Looking for me?"

"Yeah, Dad is trying to get your bed set up and he can't find the rails."

"Oh, I think they're still in the garage. I'll go get them." Then he was gone.

Rachel turned to go back inside, but Kathie caught her arm.

"Can I have a word?"

"Sure."

"What's going on between you and Noel? He's never mentioned you."

Geez. Was his entire family going to ask this question?

"Nothing. We're just friends."

"What I interrupted didn't look like just friends."

Rachel couldn't help but smile at her protectiveness. Even if they weren't in a relationship. "And if it's not, what business is it of yours? I think your brother can take care of himself."

"Yes, he can. Now. And I want it to stay that way." Kathie paused as if deciding what to say. "You didn't see what he went through with Clarissa. And so help me, God, if you hurt him I'll personally come after you."

Rachel raised a brow. "Gonna take me out to the woodshed?"

Kathie had the grace to blush and then she laughed. "I guess I did come on a little strong. But, seriously, he's a good man and he has been to hell and back with his ex. I don't know you."

"No, you don't."

"I'm just asking, as a loving sister, that if all you want is a playmate to please look somewhere else. I think he's really vulnerable and he's in the market for a mother for Claire. And…well…"

"I get your meaning." Rachel placed her hand on Kathie's forearm. "I'm not in the market and to tell you the truth I'm definitely not Noel's type. So you have nothing to worry about. I'm just the fiddle teacher."

Kathie raised both brows then turned toward the view to catch the final streaks of crimson sky. "It is beautiful. He needs this so much." Rachel looked at her and saw a single tear escape. Kathie quickly brushed it away. "If you knew him, believe me you couldn't stay away. No woman could. And I'm not saying that just because I'm his sister. He's amazing. Romantic. Kind. Knows how to take control when he has to. And he protects his family above all else." She turned back to Rachel and looked her in the eye. "That's why he deserves only the very best. He paid a heavy price with his first wife, and stuck with her longer than any of us wanted him to. He deserves only the very best."

Rachel nodded. She understood completely. She definitely was not the very best.

CHAPTER NINE

Kat pulled the blanket over her face to block out the light. She could not face yet another morning of trying to act normal. For the past few weeks she could barely drag herself out of bed to get to school. Lately she hated the fresh air, the warming spring breezes that at a moment's notice would turn to a hard rain or stiff wind. It reminded her of everything wrong in her world. It would begin by ruffling her hair, caressing her skin, reminding her of being kissed, touched, falling in love. Then it turned ugly. The thunder would roar and the lightning flashed, and she'd be drenched in fear.

She hurried through her days, trying not to connect, afraid if she did it would all spill out—her stupidity, the horror. After school, she headed straight to practices with Sweetwater Canyon. She tried to already be practicing a piece when everyone gathered, keeping her concentration locked on the music, shying away from hugs, hurrying through greetings. She didn't want anyone to know.

Of course, Rachel probably knew, even though they never talked about it. But Rachel was different. She'd made mistakes. She'd understood. The others? No way.

The phone rang, and Kat curled into her pillow to drown out the sound. She'd avoided the phone. Her friends wanted to see her, wanted her to come to parties. She had no interest in going. She didn't want to run into Chris.

At school she'd put on a good front, her usual talkative and funny self. But, inside she was shattered. She felt like a broken watch that had been taken apart, and when put back together the quartz movement was missing. She could move her hands and her feet, but the timing was all wrong.

She heard a tap on her door and ignored it.

"Kat? I know you're in there. It's your friend, Lori."

She crawled further into the corner of her bed and watched with horror as the door knob turned and her mother stepped into the room.

"I don't know what's wrong, as you refuse to tell me, but you can't keep ignoring all your friends. Either talk to Lori or talk to me. It's your choice."

She rolled her eyes and thrust her hand toward the phone. When her mother handed it to her she held it against her chest and speared her mother with eyes she hoped would burn her. Finally, she left the room.

She took three deep breaths. Think of something happy. Think of…dancing. No that won't work. Think of…Joan of Arc just before they burned her at the stake. Yes, that's it. Kat stiffened her spine.

"Hello, Lori."

"Kat, thank God. I've been trying to talk to you for weeks. So, why haven't you called? Why haven't you been at the parties? Are you okay?"

"I'm fine. Just haven't had time. You know, with the band and all."

"Yeah, but usually you at least find time to talk."

Kat couldn't find anything to say. How could she get her friend off the phone and still sound cool?

"So, how was the big secret romantic thing with Chris? Gosh, when was that? Like a month ago? I can't believe you haven't said anything yet. Was it that good? I mean soooooooo good you, like, just want to hold it to yourself?"

Kat almost choked on the acid welling in her throat. God! They all knew she was meeting him and now they thought she must be in love or something. Crap. The last thing she needed was everyone trying to keep her and Chris together.

"To tell you the truth, it was a bust. I mean his motorcycle is cool and all that, but Chris ended up to be kind of a jerk. I don't like him anymore."

"You're kidding? Are you sure? But he's so hot. I mean, he's already graduated and everything. I thought you were, like, really high on him. What did he do? I mean that was jerky?"

"Really, it's no big deal. We just…uh…didn't really hit it off that well."

They'd hit all right, she just wished she could've pushed him and his bike over a cliff afterward.

"I can't believe it. I mean, you seem so calm about the whole thing. If I decided some hot guy like Chris was a jerk, I wouldn't be calm. I'd be hoppin' mad."

"Well, it's not worth being upset about…I guess."

Only that was a lie. She'd been crying for the past three weeks. She'd cried so much she didn't think there were any tears left in her body. And even without any more tears left, she felt like she wanted to cry again.

"If you say so." Her friend didn't sound convinced, but Kat really didn't care. She just wanted to get off the phone.

"Yeah, well, I have to go. Thanks for calling, Lori. I'll catch up with you later. Okay?" She hit the disconnect button before Lori could answer and slumped back against the pillows.

God. How was she going to survive without her friends? Without her family? She could never tell them what she feared most. She wrapped her arms around her stomach, pressing it in, as if she could stop anything from growing inside her.

Her period was ten days late and she just knew she was pregnant. That explained why she was tired all the time, her stomach in knots. God, if she had Chris' alien sperm hitting on her eggs she was going to throw up. She'd have to leave. Her life would be over. No one wanted to see a seventeen-year-old prego playing with the band, ruining their squeaky-clean family reputation.

She had to do something. She had to find out for sure, so she could make plans.

She slipped on her tennis shoes and snatched a big sweatshirt out of her drawer. She already felt fat. The sweatshirt would hide any bulge in her tummy. She grabbed her purse and headed to the kitchen.

"Mom, can I borrow the car? Lori and I wanna go into Sandy and hang out at Mountain Mocha for awhile."

"Sure honey." Her mother handed the keys to her with a smile. "I'm really glad you're getting together with your friends again." She brushed a stray hair out of Kat's eyes. "Maybe she'll bring you out of the dumps. Just remember, you have to be back by 2:00 for practice."

"No prob. See ya." Kat dashed out the door, anxious now to carry out her plan. If she really was prego, maybe she just wouldn't come back. Maybe she'd ditch the car at the airport and take off for…well, she'd work that out later. What kind of place wouldn't mind having her, wouldn't judge? Maybe an island, like Bali Hai in that movie, South Pacific. They seemed free and understanding. At least she'd never run into anyone she knew there.

Kat worried all the way down the mountain. When she got to Sandy, she drove straight through heading for Gresham. She wasn't exactly sure what she was doing, but she knew enough to get out of her own town and the town of her high school.

Her stomach flipped as the light changed and she accelerated past the Gresham grocery store. That was still too close. She might run into someone there. She looked to the left and right, judging each store along the road. No, not toward the mall. Too many kids went there.

The farther she drove, the more she was sure she was pregnant. Every time her stomach gurgled she was sure it was sperm swimming around in her body, attacking her eggs—his unwanted, ugly, sticky, condomless grossness had deposited an alien baby in her, or maybe more than one. She felt like Ripley in Alien Resurrection. She shuddered at the thought.

She noticed a Walgreens. The perfect place! None of her friends would ever be caught dead in a boring Walgreens. She made a left across traffic and pulled into the parking lot. Her pulse raced so fast, she could hardly stand it. Maybe she'd get lucky and have a heart attack before anyone found out the truth.

She could already see the headlines. *Seventeen year old girl dies of heart attack. Mother devastated to learn of undisclosed pregnancy.*

A display of balloons and flowers, with greetings like congratulations and get well, assailed her as she walked into the drugstore. Kat marched past the fun stuff, directly to the shelves of medical-type things. She steeled herself, searching for the tests. Passing a shelf of Maxi-Pads, she almost cried. Would she ever need Maxi-Pads again? She prayed that she would, and soon.

Her hands shaking, she stared. She was such a virgin, or had been, until Chris. She saw condoms. God, why couldn't he have at least used one of those? She moved to the next aisle. It looked more promising—ointments for yeast infections, douches, KY jelly. Half the stuff she'd never seen before. Geez, what was wrong with just using soap down there?

She looked behind boxes, stood on her toes to search the top shelf, got to her knees to scour the bottom shelf. No pregnancy tests. Didn't they come in clearly labeled boxes that were easy to see? Soon, she was at the end of the aisle, at back of the store by the pharmacy desk. Ohmigod. This was embarrassing. Could she ask for one? What if it was under lock and key? What if they required ID, or a doctor's note?

"May I help you?" a young woman asked.

"Yes," Kat said. She unclenched her fist and pasted a smile on her face. "I can't seem to find the pregnancy tests. My, uh, husband and I have been trying so long." She crossed her fingers behind her back. "And I've missed my period, and well…we really hope this time it worked." She was sure the pharmacist could easily see through her lie. She hoped she didn't break out in a sweat in the next few minutes.

"Here, let me show you. We have them near the baby display." The woman came around the counter and pointed Kat two aisles down.

Kat followed her, placing one foot in front of the other as if she was walking to the gallows.

"Here they are. There's quite a variety. Did your doctor recommend a particular one in the past?"

"Um…no…I mean I can't remember. It's been awhile since we…I, uh, haven't been to see him yet. I…we…wanted to be sure first. You know, not be disappointed." *Please God, don't strike me down with lightening right now.*

"Just let me know if you have any questions." The pharmacist smiled and patted her shoulder, then finally left Kat alone with the shelves of colorful boxes. Some of them pictured a happy couple holding a baby, others had a kind of artsy line drawing of a woman.

Kat held her smile until the woman was well around the corner, then she sagged against the shelves. There were far too many choices. Geez, can't I get a break? Just three possibilities would have been enough. How should I know which one will be the most accurate?

She examined all the pregnancy tests. They all had names that indicated you could find the answer right away like First Response, Confirm1, Day Seven. Some required you to pee in a bottle and then dip in a stick, others you peed directly on the stick. At the moment, she wasn't sure if she'd ever be able to pee again.

She read the back of each box carefully. They all seemed to indicate similar results and worked for early detection, within the first month. It didn't take long to decide she'd rather just pee on a stick. Less stuff to keep track of and discard. Probably take less pee, too. She took her choice to the counter and pasted her smile on again for the pharmacist who had helped her.

The woman scanned it into the register. "That will be fourteen ninety-five."

Kat handed her a twenty. Money she'd withdrawn from her savings account—money she was supposed to be saving for college. Her palms were so sweaty she was pretty sure they would turn green from the money. The woman put the test kit in a paper bag and handed Kat her change.

"I hope you're pregnant. Have a nice—"

But Kat didn't wait to hear the rest. Tearing out the door, she ran to the car, popped the keys into the ignition, and went in search of a bathroom. A McDonalds or a Carl's Jr would be the best bet. They always had clean restrooms. She remembered a Carl's Jr just up the road. She sped through the next two lights as they turned yellow and then careened into the parking lot. She jumped out of the car and flew into the restaurant heading straight for the bathroom.

She slammed the stall door shut, dropped her jeans, and tore open the packet. Her hands shook as she read through the directions. She had to follow them exactly. Just as she finished peeing on the stick, she brought her hand forward and the stick bumped against her thigh. Startled, she let go and it dropped in the toilet.

"No!" she wailed as if she were dying.

"Kat?"

Omigod, she knew that voice. She choked down the sob, clenching her teeth to make sure no sound came out.

"Kat, are you okay?"

It was Rachel. What was Rachel doing all the way down in Gresham? Maybe if she didn't say anything she would go away. Maybe she would think she was mistaken.

She heard a knock on the stall door. "Kat, what's wrong?"

Oh crap! Oh crap! Could things get any worse? She knew Rachel wouldn't leave without an explanation.

"Just a minute." The strangled words brought a fresh flow of tears as she flushed the toilet. When she exited the stall, she no longer tried to stop the tears streaming down her face. Rachel immediately pulled her into an embrace.

"Oh, Kat."

Kat gulped, feeling the sob overtake her. She cried for what seemed like hours, though it was probably only a few minutes, until she was all cried out. Thank God know one else came into the bathroom.

"Remember when you came to get me on the mountain?"

Rachel nodded, stroking Kat's hair and handing her some tissues for her eyes.

"Something happened to me… with a boy…"

Rachel stiffened. "Did he hurt you?"

She nodded and hot tears poured out of her eyes again. He had hurt her so much. There was so much to say, but all she could whisper between sobs and hiccups was, "I think I'm pregnant, and I just dropped the test down the toilet." Another wail let loose.

Rachel pulled her to her chest once again. "Oh baby. You must be scared to death. Let me help you. I'll get another test and we'll find out for sure. Okay?"

She nodded into Rachel's chest.

Rachel gingerly pushed Kat back. "Wait here just a minute, okay? I have to say goodbye to someone."

Kat nodded, wondering who in the world Rachel would be with at Carl's Jr. She grabbed a tissue and blew her nose, then peeked out the bathroom door and around the corner. She stepped quickly back into the bathroom when she realized who it was. Noel and his daughter. God. Now she'd gone and ruined a date or something, too. Was there no end to the evil she was doing because of one stupid mistake?

"Ready to go?" Rachel asked when she walked back into the bathroom.

"Look, Rache. I'm sorry. I didn't mean to interrupt anything. I can do this myself. Really. I just kind of lost it there for a minute, but now I'm okay. Really, I'm fine."

"No. Don't even think it." Rachel reached for her hand. "Let's get your face cleaned up a bit first. I assume you have a car?"

Kat nodded, as she wiped a wet paper towel over her eyes. She frowned at the image in the mirror. She looked like hell—hair askew, red-rimmed eyes, dark circles, splotchy skin. What next? She'd probably break out in hives from nerves. Just great!

"Give me the keys. I don't think you're in any shape to drive."

Kat reached into her jeans pocket and handed the car key to Rachel, her hand still shaking.

"You ready?"

Kat nodded, and followed Rachel from the bathroom praying that Noel and his daughter weren't still around.

Kat laid her head back on the head rest as Rachel went in the Fred Meyer's. She was glad they didn't go back to Walgreens, and she was glad she didn't have to find the tests again. She didn't think she was capable of reading more boxes. Every time she thought she'd cried herself out, she remembered why she was here and it started all over again. Surely her entire face would be one big zit by tomorrow. This was too much stress—and all because of that jerk off, Chris.

Rachel took a deep breath as she read each of the boxes. She'd never thought she'd be looking for a pregnancy test. In fact, for the six months she'd made a point of avoiding this aisle of the store, along with the baby clothes section, or anything having to do with babies.

She really hurt for Kat. She knew when she'd called her almost a month ago to come get her on the mountain that something awful had happened, but she couldn't get her to talk then. Had she been forced? Did she have to live with the thought of being pregnant and raped? Rachel took a deep breath to stop the cold feeling on her heart. God, she hoped that wasn't the case. And Theresa. How would she ever convince Kat to tell her mother? She would have to, of course.

She shook herself. One step at a time. First, get the test. Second, have her take it, and then we'll deal with the consequences.

Rachel crawled back into the driver's seat and handed Kat another small bag. "Are you okay?"

Kat nodded her head, blowing her nose. "I think so. I still have to take the test though."

"We'll find a place for that. Waiting a few more minutes won't make you any more or less pregnant. Can you tell me what happened?"

"It's pretty obvious isn't it?" Kat stuck her chin out. "I had sex. No big deal."

"Was it your first time?"

She looked into Kat's eyes and saw them mist, but no tears this time. Her eyes were sharp, her jaw tense.

"Did it happen that night you asked me to come get you?" Kat nodded. "Then where was the guy?"

"You mean the jerk?"

"I take it he's not your boyfriend then."

Kat shook her head. Then her lip started to quiver and again she dissolved into tears. The pain came from deep inside. She sounded as if she was being destroyed each time she cried, and soon there would be nothing left. Rachel reached for her hand, wet with tears. Her own insides ached, and she remembered crying like this after Branson. She'd cried for months and months.

"I…liked him. I thought…he was…" Kat wept.

"What happened?"

"He …called… me…Sheila!"

"He didn't even know your name?"

Kat nodded. "He pretended it was on purpose, like the Australian's call all girls Sheila, like it was something special. But later….I knew it wasn't true. Especially, in the end, when…" She cried even harder, unable to finish, but Rachel got the drift. Probably when he'd climaxed he'd yelled out Sheila.

"Oh, Kat, I'm so sorry." She squeezed her hands again. She waited. Was that the worst of it? It was horrible enough, but it sounded like Kat at least went willingly. But then why did the guy leave?

"Did you think you loved him?"

"I'm not sure. It all happened so fast. In the beginning I thought so…"

"In the beginning?"

"I liked the kissing. It felt good, and when we started to round second base…I…" Kat looked up with a question through the tears. "Do you know what second base is?" Rachel nodded. "Well, when he undid my bra I wasn't sure. But somehow he convinced me it was okay, or I wanted it to be okay. I'm not sure."

Kat started to shake again and Rachel wrapped her arms around her. “It’s okay. You were following your feelings. You aren’t a bad person. You were doing something that came naturally.”

“I don’t think it was natural at all. All I wanted was to kiss. That was my first ever kiss even.”

Rachel hugged her tighter. Oh, dear God. First kiss and she ends up possibly pregnant.

Kat pushed away and wrapped her arms around her middle. “After it got started…well…I’m not sure I wanted to.”

Rachel’s heart smashed against her ribs. She struggled to stay very calm. “You’re not sure you wanted to…have sex with him?”

Kat nodded.

“Did he…did he force you?”

“I’m not sure. I thought I said no, but then I think I may have said yes before I said no. It was so confusing. I know for sure I said no before he stuck it inside me. But he didn’t stop even though I was screaming at him to stop.”

Rachel’s pulse accelerated and she dug her nails into her palm to stop herself from hitting something in frustration.

“It started off so romantic, looking at the mountain, watching the sunset, seeing the stars. He held my hand. He hugged me. It was like…the Princess Bride, all sweet and kind. Then he kissed me and it felt…good. I felt all warm, you know all over, and even down, well you know. But then…" Kat let out a choked scream.

"Take it slow. You need to talk it out, but take your time." Rachel tried to make her voice as soft as possible.

"He had me lie down on my back and I saw the…" Kat squeezed her eyes tightly shut. "The hard thing in his pants, and he wanted me to take it out, and I knew I couldn't do it. I knew I had to stop."

"Did you say no then?" Rachel asked, after a long period of silence.

"I think so, but…" Tears rolled out of Kat's tightly closed eyes. "But, I can't remember for positive. Everything was pushing at me, and my mind was foggy, and then it was out and it was ugly and it…" Kat's entire body was shaking as she sobbed. "I'm never having sex again. It's so awful."

Rachel's body and blood were burning. Kat had said no and yet he didn't stop. All Kat wanted was kisses and he had taken everything from her. Rachel wanted to pound him to a bloody pulp.

"It's not like you, Rache. It's not as bad as you."

"Oh, honey. If you didn't want it, it was bad enough. I'm so sorry. That's not the way it's supposed to be. It's supposed to be beautiful, and afterward you're supposed to lie with each other and be happy. Don't judge sex by this experience.

Someday you will truly fall in love and then it won't be all ugly and wrong."

"How did you survive, Rache? How did you get over what happened in Branson?"

Rachel closed her eyes. She hadn't survived. Not yet. Yes, she had physically recovered, but she didn't know if she would ever again have sex with the abandonment she did before. As for love? She'd given up on love, hadn't she? How could she give advice to a seventeen year old, when she didn't have any answers herself?

"You just keep getting up every day and each day it gets easier."

Kat pulled away and swiped her arm across her face. "This is pretty stupid, huh? Crying over a jerk?" She pulled down the visor and looked in the mirror on the back. "God, I'm a mess. Don't tell Mom, okay? I just can't face her about this."

"You'll have to tell her if…"

Kat was silent. Rachel gave her time.

"Yeah. But not yet." Kat looked out the window. "Look. I have to take the test. Let's find another bathroom."

Rachel nodded, then turned the key and drove out of the parking lot.

"If I'm prego, I'll give you the baby. I know you can't have one yourself, and you'd be a wonderful mother."

Rachel forced herself to keep her eyes on the traffic. There was no way she could say anything to that. She prayed Kat wasn't pregnant. Her offer was innocent, but she didn't realize how much pain that would cause both of them.

"It's a good thing I hate Chris anyway, he wouldn't stick around you know. Men don't like kids. Men don't stick around. I have first hand knowledge of that."

Rachel's heart was breaking to think that Kat would be so cynical and so young. "Not all men are that way. Look at Michele and David. They really love each other and they're truly happy. That's what you'll find too, Kat."

"No. They're the exception to the rule. Look at my Dad. He couldn't stand having a kid, so he just left."

"He didn't leave because of you, Kat. I'm sure it had more to do with the relationship with your Mom."

"No. I heard them fighting. I heard him say he didn't want a kid and it was all her fault."

"I'm sorry."

"Yeah. Well. What about your ex? You said he didn't want kids either."

Looking back, she realized that Kavan had always been selfish, both in bed and out of it. After the divorce, he'd admitted to several other affairs during their brief three year marriage. She'd never known—never even suspected. He also told her he'd never wanted children. However, when he re-married only six months after their divorce his wife was already pregnant.

She really didn't want to talk about that lying, cheating, jerk. But she couldn't let Kat become so pessimistic at only seventeen.

"Kavan probably lied about that, too," she finally said. "He was cheating on me through our entire marriage. Who knows what he really wanted? It just wasn't me. But don't judge all men by my experience. I've been a little unlucky. Some of it I brought on myself."

Kat turned toward the window, her voice choked again. "And I brought this on myself, too."

They were both silent as Rachel drove past Sandy and headed up the mountain. She'd made a decision. They would go back to her apartment and Kat would have the privacy and safety she needed. After the test, they would both talk some more and work this out.

For the rest of the trip the only sound in the car was the tires turning on the road. Rachel's heart hurt. Her chest felt like she was wearing a compression bandage around it. Every inch of her body wanted to cry out at the unfairness of it all. But instead she kept silent, kept driving.

At her apartment, Rachel pointed Kat toward the bathroom. Kat looked her in the eye and she could read the fear there. She gave her a quick hug and turned her to the door. "Bring the stick out and we'll find out together."

Kat nodded and handed her the directions. Then she stepped inside, closing the door behind her.

Rachel's hands trembled as she started to read. The printed words swam together with her thoughts. She thought of her own lost chance of motherhood. But mainly, she thought of Kat. She imagined what it had been like, expecting sweet romance and a few kisses, maybe even a movie score in the background, and then being forced into sex. Kat had said no, Rachel was sure of it. No matter what had happened leading up to it, she had meant no and the man surely would have known.

Did she say he was nineteen? Statutory rape. They could get him. For a moment she took strength in the knowledge that he would be caught and charged, stopped from taking advantage of another young women's naiveté.

She shook herself. No. Kat would never agree to that. In some ways, Kat seemed more mature than her peers. She'd been working with the band since she was fourteen and she'd seen more than her share of bad things with Rachel. But, she'd also led a sheltered life. Theresa protected Kat like a bear. Since Kat's father left, Theresa had felt she needed to be five times better than any parent on the planet.

Kat loved movies and tended to see the world through them. She remembered how Kat had used plots in movies to bring Michele and David together when they were fighting. She remembered Kat at Michele's wedding and how she was awestruck by the candlelight, the music, the love, as if the movie script she'd created was finally at the happy ending.

Rachel sighed. That's the way it should have been for Kat's first time—all soft candlelight, dancing, music, and love. She read the instructions for the pregnancy test one more time, her palms damp. She could hear the clock ticking on the end table next to the sofa.

After another minute, the toilet flushed and the bathroom door opened again. Kat stepped in front of her, holding the small, light blue stick between her thumb and forefinger.

"How long does it take?"

Rachel drew in a slow breath. "Three minutes." She punched the numbers into the stove's timer.

"What color do we want?"

"Pink means you're pregnant, white means you're not."

They both stared at the stick. Rachel was sure Kat was holding her breath as much as she was. When the timer buzzed they both jumped.

Kat held the stick out to Rachel and turned the window toward her. "I can't look. Just tell me."

Rachel reached over and gently took hold of Kat's wrist, tilting it so she could see in the small window. "It's white."

CHAPTER TEN

It was the weekend before Spring break and Noel was planting. It wasn't officially Spring yet, but Easter was early this year and he was anxious to get into the garden even if it rained as forecast. The winter had been mild, but he hadn't had a chance to do anything outside since they moved into the house three weeks earlier.

He checked his watch for the second time. Claire's lesson was going to be extra long today because Rachel had invited her to play with Sweetwater Canyon. She wasn't going to play everything they did, but they were planning a concert in Meinig Park this spring and they had two songs Claire could play with them. She was so thrilled with the invitation that she'd talked about it all week. He was so proud of her. Since Rachel had taken Claire under her wing, she'd again become the sweet, happy child he remembered before all the trouble with his ex.

Noel frowned as a stiff breeze picked up and pushed through his lose hair. He was worried about Claire's relationship with Rachel. On the one hand, it had brought her such happiness. On the other hand, he was concerned with that attachment. There were no guarantees in life, and he wasn't at all sure where he and Rachel stood romantically.

He walked over to the wild rhododendron. New buds were already formed. He traced the new green branches with his finger. It would be beautiful when it leafed out next month, and it looked like there would be plenty of blossoms for April and May.

Back at the garage, he fetched his shovel and a box of ferns. While Claire was at her lesson last weekend, he'd scavenged for the ferns in the national forest. Rachel had told him how he could get a free permit and gather up to fifteen plants, including ferns and rhodies, if they were to be used for transplanting at home. He'd found some large specimens. Without Claire underfoot, this was a good time to get them in the ground.

Noel dug holes a foot to eighteen inches deep and twice the diameter of the plant's root systems. He dug the entire hole first and then threw some loose soil back in the bottom to make it easier for the roots to penetrate. With each plant, he took care to place it in the hole with the roots stable in the loose soil. As he replaced the soil around the roots, he first firmed it with his hand, then with his foot, making sure there weren't any air pockets. Patting the soil he thought about how spring could make something old new again, and how it always signified such hope for the full blossoming of life in the summer. It seemed Claire was already blossoming and he couldn't wait to see the full fruit of that soon. He only wished his heart could experience that same kind of transformation this year.

He felt a splash of water on his back and looked up. The rain fell hard and fast. Within a short time the loose soil was mud. Noel kept working. He wanted to get everything in the ground today, before Claire left for a break with his parents. He wanted her to see the new plants and to think about coming home to something growing. He got lost in the roots and the soil and the falling rain, barely noticing his clothes getting drenched.

"Hello."

He looked up. He hadn't heard the Daewoo come up the drive. Rachel leaned out the window and smiled. "I decided to bring Claire home. We ended the rehearsal a little early because Kat had a prom date and she needed to get ready.

Claire crawled over Rachel and leaned out the window. "Hi Daddy. You're all wet."

"Hi sweetheart." Noel stood and looked down at his clothes. He was a mess. His shirt stuck to his skin and his hair was matted. "Why don't you two go on up to the house. Claire, show Rachel where the hot chocolate is and I'll join you in a few minutes."

"Yippee!" Claire clapped her hands and scurried back to the passenger side of the car. "Chocolate. Come on, let's go." Rachel moved the car past him and the rest of the way up the drive.

Rachel chuckled when Claire jumped out of the car and raced to the house, oblivious of the rain. In contrast, she took her time, trying to calm her nerves. Her hands shook and her heart beat a staccato rhythm in her chest. She hadn't seen Noel since the move, except to drop off and pick up Claire. She'd had the distinct impression he was avoiding her and now he'd invited her for hot chocolate. *Don't get your hopes up.*

She ran her fingers through her short hair and turned toward the car window, then jumped back, her eyes wide. His face was staring in, water cascading from his shoulders to the ground. She hadn't heard him tapping.

"You okay?"

She nodded and opened the door as he stepped back. "Sorry. I was in music land," she lied. "Going over a new piece in my head."

Noel grabbed her hand and pulled her across the drive and under the cover of the porch. "Don't want you too wet."

"I won't melt. I'm not the Wicked Witch of the West."

He looked at her with a question.

"You know, Wizard of Oz. Wicked witch, water?"

"Oh." He pulled his t-shirt over his head and wrung the water out of it. "Excuse me, I'm soaked."

She couldn't stop herself from staring. His broad chest looked strong, like he could hold her really tight and take control of pleasuring her for hours and hours. She blinked and cleared her throat. "You, uh, gonna remove those soaked pants too?"

His eyes looked deep into hers and for a moment she thought he would not only take off his pants but take her right there on the porch. Then he laughed, a long, low laugh that was so sexy she thought she could climax right there without him even touching her.

"Don't tempt me," he said, his eyes roving over her in appreciation. "But right now I think Claire's waiting for us to make cocoa."

She turned quickly and stumbled toward the door, almost running into it. He reached in front of her and turned the knob, his hand under her elbow as she stepped across the threshold. "Kitchen?" She pointed in the direction she remembered.

"Yup. I'll be there in a few minutes. I want to take a quick shower to warm up and put something dry on."

She nodded and hurried toward Claire's voice, not daring to look back at him. She didn't want to imagine him in the shower, or even better her *with* him in the shower.

Claire was carefully spooning chocolate into each mug. She looked up at Rachel's entrance. "I've already made it, but you have to make the hot water. Daddy doesn't like me to make the hot water without him. But I already filled the pot."

Rachel bent over the mugs and looked inside. "How many scoops?"

"Three. Daddy showed me before. You use this spoon." Claire pointed to a measuring tablespoon. "And you count one, two, three." She pantomimed putting the chocolate in the mug. "Then you add the hot water. And then you stir it. But not with this spoon, with a different one."

"Sure looks like you've done this before." Rachel lifted the teapot toward the smaller front burner and turned on the stove. "Shouldn't be too long now."

Claire crawled onto a stool on the other side of the island and smiled. Neither of them talked for several minutes as they listened to the water in the pot heat.

"When I grow up, I'm going to play with Sweetwater Canyon all the time."

"Are you sure you want to hang out with all us old folks?"

"You're not all old. Well maybe a little old. But Kat isn't old."

Rachel smiled. “That’s true. She’s only seventeen.” And going on twenty-five it seemed sometimes.

“Oh, seventeen? That is old.” Claire put a finger to her lips and furrowed her brow. “How old do I have to be to play in the band all the time?”

“Probably at least eighteen.”

“But, you just said Kat—”

“Kat is different, because her mother plays in the band and can watch her all the time.”

“Well, you can watch me all the time. You can be my mother.”

Rachel gulped.

“Well, can’t you?”

“Can’t she what?” Noel walked in the room and lifted Claire off the chair in a big hug, swinging her around the room. “Can’t she what? She can do anything she wants.”

“See,” Claire leaned forward and looked at Rachel over Noel’s shoulder. “See, even Daddy thinks you can be my mother.”

“Whoa.” Noel set Claire back on the stool. “I’m not sure what I walked in on here.” He sent an accusing glance to Rachel. “You already have a mother, Claire.”

“I know. Not my real mother. My second mother. You know, like my friend, Megan. Her mommy and daddy got divorced and her daddy married a new mommy. So, Megan has two mommies now. See? Rachel can be my second mommy. Okay?"

Rachel cleared her throat. "Honey, I…uh…don't think that would work out."

"Why not, don't you like me?"

Rachel glanced at Noel then took Claire's face in her hands. "I love you, Claire. But can't we just be good friends instead?"

Claire looked at her, then looked at Noel, and then back to Rachel. "Do you love my daddy, too?"

"I think your Daddy is very nice, but it takes a long time for adults to fall in love. It's different with grownups. You see, I fell in love with you the first day I met you because you're little. But your daddy is grown up and …well…it just takes a long time."

"Is that true, Daddy? Does it take a long time for you, too?"

"That's right, sweetheart. And sometimes grown ups never fall in love." He looked over Claire's head and mouthed a "thank you" to Rachel. "But don't worry. Everyone loves you and that's what's important."

Claire furrowed her brow again, as if making a big decision.

"I can wait for awhile for you to fall in love, 'cause I'm still kind of little. But when I go to second grade, then I'll be big. So, you better hurry up."

The teapot whistled and both Rachel and Noel reached for it at the same time. Rachel laughed nervously and withdrew her hand. “Be my guest.”

Over the next fifteen minutes, it seemed they both did everything in their power to keep Claire’s mind on other things. Rachel asked about first grade and what she was learning. Noel talked about music and school and gardening. Before Rachel noticed the time, Claire announced it was time for dinner and asked if Rachel could stay and eat with them.

The dinner was awkward and exciting. Noel made a wonderful chicken and mushroom casserole, and Rachel helped put together a salad. Claire set the table with great pride and they all chatted like a real family. In fact, Rachel could almost let herself believe they were a family if it weren’t for her past. She remembered his sister’s statement to her, he deserved only the best.

There was no way she should even consider being Claire’s step-mom. Not that she was seriously thinking this relationship had any chance at all. That kind of thinking would only hurt her in the end.

After clearing the dishes and helping to load the dishwasher, Noel asked Claire to say good-night and directed Rachel to the family room to wait while he got Claire ready for bed.

“Really, I’ll just go and you two can have your usual routine. It was nice of you to invite me to dinner, but I should just go.” She kissed Claire on the forehead. "Good night, sweetheart, I'll see you next week."

She turned and Noel grabbed her wrist. "Please. Wait. It will only be fifteen or twenty minutes."

She couldn't deny the urgency in his eyes. Holding her breath, she nodded. She didn't let it out until he and Claire were in the bathroom. What could he possibly want? Maybe he'd decided a little companionship would be nice. After all, they were friends—kind of. Well, she was friends with Claire and Noel was part of the package.

She curled her feet under her and pulled the afghan from the sofa up to her waist. Could she indulge in an affair without any chance of love or marriage? Before the rape, that had been her M.O.—short, pleasurable affairs. No strings, no expectations. But that was then. Now? Everything had changed.

She certainly felt attracted to Noel. She smiled. Big time attracted. But sex? It would be her first time since…and she wasn't sure she was ready. Or was it that she no longer wanted sex without commitment? Well, if that were the case, she'd probably never have sex again. Maybe Noel would be the easiest transition back to that world—even knowing they would never become permanent.

Rachel listened to the bath running, the shared giggles, and then the safe, low voice as Noel read a bedtime story. She closed her eyes and listened, impressed with what a wonderful father Noel was. He seemed completely unselfish, definitely protective, and obviously loyal as he'd stayed with his ex through thick and thin. He seemed everything Kavan was not.

Why couldn't she have met someone like Noel first? Life would have been so different.

"I think she's finally asleep." The door framed Noel's form, the dark of the hallway behind him cast him in shadow. "Can I get you a beer? Wine?"

She raised her hand as if to decline, but changed her mind. "Okay. I'll have a beer then. What do you have?"

"Dark or light?"

"I'm fond of good Scottish ales."

"You're in luck. I have a MacTarnahan's Amber." He disappeared into the kitchen and she heard the twist of the cap and then liquid pouring into the glass. He appeared again and held out the glass to her. It looked like he'd chosen the same thing.

"To Claire." He clinked his glass against hers.

"To Claire," she echoed and sipped, looking over her glass through her eyelashes.

"I suspect you want to talk about this whole mother thing."

He motioned for her to sit. She lowered to the sofa and he did the same, about two feet away from her.

"Yes." He set his glass on the coffee table. "You are a wonderful woman and I can tell you care about Claire, but I'm concerned about her growing attachment to you."

Rachel gulped. She loved Claire and she didn't want her out of her life. But, if he really felt that was best for her, who was she to argue?

"What do you want to do about it?"

"That's the problem. I'm not sure. She loves the fiddle and I think if I changed teachers right now, she'd regress. She's come back to her old self since she's met you and started playing. You've been so good for her."

"She's a special child. I really do love her." Her eyes misted as she allowed herself to imagine having to say good bye.

"I know." His gaze settled on her eyes. His hand reached for hers, then withdrew before they touched. "I wish…"

"What?" she whispered. Did he wish they were a couple? She suddenly realized that was her wish. In fact, she hadn't wanted to be part of a couple this badly since Kavan left.

He raked a hand through is hair and sighed. "I just wish you were the one. It would be so much easier."

She took another sip of her beer, swallowing it slowly.

"Is there something wrong with me?" She tilted her chin in a dare.

"Wrong?" He looked from side to side as if the answer were somewhere else in the room. "No, you're wonderful, it's just that…"

"Are you not attracted to me?" She crossed her legs and sat taller. She knew she wasn't beautiful in the traditional sense, but most men found her attractive. Surely there was something Noel liked about her.

"No, it's not that. It's…oh hell." He took her hands in his. "The truth is I'm very attracted to you. Too much, probably. But, I can't afford to have a … a meaningless affair. I can't do that to Claire."

She flinched. That had been exactly what she'd been thinking about a few minutes earlier. Using him to help herself heal. Of course, she wouldn't have called it meaningless; but she knew it couldn't last either. Or could it?

"And what makes you think that's what I would want?" she whispered, not daring to hope for anything different.

His eyes searched hers, but she looked straight back. She didn't want to make it easy for him. She wanted the truth. She wanted it out in the open. Was there a chance for them?

Dropping her hands, he again raked a hand through his hair. "I'm handling this badly, aren't I?"

She held to her silence.

"Oh hell, I don't know what I mean. It's complicated."

"I can take complicated." She held her breath for a moment. "Believe me, I understand complicated really well."

Her heart beat erratically as she waited for him to move, to say something. Just as she thought she couldn't stand it anymore he sat forward, picked up his beer and finished the rest of the glass in three large gulps, then set it down.

"It's not about you…exactly…it's about Clarissa."

Rachel let out the breath she was holding. She tucked one leg back under her and held her beer in her hand, taking slow, steady sips. "You're still in love with her."

"God no. She killed that forever."

"Then?"

"You already know she's in prison."

Rachel nodded.

"It was drugs. Cocaine. I went through rehab with her several times, but she always relapsed. I didn't want to give up. The truth is I stopped loving her when Claire was only a year old."

Rachel shrunk into the cushion. Was he comparing Rachel to Claire? Rachel never did drugs.

Noel continued. "It had nothing to do with Claire. I loved her. I was ecstatic when Clarissa told me she was pregnant. But Clarissa didn't want her.

She hated being pregnant and she hated the responsibility of a child. For the first time I recognized how selfish Clarissa was. I don't know how I'd missed it before."

Rachel looked over his head toward the picture of Claire, Noel and Clarissa so prominently displayed on the shelf behind him. Clarissa was beautiful. She could see how a woman like that could hold any man. "It was all sex," she said.

Noel followed her eyes to the picture and shook his head. "Maybe that was part of it," he said, turning back to Rachel. "At least in the beginning. But that wasn't the reason. I would do anything for Claire. I knew that taking her away from her mother wasn't right, but I couldn't leave her there either. I never knew when Clarissa would backslide again. So, I tried to support her in rehab. I tried to keep us together as a family."

Rachel saw his jaw clench when he paused. His eyes narrowed and she saw a deep sadness she knew all too well. The type of pain that screamed of failure, of giving up on believing the world would ever be right again. She reached for him but he withdrew, crossing his arms across his chest like a shield. She waited, quiet.

"I was forced to give up when…"

She leaned forward. She could barely hear him.

"When Claire told me about the men Clarissa had over to the house. Men that frightened a four-year-old child." His hand fisted into the cushion, as if he was going to tear the stuffing out of it. "While I was at work, she was selling her body to get money for her next fix."

"Oh, God." Rachel laid her hand on his knee. "I'm so sorry."

How could anyone do that with their own daughter in the house? She couldn't begin to imagine. Her troubles with Kavan, all the men in her life, even Drake paled in comparison to this. Everything she had done was out of her adult decisions, but to expose a child…

Noel let out a big sigh and closed his eyes. "I moved out immediately and took Claire with me. Clarissa was so high she didn't even care. It was only three weeks after I filed the divorce papers that she was picked up for robbery. Three months later she was in prison, and poor Claire didn't know what hit her."

"I'm so sorry, Noel. I can understand that you're not ready for a relationship. I know what it's like to need time. And you have Claire to consider."

He covered her hand with his and looked deep into her eyes.

"You have a calm surface like Mt. Hood, but I can see a deep churning magma underneath waiting to erupt. I think you draw energy from that magma.

Energy for your music, and maybe that is where your love for Claire comes in. But I'm afraid of what else lies in that passionate pool of molten lava. What I don't know about you. What will hurt Claire."

"And hurt you?" she whispered.

He withdrew his hand and fisted it on his thigh. "Maybe."

She sat without moving. He was right. Her pool was so deep, so turbulent underneath, that she'd probably pull him under and drown him. Okay, so they couldn't have that permanent, fall-in-love, kind of relationship. But they could enjoy each other's company. Maybe, they could even pleasure each other—when Claire wasn't around, of course.

She drew in her disappointment and pasted on a come-hither smile. She placed her hand on his chest and walked her fingers to his lips. When they parted slightly, she leaned in with the intent of a quick brush—a hint of seduction, but not a full invitation.

His lips were soft, warm, and sweet, like solid honey ready to melt. She brushed hers across them but couldn't stop there. When he opened a little more she couldn't help herself, she pressed in. Her body melted and her heart and mind followed.

He moaned that helpless, I-must-have-it sound and firmly drew her into an embrace. Now he led and she followed. His mouth building tension and excitement through a symphony of complex rhythms carrying heat from her mouth to her stomach and to her center.

"Noel." She said it on a breath when he shifted her on top of him, and rolled so that she was lying on her side trapped between him and the back of the sofa. She shuddered out another breath as he assaulted her lips again. Then his mouth slid to her neck and she couldn't help but stretch to luxuriate in the sensation and warmth overtaking her. "Oh!" she moaned, as his hands moved under her shirt. The warmth of his caress sending signals directly to her pleasure center.

"Daddy."

Rachel barely registered Claire's call.

"Daddy, I want a glass of water."

Noel groaned and rolled off the couch. "God, what am I doing. I'm sorry, Rachel, I …"

He didn't finish the sentence. Instead he turned and walked down the hall to Claire's bedroom. She heard a mumble of soothing words. She couldn't quite make out what they were. Rachel sighed at the loss of his warmth. She sat up and rearranged her clothing. She smiled. Evidently, she could have sex without a commitment. She sure wasn't going to stop him a minute ago, and she wasn't at all scared. Worked up. Excited. Wet for him. But not scared. Her grin expanded until her cheeks hurt.

Noel came back into the living room and sat near her on the sofa. "I'm sorry, Rachel, I shouldn't have let that go so far. This is exactly why we can't spend too much time together."

"Did you see me complaining?" she asked.

His lips curved up in a combination of non-repentant rake and wistful regret. "I can't just sleep with you. I want to—oh, God, I want to—but I can't do that to you, knowing you'll be hurt in the end. I have a lot of need stored up and it'd be so easy to let it loose with you. But that would be all it is. I don't have anything else to give."

"I'm a big girl, Noel. Don't you think I can make my own choice here? What if I'm willing to just be a friend and a lover, without the extra complications?"

Her heart beat double-time. She wanted more. Oh, God forgive her, she wanted the whole package even if she didn't deserve it. But, for now, she would take whatever he was willing to give.

"Rachel, I can't. For me it's all or nothing. With Claire, I have to think that way." She shook her head, unwilling to accept defeat. Before she could say anything, he put a finger to her mouth. "Suffice it to say that if you and I … had sex … it would be a relationship."

She closed her eyes and took two deep breaths. No! She would convince him otherwise. She'd always been able to convince men to have a fling. She squared her shoulders and her breathing quickened. She wasn't going to walk out of here in defeat, not when it was obvious he wanted her.

She stood in front of him, her teeth clenched. "What is it you were offering just a moment ago? Sex or love?" She leaned toward him, making sure he could see down the scoop neck of her shirt.

He smiled and sat back, wresting his eyes from the view. "Come on, Rachel. You know we both got carried away. Don't make this a wrestling match neither one of us can feel good about."

"If Claire hadn't called, would you have gone all the way? Would you still be inside me now?"

He stared at her, then nodded, but he didn't move even an inch toward her.

She straddled him on the sofa, her knees trapping his legs, her hands on each side of his shoulders. She leaned into him, her breasts grazing his mouth, and whispered into his ear with a sultry voice. "I want you. You want me. What's wrong with giving each other pleasure? What's wrong with helping each other forget the complications in our lives?" She ran her tongue along the inner flesh of his ear. He groaned. She nuzzled his neck and rained it with kisses.

"I can wait for another night, if you want. I can even wait until you get a babysitter for Claire and we meet somewhere else." She lowered to his lap and moved against him, feeling the hardness build. "But there's no reason for two adults who like each other not to help each other in this way. If it grows to something more, great. If not, we both entered into it willingly." She looked into his eyes and could see the desire warring with something else.

He put his hands firmly at her waist and held her still. He brushed a kiss across her lips. "God, you drive me crazy." He took a deep breath, then lifted her off him and stood, placing her feet safely on the ground a good foot away from him. "Rachel, it's not you. It's me. I just…can't. I need…"

The words seemed to catch in his throat. He opened his mouth to complete the sentence, but he couldn't. She saw him clamp down on the words and the thoughts. He stood, silent. Rachel felt that silence deep in her soul. How often had she wished for a good man? A man who could love her forever, and for a child, a daughter? Now, he was staring her right in the face and she couldn't reach him. All the running she'd done. All that time trying to prove to herself that she was woman enough for any man.

She looked down. What did she think she was doing, coming on to him so strong? That was the exact wrong approach. That was her old M.O. wasn't it? Exchange sex for love. Deep inside, she knew she could never hold on to love, so sex was what had kept her together.

Now that she'd found the right man, she wasn't right for him. She never would be. In fact, if he knew about all that proving she'd done in her past, it would drive him even further away from her.

He reached for her hand. "I'm sorry."

Her heart pounded. She felt his pain through her skin, like the drone of bagpipes at a funeral, the funeral of his soul. And it hurt so much she couldn't move. She couldn't find any words of comfort for either of them. She knew what it was like to feel completely abandoned, to wonder if it was something you did wrong. Drake had taught her that lesson when he raped her and left her to die. What Noel's wife did was like that—a rape of his soul, and with Rachel he feared for his daughter's soul.

Noel let go of her hand and her heart dropped. She wanted him. She wanted Claire and she didn't know how she could make it right.

She stared at Noel, begging him to say something. Do something. He looked away, no longer able to meet her eyes.

"This isn't over," she said. "I'm not Clarissa. I admit I have my problems, but I'm not selfish and I don't offer myself lightly. Well at least not anymore." She walked to the kitchen, her spine straight, and slung her purse over her shoulder. She returned to stand only a few inches from him. "I love Claire. I've loved her since the moment I first saw her. I would never hurt her." She bent forward and brushed her lips on his cheek. "Or you."

She turned and let herself out the door.

CHAPTER ELEVEN

Rachel awoke with a sad melody in her head. It had been three days since that evening with Noel and she'd only left her apartment for rehearsals—rehearsals that had lacked energy or harmony on her part. Though her bandmates tried to help, tried to get her to open up, she couldn't. How could she talk about feelings that seemed so ludicrous even she couldn't believe them? How could she admit she'd fallen in love with a man she hardly knew, a man who wanted her but refused her?

She walked to her fiddle, tightened the bow, and without tuning began to play *Caledonia* as the lyrics echoed silently in her head and transported her home to Dunoon. *I don't know if you can see / the changes that have come over me./ In these last few days I've been afraid/ that I might drift away.* She played it through several times, with each rendition a little stronger and each lyric reinforcing her roots. It was a song of Scotland, of struggling to remember the old stories and the old ways. A song that exhorted her to share the tunes and lyrics and thus return her to her home.

After several minutes, she stopped and tuned her fiddle. Feeling stronger she launched into the *Uist Tramping Song* of the Outer Hebrides. *With the hills of home before us / And the purple of the heather,/ Let us sing in happy chorus, / Come along. Come along.*

Soon a reel, then a jig bubbled up from her heart and into her fingers. Before she knew it her feet were dancing as fast as her bouncing bow, pushing her from one melody to the next. After an hour of playing and dancing she knew what she had to do. It was Spring break, and it was time for things to bloom. She wasn't giving up and she wouldn't let him give up either. For the first time since Sweetwater Canyon left Branson last October, she would ask for their help. She would depend on her bandmates to come through for her.

With a broad smile she dialed Sarah, then Theresa, and finally Michele to set the plan in motion.

* * * * *

Noel woke at ten with a headache. His head throbbed with every heartbeat. But that was nothing compared to the way the rest of his body felt. His tongue was clearly too large for his mouth and saliva production seemed to have shut down, leaving his teeth feeling furry. He sat up and put his feet on the carpet, his head hanging low, and groaned. His bladder was screaming for release but he wasn't sure he could stand. He took a deep breath and pushed himself off the bed and stumbled toward the bath. Clutching the door frame, he steadied himself, and then stepped again to the toilet.

Five minutes under a hot shower made him feel a little more human. He wanted to stay until the water turned cold again but he desperately needed rehydration, and gulping down hot water in the shower was not an inviting thought.

Noel toweled dry and wrapped it around his waist as he moved cautiously to the sink to brush the fur off his teeth and tongue. Finally, feeling a little more human he moved toward the kitchen. He leaned against the refrigerator before opening it. Gasping, he pressed a hand to one temple and closed his eyes on a wave of nausea. He should know better. He hadn't been this hung over for more than ten years. He hadn't even gotten drunk when he divorced Clarissa.

The nausea temporarily under control, he opened the fridge. His hand grasped the orange juice then released it. Acid. Not wise. Instead he pulled out the milk and poured himself a tall glass and gulped it down. Food. He couldn't handle cooking, and nothing seemed appealing at the moment. He settled on putting two pieces of bread in the toaster. He'd start small and see if he could keep it down, then work up to something more substantial by noon if he could get the loud noises in his head to stop by then.

Noel hadn't seen Rachel for two weeks and two days, not that he was counting. Four days ago, Noel had come home to an empty house after ferrying Claire to Yachats the day before. He could have stayed with his parents and enjoyed the week with them, but Claire needed some time to be the center of attention and he needed some time alone. Or at least he'd thought that was what he needed. He kept himself busy in the yard during the day, planting and cutting. He'd made two trips up the mountain for more ferns and rhodies. He worked hard, kept in constant motion, hoping to be so tired he would just fall into bed. But as darkness closed around him, he wasn't able to sleep.

He missed having Claire's energy and her constant questions. He missed reading to her as she went to sleep each night, continuing the story of unicorns and magic they were immersed in this month. He realized this was the first time they'd been separated for more than one night since he'd left his ex two years ago.

The past week had been filled with sleepness nights. Racked with sexual dreams of Rachel, nightmares of his ex-wife, and Claire somehow caught in the middle of everything kept him awake, dreading falling to sleep. For the last two nights, he found himself working on a poem—something he hadn't done for more than a year.

He wasn't sure why he needed to write it, but it captured something about Rachel…something he couldn't quite get from his heart to his head. Each night he'd fallen asleep on the sofa, pen and tablet in hand, as dawn lit the sky.

Last night it all came to a head, when he found himself in the kitchen staring at a bottle of whiskey. When it was time to make dinner he couldn't decide what to cook for only one person, and ended up starting with a drink instead. He didn't remember ever having dinner. He did remember finishing the bottle and wishing he had another one to start. Thank God there wasn't any more in the house.

Noel looked at the clock when he heard the knock on the door. Two. He wasn't expecting anyone. His bare feet slapped the tiles at the entry and he peered through the peep hole. Crap. Rachel. Resigned, he opened the door.

"Hi. I know I should have called but I wasn't sure you'd invite me over, so I decided to take a chance and make you miserable face to face instead." Her smile was tentative. He felt a stab of guilt as he realized he had been the one to make her feel unsure.

"Good to see you." He was surprised, but he actually meant it. "Come in." He gestured toward the kitchen but she didn't move, her eyes fixed on his bare chest and his open shirt. "I'm…uh…being pretty lazy today. Spring Break."

She tore her gaze away and moved past him. "Yeah. It's good to relax."

He hurried ahead of her to the family room, and picked up the shot glass and the empty bottle from the coffee table. He whisked the glass into the dishwasher and shoveled the bottle into the recycling bin.

Rachel laughed. "Good night, huh?"

"Bad morning."

"I'll bet." Her eyes scanned the kitchen and living room. It was a mess but he at least he hadn't turned the place upside down. Then her eyes returned to him as she looked at him from head to toe and almost purred. "You look okay now, though."

"Yeah, if you consider a two-day-old beard, no shower, and a house that smells like a college fraternity, everything's just fine." Noel stood at the sink. "Can I get you something? Coffee? Juice?"

"Coffee would be great. Black." She leaned against the island counter.

He felt her nearness all through his body, like an electric current. He took down mugs from the cupboard. Everything seemed casual, but every muscle in his body was tense, reaching toward her. He filled both mugs with coffee. He added sugar to his and stirred. She reached for her mug and slid it across the counter, her eyes eating his every move. When she lifted the mug to her lips without dropping her gaze, he was ready to climb across the island to have her. Then, as she tipped the mug to sip, her lashes dropped and he felt the pit of his stomach drop at the same time. What the hell was he going to do about this?

He tore his eyes from her and drank deeply from his mug, scalding his tongue and throat. "Shit!" He slammed the mug back to the counter.

Rachel moved quickly to his side, her fingers caressed his jaw and then his throat. "Hot. Have to be careful."

A bolt of electricity slammed from his lips to his groin.

"Rachel," he said, struggling not to reach for her.

"I couldn't help myself." She looked up, her eyes wide and accepting.

"Thank you."

She turned her face into his chest and he was content to just hold her. Nothing more. No expectations.

Then everything changed.

Noel knew the precise moment when the softness became something else. He made a half-hearted effort to extract himself, but her cheek against his bare chest felt good. When he felt her mouth open to place one soft kiss against his collarbone, his growing hardness went rigid. She must have felt it, too. When she raised her face to his, her lips inviting and her eyes begging, nothing on earth could have prevented him from covering her mouth with his.

He surged into her mouth as the hunger flared within him. His thirst for her made him drink long and deep. He backed her against the counter and he lifted her to sit on top of it so he could feel her everywhere. He lifted her t-shirt out of her jeans and over her head. Within seconds he had removed her bra and was feasting on her breasts. She groaned and arched toward him.

When he moved back up her neck, she wrapped her legs around him in a vise as her hands worked his shirt off his shoulders. Filled with a need to have as much of her as possible, he alternated between caresses along her sides, kisses to her neck and lips, and licks to make her nipples stand and beg for more. She murmured directions, guiding him to those things that pleasured her. Arching toward him when he took her breasts full in his mouth and suckled, her hands slaked across his bare back, followed by nails bringing him to a frenzy. When he came up for air, her nimble fingers had unzipped his jeans and she was shimmying out of her own. He helped by stepping out of his and pulling hers away as she raised her hips toward him. Her smell drove him wild and he raised her hips to his mouth, diving into her center and inhaling deeply before drinking her essence.

He felt the orgasm slam into her, but he kept eating as if he were a starving man.

"Please, Noel. Take me now."

He raised his face and moved his hips to her, his cock begging to be inside her. She reached down to stroke him, at the same time opening herself wide, guiding him to take her.

"Now." She repeated. Her hips gyrating. "I want you inside me."

He plunged and pumped.

She wrapped her legs around his back an moved against him. "Yes. Yes. More. I don't care if it's only once, or forever. I want you. More. More."

He froze. "Oh, my God." He gulped air as if he had no oxygen. "Oh, my God." But he couldn't stop. She felt so good. He heard her scream his name when she came and he finished only moments later and immediately withdrew. God, what had he just done? No planning, no condom. Shit! Shit! Shit!

Rachel pushed herself up and reached for him, but he stepped away.

"What's wrong?"

Noel bent and picked up her shirt and her pants and flung them at her. "Get dressed." He turned away and found his own clothes, and put them on as quickly as possible, making sure he buttoned his shirt.

Christ, he'd just taken a woman in the most hedonistic fashion ever—a woman who he barely knew. After all he'd promised himself. After all he'd said to her two weeks ago, he'd taken her right there on the kitchen counter without any thought to the consequences.

He shoved both hands through his hair and turned back. She was still sitting on the counter, naked, clutching the clothes to her breast, tears streaming down her face. Shit! What kind of man was he? He walked back to her and put his arms around her.

"I'm sorry, Rachel. I shouldn't have gone so far."

"What…do…you…mean," she gasped between sobs. "I wanted it as much as you. Am I so offensive to you that you can't take advantage of mutual pleasure?"

Yes, that was exactly it. He couldn't take advantage. He released her and stepped back again. He moistened a washcloth and handed it to her. "I'm sorry. Please, get dressed. Then we'll talk."

He watched her awkwardly lower herself from the counter. He turned and headed to the bathroom. He needed a moment. If he watched anymore he'd probably jump her again.

When he came back she was fully dressed and standing by the open front door, her posture unyielding. She didn't look at him. Instead she stared straight ahead.

"I didn't come here for this."

"I know. It's just that—"

"Let me finish." She paused and he didn't say anymore. She continued to look straight ahead. "I didn't come here with the thought of having sex, especially after our talk…before. I wanted to give you time. But I can't say I regretted it when we started. I'm sorry that you don't feel the same way."

"I didn't—"

"Please, just let me finish."

She turned then and stared straight into his eyes. He could see the streaks tears had left on her cheek, even though her eyes were dry now. He was sure she grew two more inches as her spine stiffened further.

"I came here to offer a suggestion, so we could get to know each other during the break. And maybe take a chance that you would come to at least like me…I mean more than for a teacher for Claire."

"I do like you, I—"

She clenched both fists. "Don't patronize me. I'm not a child that you have to soothe. It's obvious how you feel. It couldn't be any more obvious after what just happened." She nodded toward the kitchen.

He reached for her hand, but she stepped away.

"Rachel. It is *not* obvious to *me* how I feel, so how could it be to you? Please, let's take a moment. Take a couple of breaths. We can sort this out."

"I can't." She looked down to the floor again. "I came here to tell you Sweetwater Canyon would be touring in Washington, Idaho, and Oregon this week. I thought you might come with us. No expectations, just give us a chance to get to know each other."

"I couldn't do that."

"Yeah, well I can see that now."

"Not for the reason you think." The real reason was because he knew he couldn't keep his hands off her. And that wouldn't be fair. He didn't completely understand how she got sex and love mixed up, but he knew she did and he wasn't willing to take the chance that whatever she thought she felt for him would never turn into love.

"I have to go." She stepped off the porch and headed toward her car.

"Rachel, wait." She turned back. "Please. Just a minute. I gave you a chance to talk, now you have to give me a minute." He ran into the house and searched through the papers on his desk. Where was it? It had been written when he was half drunk, but maybe it could explain. Maybe it could be a start. He found it in the trash, crumpled in a ball. Shit. Would she take it as one more rejection? What did he have to lose?

He unfolded it, his hand tried to flatten it against the desk, but the wrinkles wouldn't ever come out again. He hurried back outside and handed it to her.

"What's this?"

"Something I wrote over the last couple of nights. It's not very good, but maybe it will help you understand. Maybe it's a start."

She held it up and lowered her eyes to read.

He covered her hand and pushed it toward her chest. "No. Not now. I don't think I could explain now if you asked. Read it while you're on the road. Then if you want…when you get back…maybe we can get together."

"You mean…you and me…even after what just happened?"

"I don't know. I have to think about it too." He brushed his lips across her forehead and lingered just a breath from her lips. He wanted to taste her again. To pull her to him and finish what they'd started—finish in a proper, loving way. "Maybe," he whispered. "Maybe when you get back." Then he backed away from the only woman who had made him come alive in the past several years.

CHAPTER TWELVE

Sweetwater Canyon gathered on stage as the first act of a double billing in Pocatello, Idaho. This was one of the largest venues they'd booked this year. It was sold out with over five hundred people in the audience. Rachel's pulse raced as they readied for their final concert of this whirlwind week. She was anxious to get home, but even more anxious for this last concert to be a great success.

She checked her fiddle one more time as she scanned her bandmates. Kat sat on a stool to her right, her left leg dangling and tapping against the lower rung as she ran scales on her accordion. Michele, definitely showing her pregnancy, stood to Rachel's left fingering a bass run for one of the jigs. Rachel caught her eye and winked. Theresa on the far right was ready with her banjo, the mandolin on a stand nearby. She was tapping a foot in front of her chair, as if counting time. Center stage was Sarah with her dreadnought guitar. She was the only one standing completely still. Her eyes closed with a serenity about her that Rachel would never understand.

The stage manager tapped Theresa on the shoulder and she turned to signal them all with a thumbs up. Kat shouted "Break a Leg," and all five of them stepped forward to their microphones. Rachel felt the energy rise from the audience and consume her as the curtains opened and the stage lights came up.

They began *a capella*, in five-part harmony, with the first verse of Townes Van Zandt's song, *If I Needed You*. Their voice blend was so sweetly potent tonight that Rachel fought a stray tear threatening to fall as she imbued each word with thoughts of Noel. When it came time to take up her fiddle and blend with the other instruments, she attacked it with abandon.

They moved through the play list, taking the audience with them as they molded their emotion like a warm, soft wax, malleable to their every whim. The songs ranged from heartwarming, to pensive, to funny, to rollicking. Even the stage patter and laughter emphasized the kinship of the band and that in turn infected the audience.

Home Grown Tomatoes brought out the spunk of each member, and the audience clapped along showing their appreciation. Their cover of Lyle Lovett's *If I Had a Boat* had audience members singing lustily on the chorus. Chris Kokesh's *As Real as a Dream* again brought tears to Rachel's eyes as she thought of both Claire and Noel. *I brought you the winged horse/ gave you the treasure / showed you the fairy tree / I pointed out dragons / showed you our kingdom / thought you could share it all with me*. At the end of their fifty-minute set, they returned to signing *a cappella* with a special rendition of Rory Block's *Heather's Song*. It felt as if the audience held their collective breath, not wanting to disturb the profound grace of that moment.

When the curtain closed, the applause was deafening and the women all held hands as it opened again for an encore—this time an original composition by Michele, *Breaking the Bonds*. Though it was about women overcoming abuse, Rachel's voice was particularly strong on the final lines of the chorus: I will be what I am / I will make my own way / I am breaking the bonds.

* * * * *

The next morning Annabelle, the affectionate name given to their motor home, lumbered down I-84 toward home. It would be another ten hours of driving, but with each of them taking turns at the wheel, they would make it without stopping again to spend the night. Michele had the first shift, and Kat was keeping her company in the front. Theresa and Sarah were at opposite ends of the sofa reading—Sarah had a romance by Kristine Grayson and Theresa was immersed in a thriller by Dean

Edwards—while Rachel cleaned up the dishes from breakfast.

As she stacked the final plates in the drainer, Sarah closed her book with a sigh. "She's such a good writer, funny and arresting. Best of all, the romance is sweet. Not all those tongues and body parts."

Rachel chuckled. "Only you would be turned off by tongues. The quintessential virgin."

"I am not a virgin, and you know it."

"You might as well be. You do know if you go more than seven years without sex you become a virgin again, don't you?"

Sarah stuck out her tongue.

"Better watch out. You leave that out and someone might kiss it."

"Just because you aren't getting any is no reason to take your frustration out on the rest of us."

"Who says I'm not getting any?"

"We all do," the other four women said in chorus, then they broke out in giggles.

Rachel couldn't help but join them. "Yeah, your right. Though I was close before we left."

"What's up with that anyway?" Theresa stuck a bookmark in her novel and laid it on the table. "I thought the plan was for Noel to join us this week."

"That didn't exactly work out."

"Obviously." Kat rolled her eyes.

They all looked at Rachel and waited. She pushed herself into the chair across from the sofa and took a deep breath. "When I went over to talk to him, things got kind of out of hand and …well…the timing just wasn't all that great."

Sarah leaned forward, her arms on the table between them. "So, is it so out of hand you aren't going to ever date? Or is it the kiss and makeup later kind of out of hand?"

"I'm not sure." Rachel furrowed her brow. "I think there's hope, but we're both pretty screwed up."

"We know you're screwed up," Kat teased as she turned her seat toward the back of motor home to listen. "But he struck me as pretty cool."

Rachel wrestled with how much to tell. She didn't want to betray his confidence, but she really needed some advice too. She decided to go with what was probably public record if anyone cared to look.

"His wife, I mean ex-wife, was hooked on coke and she actually prostituted herself to get money."

"Holy Crap!"

"Watch your language, Kat," Theresa warned.

"Geez, Mom. Can you imagine? Did that little girl see this?"

"It's hard to know. Noel said the way he found out was when Claire complained about the men coming over while he was at work. She was pretty scared of them."

"That poor child." Sarah shuddered and wrapped her arms across her chest.

"So, he's pretty reticent to have a fling. He has this idea of somehow knowing when he's met the perfect woman, and just not having sex until that happens.

"So, what's the problem? You are the perfect woman," Michele offered.

"Hardly," Rachel said. "I'm too much like his ex."

"What do you mean?" Sarah said. "You are a wonderful person, and the way you treat his little girl you'd think she was your own daughter."

Now that she was really into it, she wasn't sure how much more to tell. Did she admit her fears? How her past would kill any future with someone as wonderful as Noel? She looked at Theresa and then Sarah, then delved in.

"The problem is, he doesn't really know much about me. If he did he'd run."

"Why? He doesn't like the life of a musician?" Kat asked.

Rachel paused for a moment. Could she share her fears in front of Kat? Not that Kat wasn't aware of her past, it was just never really discussed by any of the band members. She looked at Kat, trusting her, urging her on. She might as well. After all, Kat had entrusted her with the biggest secret of her life to date.

"He doesn't know I used to sleep around when we were on the road."

"Ah shit!"

"Kat!" Theresa speared her with a look. "Where do you pick up this stuff?"

"Come on, Mom. This is serious trouble here."

"Sorry, Theresa. I'm probably to blame for saying worse within her hearing."

"Forget it. So, what does he know?"

Rachel wriggled in her chair. "Suffice it to say he probably figures I've slept with two or three guys since my divorce. The truth is it's never come up. I really didn't think there was a chance of us ever…having a relationship. Sex maybe, but not a relationship."

"Holy…" Kat clamped her mouth shut before she could let loose with another swear word and Rachel laughed as Theresa looked over with another warning.

"Oh, Rachel," Sarah patted her arm across the table. "I knew one day it would catch up with you. Now you're in love and he doesn't want you."

"Who said I'm in love?"

"No one has to say it, we can all see it in your eyes when you talk about him," Sarah said.

"I can't be in love. I hardly know him."

Sarah looked at her with that open smile and those trusting eyes, and it undid her. She wondered how any twenty-nine year old could still be practically a virgin with a look like that.

"Okay, maybe I'm a little in love."

"Duh. You can't be a little in love. Even I know that." Kat rolled her eyes again.

"I know I love Claire for sure. I'm just not sure if I really love Noel, or if I just love the idea of Noel and Claire and me as a family."

"Do you have the hots for him?" Kat asked.

Rachel laughed. "Of course. Let's face it, when have you known me not to have the hots for any good-looking guy."

"There's a point." Michele tossed over her shoulder from the driver's seat.

"Yeah, but I mean the hot hots," Kat insisted. "The kind that when he starts to do stuff to you, you really want it to continue. The kind where you never even consider saying no."

Theresa turned, her eyes wide. "Kat, you talk like you know about this? Is there something you haven't told me?"

Kat spun her chair back to the front and started humming.

"Don't turn away from me. Kat?"

Rachel reached across the table and grabbed Theresa's hand and shook her head.

Theresa's lips began to quiver and she held Rachel's eyes in hers. She mouthed a silent plea "No." Rachel didn't nod or deny it, she just held tight. It was for Kat to say, but she wouldn't lie to Theresa either. Theresa withdrew her hand and swiped at her eyes.

Rachel swallowed the lump in her throat. "I guess I am in love with him after all, but he is definitely *not* in love with me."

Kat turned back, her eyes searching between Theresa and Rachel. Then she looked down to her feet. "How do you know? How do you know when someone's in love with you for real?"

"I'm not the best person to ask. Look at my track record. One divorce and a whole string of guys over the last four and a half years."

Michele glanced toward Rachel and then set her eyes back on the road. "If Noel is anything like David, he is probably fighting it too. You remember all that back and forth David and I did on our tour last summer? I didn't know he really loved me until the last minute."

"I remember." Kat's eyes took on a dreamy quality. "You were singing that song at the end of the concert and David joined you. It was just like when Captain Von Trapp and Maria were reunited and they both sing *Something Good.*

"So, what are you going to do about it?" Sarah's voice was soft and understanding.

"I'm thinking of taking him to see Brigadoon at the Schnitz."

"The Schnitzer Concert Hall," Kat screamed like it was a revelation. "That's purrrfect! Your Scottish, he's American. How? When? Can I come too?"

Rachel laughed and pushed a stray piece of Kat's hair behind an ear. "I don't think you would help with the romance part."

"I'd always heard the Scots hated that play because it's so stereotypical of Scotland." Sarah said.

Rachel laughed. "I guess some hate it, but truth be told it's brought lots of tourist dollars. Perhaps when the movie was released in the late 40's there were more people upset by it. World War II had just ended and the European continent had been devastated. Much of Scotland was spared, but the mood was to become a center for culture, the arts, and to prove to the world how modern she was. There weren't many who wanted to be thought of as kilt-wearin' bagpipe-playin' sheep-herders. But times have changed, and now many of the young people embrace the old ways. And we still make plenty of money on it."

"When is the run?" Theresa asked.

"It opened at the Schnitz Friday, and I have tickets for the second matinee on Sunday."

"That's tomorrow!" Kat said.

"Yeah. I bought the tickets before we had our falling out. Three. I think Claire would like it too. I figure what can I lose? If he says no, I'll take Kat." She smiled at Kat. "And someone else."

"Me, me, me," the other women shouted.

Kat giggled. "I won't be such a good kisser, but if he's stupid enough to say no, I promise to keep you laughing."

"Then it's a deal."

* * *

It was almost midnight when Rachel finally crawled into her own bed. She plumped the pillows behind her and drew out the folded piece of paper marking the last entry in her diary. She held the single sheet of paper to her breast.

Sweetwater Canyon had been on the road for four days, and Rachel had read Noel's poem several times each day and each night before she went to sleep. It was so sad and yet so beautiful. She still wasn't sure if his writing had any hope for the two of them. It was also frightening how well he'd captured her part in this melancholy duet they seemed to be playing. She unfolded the paper again and read it aloud, even though she could probably recite it by heart now. It was titled "Rachel's Walk."

I walked in dark silence, transparent.
You bent low from the sky to my side,
while all the stars looked on.
We wandered together the solemn night,
exchanging your woe for mine.
A touch not felt, a breath not full,
our lives not quite intertwined.

Fingers of dawn approached, toyed with me,
but the night clutched you still in darkness,
conscripting you aloft.
I stood on the rising ground and watched you pass,
lost in the anguished black of night.
A sad orb waning, the cloud encircling.
My soul reached, but you were gone.

CHAPTER THIRTEEN

"Hello, this is the…the Kershaw residence."

Rachel smiled at the voice trying to sound so grown up.

"Hi, Claire. This is Rachel."

"Really? Hi! I was at grandma and grandpa's and we had a picnic, and we went fishing, and we found a starfish, and I got to watch movies, and Daddy came to get me yesterday, and he was really happy to see me, and he brought me home and gave me a big ice cream cone."

"Wow. Sounds like you had a big week."

"Uh huh." There was a pause as Rachel heard Noel in the background asking who it was. She wished she could see his response when Claire told him. "Do you want to talk to my Daddy?"

"Well, I don't know, I'm having fun talking to you."

Claire giggled. "When are you coming over? I want to show you my sand dollars. Do you know they aren't really made out of sand? They have a star on them. They are kind of like a shell, but not. I got to bring them home. Daddy wrapped them up in Kleenex and then he made a special place for them on the table so everybody could see."

"I'd like to see that." Rachel could picture Claire dancing around the room, so proud of all her special finds.

"So are you going to come over now?"

"I'm not sure yet. It depends on my schedule. Let me talk to your Daddy and he can help me decide."

"Okay." Rachel heard the phone drop, then a shout. "She wants to talk to you now, Daddy. Tell her when she can come see all my stuff. Okay?"

She heard his intake of breath before he spoke. "How was the trip?"

"It was better than we could have hoped. We had sell outs at each place, and the last one was like a dream come true. We played to a packed house, and when the headliner finished their set, they asked us to play a couple encores with them."

"I wish I could have seen that."

Rachel blinked. He sounded sincere. Had he had a chance to think while she was gone?

"I have a proposition."

Noel laughed. "I'll bet."

"Not that kind. This one involves both you and Claire."

"I'm listening."

"I have three tickets to Brigadoon for the four o'clock show. It's one of my favorite Broadway musicals and it opened Friday, downtown. Do you think…"

Suddenly, she was unsure. She felt like her heart was beating so loudly it would deafen him on the other end. She had really stepped into the abyss this time. What was she thinking? Why was she so obtuse sometimes? Oh God. Would he think she was using Claire to get to him? Was she?

"That's a great idea." She caught her breath. Did he just agree to go? "Claire will love it, and I have a soft spot for the musical myself."

"Really? I mean…I didn't mean—"

"Rachel?"

She stopped stuttering. "Yes."

"Things have changed. I've had some time to think, to put things together."

"Yes?" Her heart sped up and she held her breath, hope balancing on the exhale.

"This is a great start," he said.

She raised her eyes to the heavens in a silent prayer of thanksgiving.

* * * * *

When she arrived at his house later, Claire greeted her at the door dressed in a sweet, gingham kilt-style pinafore that Noel said she insisted on wearing. A bright, white long-sleeved shirt with a peter pan collar highlighted the blue and grey colors of the gingham pattern. She proudly pointed to her shiny black patent leather shoes. "See, I'm Scottish now, too."

Noel greeted Rachel with a quick brush of her lips. His arm around her waist, he shepherded Claire and her to his car. "Hope it's all right if I drive. My car is a little larger." Rachel nodded, unable to speak as all her nerve endings were interweaving three pipe jigs in double time.

The musical was fun, charming, and romantic. Rachel cried at the near loss of true love when Brigadoon disappeared and Noel squeezed her hand and passed her a hankie. When Fiona and Tommy reunited, tears escaped again as she rejoiced in their love and Claire clapped with glee.

They all sang parts from the musical on the way home, with Noel goading Rachel into singing all the amusing lyrics from Meg the milkmaid's song, *My Mother's Wedding Day*. Afterward they stopped at the Elusive Trout, a Sandy pub, for dinner. They each enjoyed selecting a gourmet hamburger and homemade soup. Noel and Rachel haggled over the large selection of craft beers, determining what would be the best choice for each hamburger.

When they got back to Noel's house, Claire had drifted off. He easily lifted her from the car and carried her to the front door. "The keys," he whispered and nodded toward his left front pocket.

Rachel slid her fingers in, and extracted them, lingering only a moment as she debated and then decided not to extend them for a brief caress. She wasn't going to blow it this time. She tried one key and then another until she found the one that fit the front door. She pushed it open and he went ahead of her, taking Claire directly to her bedroom.

It had been a wonderful evening. Rachel didn't want it to end. She opened a cupboard near the sink, remembering how she'd helped him move and unpack only a month ago. She found the Grand Marnier on the top shelf and took it down. Maybe she could convince him to have a nightcap before she left. As she was searching the cupboard for the proper glass, she felt an arm go around her and he pressed against her back as he reached above her head and to the right.

"If you drink this you can't drive home," he said, extracting one glass from the cupboard and putting it on the table, his other arm still around her waist. Then he opened the bottle and poured. He turned her toward him as he handed her the glass.

She took a good sized swallow, letting the warmth slide down her throat to her belly and pool between her thighs. "Now that's a difficult decision."

He hooked a finger under chin and lifted her face. His eyes bore into hers. "If you stay, I won't stop this time."

She didn't say anything. She searched his eyes, wondering what had changed and what it really meant.

He kissed her. At first it was a light, sweet kiss, just the barest of touch to her lips. Then he groaned and deepened it, sucking the taste of orange from her lips, from her tongue, from every part of her mouth. She felt her legs start to give way, but he held her firmly to him. Then she noticed the hardness of his arousal.

"What I'm thinking is," He took a sip of her drink. "I want to taste this on you. On every part of you. I want to take you down the hall, lay you on my bed, and make love to you. Not have sex. Make love."

Her hand trembled as she brought the drink to her lips and sipped again. She nodded, unable to speak. He chuckled and lifted her off her feet, placing one arm beneath her knees. She nuzzled under his neck. She was a fool, and she knew it. She knew it wouldn't last, but she didn't care. She wanted this. She needed this, and she wasn't going to stop him now.

He flicked off the kitchen lights with his elbow as they passed the switch and entered the darkened hallway. The door to his bedroom was open, and he closed it with one foot once they were over the threshold.

The queen bed was covered with a dark blue comforter. Moonlight spilled through the trees outside the window, sending diagonal shafts across the room—one at the pillows, one in the center of the bed, and another on the floor.

Noel stood her next to the bed and pulled back the comforter. His fingers reached for the zipper at the back of her dress, and with a slow, steady pull he slid it down to its base. She didn't move, couldn't move as the barest touch of his lips to hers set the rhythm of her heartbeat to *largo*.

His hands pushed the dress off her shoulders and it pooled at her feet. He dipped his finger in the Grand Marnier and traced it along her neck, then across the top of her breasts. She first felt the tickle of his breath, followed by his lips and tongue, licking, tasting, suckling, drawing the liquid from her skin as he unclasped her front hook bra. She heard his intake of breath and her knees began to shake. He lifted the bra off her arms and gathered her to him, while at the same time lowering her slowly to the bed. He moved her into the center and hovered above her taking her in. She reached for him, but he shook his head and removed her panties, flinging them across the room. Then he stood and stared.

"You're beautiful," he breathed.

She felt ravishing, his eyes drinking her in with frank desire. She was sure her skin glowed with her willingness, the moonlight highlighting her erect nipples straining for his touch again.

She couldn't keep her hands off him now. She reached to draw him to her. Her fingers made quick work of his shirt and he seemed equally eager to remove it after crushing her mouth to his once more. When he came up for breath, he hurried to unfastened his pants, slipped them down and kicked them aside. To her surprise he was wearing briefs. The last time they were together, she never saw what he wore. Somehow she had assumed it would be boxers.

He stretched out beside her, the bed sighed as if enraptured with the additional weight. His feet pushed the comforter toward the footboard. Then he wrapped an arm beneath her and rolled to his back, carrying Rachel on top of him as he kissed her breathless.

The kiss set a new tempo to her pulse, an *allegretto* as fire streaked through her. The size of his erection, straining through his briefs and to her belly, took her breath away. She broke the kiss and reached to remove his underwear, rotating her hips to indicate she wanted him inside her now.

He chuckled, his hands grabbing hers as he intertwined her fingers. "Oh, no you don't. I'm not even close to entering you."

She whimpered as he drew her arms out to each side and then rolled her beneath him, stopping her from touching him. He kissed her forehead, her eyes, the tip of her nose, nuzzled her ears. Her arms firmly out to each side, fingers entwined he followed the line of her jaw with his torture, slowly tasting the full length of her neck. He loosed one hand and dipped his fingers in the Grand Marnier again, sprinkling it across her breast, then encircling her nipples. She arched to his touch and he fell to them, teasing, and tasting with the tip of his tongue.

"Oh God," she moaned, arching again and pushing him closer with her free hand. A fine sheen of perspiration broke out all over body.

He dipped and suckled, tasted and teased until her hips were grinding against him begging, then he dipped his fingers into her and caressed her center with the pad of his thumb until she crescendoed in successive waves, gasping and crying out for him to take her completely.

Instead he kissed his way down her rib cage and across her belly. He stopped at her navel and explored it with the tip of his tongue, and she trembled anew. "Please, I can't take any more," she begged.

"Yes, you can. This is only the beginning."

He parted her, touched her with his tongue, and she jumped, her hips shooting straight toward the ceiling. He pulled her back down and held her firmly, positioning her for pleasure, his hands and his fingers driving her up.

"Oh, God. No one has ever…"

He pushed her knees wider and inhaled her smell. He nuzzled and teased, suckled and ate greedily.

Her head tossed side to side on the pillow, unable to cope with the dizzying sensation. Tears streamed down her face as another orgasm hit her. She couldn't even cry out, the sensations were so overwhelming. Ever so slowly, he worked his way back to her thighs. He lifted a leg and kissed her beneath her knee drawing her further into the center of the bed, then he draped her leg over his shoulder.

She opened her eyes and looked down. Somehow he had divested himself of his underwear. She had no idea when, and she saw that he'd already put on a condom. In a continued haze of pleasure, she felt him lift the other leg and kiss the back of her knee there. As he arranged that on his shoulder he slid two pillows under her. His erection pressed against her thigh, stroking and teasing. Then he entered her slowly. But she couldn't be patient. She pushed her hips up and he groaned as he fell into her waiting wetness.

"Yes," she whispered in triumph, grabbing his backside and pulling him in as deep as he could go.

She rotated trying to wrest control from him, but even now, when she knew he must be at his limit, he didn't let go. He moved in long, deliberate strokes, each one harder and hotter than the one before. The fire inside her was so strong, she thought surely it would burn her clear through. Just when she thought she could take it no longer he moved against her with a fierceness that changed the dynamics of their love making to a *vivace* as he slammed into her again and again.

A low, keening sound, she barely recognized as coming from her own voice sent her soaring once again. Then, at last, she felt him stiffen and let himself go as he called her name.

They laid holding each other, until the perspiration from their bodies evaporated. He rolled away from her and disposed of the condom, and she shivered at the lost of his body heat. Noel pulled her to his side, spoon style, and moved the comforter over them. It seemed that a long time passed as he held her to him, his breath slowing on her neck. She fell asleep that way and sometime in the early morning, before dawn, she awoke to him caressing one of her breasts. She trembled and he turned her on her back as Noel bent over her, tasting her nipple.

"What time is it," she asked, sleep still chasing her.

"The right time." He bent to the other nipple.

"Meaning?"

He drew more of her breast into his mouth and took the time to suckle. Rachel was already responding. Her blood heated, her body writhed with need.

"Again?" she asked, her breath catching as he moved down to her stomach.

His answer was to part her legs and use his fingers on her again. She tried to close her legs, to indicate they should just sleep, but that only made him move more insistently. His fingers inside her, his mouth on her breasts, her neck, her lips. Noel held her firm, wringing every last response from her until she couldn't move, couldn't think, could only die the sweet death of pure pleasure.

The next time she awoke, the bed was empty. She searched for a clock. It said nine-thirty and she sat up with a start. Omigod, Claire. What if Claire had come in looking for her father? Rachel had meant to leave before morning. She saw the door was still closed. She searched for her clothes and put them on. She looked out the window and saw that his car was gone. Of course, Noel had to be at the high school by seven thirty. He must have gotten Claire up and taken care of everything, so Rachel wouldn't be discovered.

She gathered her purse and turned to look at the bed once more. The bed that had brought her more than pleasure. It had given her healing through a miraculous blending of sex and love. It had delivered her a dream, however short. Then she saw the note card pinned to the pillow next to her. It was a single line. *Love consists in this, that two solitudes protect and touch and greet each other*. He'd added the poets name at the end, Rainer Maria Rilke.

CHAPTER FOURTEEN

In the throes of love's first blush, Rachel danced on a euphoric cloud through the next few days of rehearsals. Noel called her every night after Claire went to bed and they talked for long hours. They talked of poetry and music, of children and lives entwined. Though they didn't plan to see each other again until the weekend, their long conversations built a bridge in her heart—a bridge from insecurity and confusion to a realistic hope for love and family.

She looked forward to seeing Claire Saturday morning for her fiddle lesson, and this time she knew Noel would stick around to listen. Sweetwater Canyon had a benefit concert scheduled in Portland later the same day, to support the Oregon Food Bank, and they had invited Claire to play with the band again. Noel had already suggested Rachel ride with him and Claire. Afterward, they would return to his home and she would spend the night.

Looking forward to the day with Noel made doing mundane things like laundry all the sweeter. Rachel poured a cup of laundry detergent into the machine and turned on the water, letting it fill while she separated the whites from the rest of her clothes. When the water had dissolved the granules she stuffed the darks in, making sure the load was balanced.

She closed the lid and turned to gaze out the front window of her apartment. Bruised purple and grey clouds covered the sky. Rain poured in large heavy drops and continued its relentless tapping on the metal roof overhead. In another month the sun would shine more often and she could switch from the heavy jeans and sweatshirts, warm jackets and wool dresses to the soft pastels of t-shirts and shorts that she favored. She shook her head and turned her frown into a smile. Nothing was going to get her down today. It was April after all, and April in Oregon meant rain—rain that nourished the ferns and the evergreens and brought about magnificent May blossoms. She smiled and danced back toward the laundry room. Her life was in its spring now. She had suffered the winter, took in the nourishing rain of Noel's loving, and for once she had a chance to blossom. It had been a long time coming. She was going to savor every moment.

Rachel jumped when the phone rang, interrupting her thoughts. The sound jarred against the soft hissing rhythm of the agitating washer.

"Hello?"

"Is this Ms. Rachel Mackenzie Cullen?"

"Yes." She tensed. No one ever called her by her full name, not even her parents.

"This is Sergeant Gaines of the Branson, Missouri police department." She sucked in a breath. "I believe we've located the cowboy you reported who participated in the rape of September last year."

She froze as memories flooded back. He'd said his name was Flint, only later she found out there was no man with that name, and the band he played with didn't exist. She'd never forget him. The hard angles of his face, the way he'd slapped her and forced himself on her, his eyes berating her even as he emptied himself. But he hadn't been the worst of it. He was only the warm-up to Drake. Flint had been the one to drug her beer and to take her first, before Drake took his time killing her little by little.

She shuddered. She had closed that experience in a dark corner of her mind and thrown away the key. After the rape, when the trail grew cold, they'd told her the likelihood of finding either man was slim—particularly Flint—as it wasn't even his real name. But she'd provided a description to the police artist all the same. And now, maybe they'd found one of them. She wasn't sure if she wanted to go back and face him, to remember in detail everything that had happened—not now, not when life was just starting to make sense again. Not now that she and Noel were just getting to love each other.

"Ms. Cullen? Are you still there?"

She cleared her throat and found her voice, but couldn't get it beyond a whisper. "Yes, I'm here."

"We need you to identify him. We need you to pick him out of a line up."

"I'm not sure I can do that. Can't you just send pictures or something? I don't know that I can go back to Branson." She sank to the floor and drew her knees to her chest, unable to control the shivers.

"The D.A.'s office will pay to fly you out here. If this is the right guy, we want to get him. He has a rap sheet a mile long for assault and battery, but never a rape conviction although he's been a suspect in a couple of other cases. We could never get anyone to go the distance in court."

Oh God. He'd done it before. She wasn't the first and probably not the last. She had to stop him before some other woman suffered as she had.

"Have you found…Drake?" She hesitated saying the name of the man who had orchestrated it all, the man who had left her to die in that hotel room.

"I'm sorry, Ms. Cullen. No sign of him yet."

"Do you think this…this…what is his real name?"

"Frances. He goes by Frank."

She held the phone with both hands so it wouldn't slip from her ear. "Do you think this…Frank," she wanted to say his name, to keep it in focus, to know who he really was, "would tell you how to find Drake?"

"I can't answer that, m'am. With his rap sheet it's hard to tell. Sometimes they wanna make a deal. Other times loyalty to the filth they run with is paramount."

A squeal of disappointment and frustration escaped her lips. Hot tears wet her cheeks.

"I know this is hard for you, m'am. To remember it and all, but if you can't identify him we have to set him loose."

"I'll…I'll come." She closed her eyes and began to rock.

"Good, I'll have the D.A. call you and get you on a plane first thing in the morning."

She couldn't speak. She couldn't think. Sobs rolled out of her now and she couldn't stop them.

"M'am? You have someone who can come over? A friend? Do you need me to call someone?"

"I'll take care of it," she whispered. She pressed the off button and the phone dropped to the floor with a thud.

She wasn't sure how she got through the next two hours. The D.A. called and told her the airline tickets had her leaving Portland at five-thirty tomorrow morning and arriving in Branson just before noon. A police woman would meet her at the airport and escort her to the jail. The lineup was scheduled for one, and that was cutting it close. Without a positive I.D. they wouldn't be able to hold him past three.

She wandered from the laundry room to her bedroom in fits and starts, unable to keep her concentration. When she found herself folding wet underwear to put in her dresser she knew she'd lost any semblance of control over her actions. She yanked the drawer out and flung it against the wall. Three pairs of red panties spilled a trail from the dresser to the wall. Blood red. Her blood. The blood that was meant to seep from inside her until her death. She dropped to her bed and curled in a fetal position, unable to stop trembling.

* * * * *

Noel was worried. He'd called Rachel during his lunch break to remind her they'd have the house to themselves the next three nights. Then he tried again at two-thirty when school let out, and at three when he got home. He'd left messages each time. It wasn't like her to ignore him.

His parents had planned a three-day camping vacation—their special grandparents time with only Claire. They'd rented a motor home and were going down to the redwoods. Claire promised to bring home a couple of trees to plant in the yard. He and Rachel were looking forward to this uninhibited time together. He had to teach on Friday, and she had a gig scheduled for Friday night that he was going to attend. Other than that they were free to spend every minute together, alone.

He checked his watch again. Four. He dialed Theresa. Maybe they'd scheduled an extra rehearsal before the gig tomorrow night. After only a minute on the phone he'd confirmed she wasn't there either. Shit!

Now he was worried. Rachel would call if she could. Maybe she had a car accident. Maybe something was wrong with her family and she had to rush to help. He'd check her house first and then go from there. He grabbed his car keys from the hall table and rushed out of the house.

During the entire sixteen mile drive up the mountain he built up the what-ifs until he was chewing the inside of his cheek trying to tamp down the worry.

He pulled into the parking lot and spotted her car in the usual spot. Without bothering to lock his door he rushed to her apartment and pounded.

No answer.

"Rachel. Are you Okay? I saw your car. Are you hurt?"

Still no answer. He tried the door and the knob turned easily in his hand.

When he stepped into the room it took a moment for his eyes to adjust to the darkness. The folding doors to the laundry stood opened with wet clothes strewn half in and out of the washing machine. Two pairs of sky blue panties were on the floor. What the hell?

He ran toward her bedroom, horrible images in his mind. A drawer was overturned in the corner and feminine silks of white and red, green and blue were scattered across the room. The covers of the bed were twisted around a small form curled into a tight ball, shaking and rocking without a single sound.

Noel sank to the bed and unfurled his length beside her. He wrapped his arms around her, warming, holding, his heart aching with whatever pain had stripped her so raw. Her pain was so palpable his words disappeared, inconsequential, like pebbles before a mountain. He couldn't even ask what was wrong.

A desolate sob erupted from her and she reached for him, clung to him as if letting go meant death.

He stroked her back and her hair. He listened as in fits and starts she told him a story of a rape so horrendous he could barely take it in without screaming. For the first time in his life he actually wanted to kill somebody. More than that, he wanted to kill Drake slowly and with as much pain as possible. He had to concentrate so as not to crush Rachel with his anger.

After what seemed like hours she quieted in his arms.

Her voice barely a whisper, she looked up to him. Tears streamed down her face. "Now that you know…" She choked on a sob. "If you don't want me…I'll understand."

He crushed her to him. Oh, God! How could she think he didn't want her? He held tight, kissing her hair, her shoulders. He held her face in front of him and kissed each of her tears, his own eyes misting at the pain and anguish she must have borne. What words could convince her of his love, his continued desire for her? None could carry all he wanted to say so he kissed her. Slowly, deeply, thoroughly.

"I love you, Rachel," he whispered in her ear. "I'll never let you go."

"Show me," she begged, pulling her clothes off her. "Show me you can still want me after knowing this."

And he did. With soft and tender kisses he worshipped her every hill and crevice. When she begged for him to be inside her, he took her with a slow, rhythmic exploration of the very core of her womanhood. He made love to her with an absorption far beyond anything he'd ever experienced with anyone else. When she was finally sated he held her until she slept in his arms, their arms and legs entangled so that it was hard to tell where one stopped and the other started.

Her soft breaths sighed against his neck. Her breasts rose and fell against his chest. He would find a way to go with her tomorrow, even if he had to fly on the wing of the damn plane.

Sometime after midnight, he awoke hard as a rock and realized it was the touch of her fingers along his shaft that had made him that way. He groaned and she looked up to his eyes with complete trust and triumph. Then she slid on top of him, taking complete control of his mouth. As she rubbed her mound against his shaft, his only thought was being inside her as quickly as possible. But then she surprised him. She turned around and straddled his face, offering her center to him as she took his shaft full in her mouth. He'd never before experienced the sensations of simultaneous pleasure. He inhaled her full scent and gripped her hips as he raised his mouth to part her.

The feeling of her slick mouth on him at the same time was almost overwhelming. His own pleasure heightened with hers as he tongued and nibbled, focusing on her, hurrying her to orgasm, afraid he wouldn't be able to hold out long enough.

Just as she climaxed, her mouth released him and she screamed his name. Then she clamped her hand at the base of his penis and effectively stayed his own release. Unable to wait any longer, he guided her hips to settle her wetness down the length of him. Her hands covering his, she moved in a rhythmic motion, her inner muscles stroking and clinching as she picked up the pace, daring him to match her tempo. Her face glowed with satisfaction as she rode him until he could barely breathe. With her arms stretched to the ceiling in conquest she cried out once more and he exploded into her.

* * * * *

In the shower, Rachel relished the feel of Noel's hands as he soaped her body. He loved her. He'd said so many times last night and he still wanted her. Those moments of passion had helped her put away what she had to do today. She moved into his arms again and wriggled with invitation.

He chuckled and crushed his mouth to hers. "I don't think we have time for that. Do you?"

"If it's fast." She teased his flaccid penis with her fingers.

With a groan he removed her hand. "Give you an inch and you want the whole ten acres."

"Ten acres? Think that much of yourself do you?"

He laughed and turned her to face away from him as he took the shower nozzle from its holder. "Rinse before we're late."

She turned in a slow circle, letting him rinse the soap off her. When she was clean, she did the same for him with a few playful grabs and pokes along the way. Then, serious, she looked into his eyes. "Are you sure you want to come with me? I know I was a wreck yesterday, but I think I can handle it without you."

He drew her against him again and stroked her back, nuzzling her wet hair. "I'm sure you can handle it without me, but why should you? I want to be there. I want to see this guy with my own eyes."

She drew away and saw his jaw constrict and his eyes flare. His grip tightened around her waist and she felt the violence build inside him. She'd felt it last night too when she'd first told him about Drake. On the one hand, she relished his desire to protect her; but that pure male aggression scared her too—even if it was aimed against someone who had hurt her.

She turned her head and nuzzled into his chest, her hands splayed across his back. She rubbed her slick breasts along his chest and then kissed the water off him. She worked her way down his stomach, her fingers working their magic along his back, his butt, his thighs. Then she took him full into her mouth, teasing and tugging until his shaft was taut and firm once again. She just wanted a few more moments with him—a few more moments to forget the past and savor the now.

* * * * *

Noel chewed on the inside of his cheek as he stood next to Rachel, his hand clasped in hers. It was just like all the Law and Order shows on television. The policeman explained how Rachel would see the men but they would not see her. How she would be asked if she recognized anyone. Then she would be asked to confirm it for the record. If she was unsure, they would have each person step forward, turn in profile, and step back. She could even ask them to walk if it would help. Then the police officer asked if she was ready.

When Rachel nodded, he signaled a guard.

Noel held fast to her hand as the six men entered the room and lined up behind the one-way glass. Within seconds she went stiff beside him. She gasped and squeezed his hand so hard he thought it would break.

"That's him," she whispered.

"Which one?" the policeman asked.

"Number two."

She shook and Noel enfolded her in his arms.

"Are you sure?" the officer pressed.

"Yes. I'll never forget him."

Her lips pinched pencil thin and her jaw clinched as she held herself tight, trying not to cry. Noel rubbed her back and whispered in her ear, "You're doing great, Rachel. It's almost over. Hang on now. You can do it."

The policeman stepped in front of Rachel, blocking the view of the six men behind the glass. "You have to be one hundred percent sure."

She opened her mouth, but no sound came out. She squeezed his hand harder.

"She's sure, dammit," Noel said, his teeth clenched. "Is that all?"

Satisfied, the officer nodded to the guard and the men exited the viewing room. He turned to the court reporter. "Note that she identified Frances William Hunter." Then he looked at the D.A. and the suspect's attorney. "Are you both satisfied?"

"All this proves is that she remembers who she had consensual sex with," Hunter's attorney said. Rachel let out a squeal and the attorney smiled. "We'll see you in court."

Noel stiffened beside her. He sent daggers from his eyes to the attorney's. If he wasn't so worried about her collapsing, he'd have liked to deck the guy. Of course, being in jail for assault wouldn't support Rachel. It wasn't until the attorney let himself out of the room that Noel relaxed.

"Ms. Cullen?" The D.A. pointed toward a chair. "Would you like to sit down? We need to talk about the court schedules and what you can expect over the next several months."

"Can't this wait? Let her catch her breath, maybe come back in an hour," Noel said.

Rachel leaned on him and whispered, "No, I want to get it over with. This is our only day here. I don't want to stay any longer than I have to."

Noel guided her into a chair and then took the one next to her, sitting as close as possible. He never lost her touch, never let go, making sure she knew she could lean at any time, she could send any signal that she wanted to stop and he would act immediately.

After the preliminary outline of what would lead up to the court case over the next four months, the D.A. got down to the nitty-gritty description of how the case would go—in particular how the defendant's attorney would present the only case possible, that Rachel was consenting.

"But I didn't consent. Do you think any woman would consent to being drugged and used by two men, especially after what happened to me? Look at the hospital records. I almost died."

For the first time, anger rose in her voice instead of defeat. Noel hoped she could hold onto that anger. It would help get her through the long months ahead.

"The hospital records do hold up well in court, Ms. Cullen and that is why we are prosecuting based on forcible rape. However, the defense has several options. First, they will try to prove either that you wanted to be drugged or that the defendant didn't know there was a drug in the drink."

"But what about the gun? What about Drake? The records document how he used that gun on me."

"That's a different issue. The defendant will say that he didn't know what Drake was going to do, that he had already left the room when Drake raped you. He will say that you consented to come up to his room and let his friend watch. He will say that you accepted the drink willingly. All of this goes toward consent."

Noel slammed his fist on the table. "But she didn't consent to anything."

"Did you ever say no to the cowboy, Ms. Cullen?"

Rachel lowered her head, her voice a shaky whisper. "I'm not sure, I don't remember."

Noel turned her toward him, took her face in his hands and looked directly into her eyes. "Rachel, you did not invite this. You did not want it to happen."

"Mr. Kershaw, please don't coach her. If you do, I will have to ask you to leave."

"I'm not coaching her, I'm protecting her. You're purposely confusing her. You're purposely making it difficult to answer. Can't you see how hard this is? Can't you see her shaking? How tight she is holding herself?"

"I'm doing what the defense attorney will do and I haven't even done the worst. She has to stand up to this or we will lose. I want to prove forcible rape and I think we have a good case. With a forcible rape conviction, the defendant does a minimum of ten years and could receive life. If all we can get is sexual assault he could be out in a year; and if there is even a hint of consent he could go free. Is that what you want for your girlfriend? For the men who did this to her? Do you want him to go free?"

Noel paused, but only for a moment. “Of course that’s not what I want, but I don’t want to see her in any more pain.”

“Stop talking about me as if I weren’t here!” Rachel stood and moved away from them. “The truth is I did accept his invitation to join him later that night, and I did go with the intention of having sex.”

CHAPTER FIFTEEN

Noel watched Rachel as she went over the case with the D.A. She seemed strong. She was looking straight at the D.A. as he questioned her, prepping her with the type of questions that the defense would probably ask. Noel knew she'd gone up to the man's room willingly. They'd already talked about this. But it was still hard for him to hear. After staying with her last night and hearing the whole agonizing story, Noel also knew she had to have said no at some point. She just didn't remember.

The D.A. raised his voice and picked up speed. "When you got to the room, what happened?"

"He offered me a drink and I accepted. I remember sitting on the bed and I'd barely taken a sip, when he started..." She looked over at Noel again and hesitated. The D.A. glanced at him as well.

"I think it would be better if you left, Mr. Kershaw. It's obvious she feels uncomfortable discussing this with you here."

Noel covered Rachel's hand on the table and looked her in the eye. "I'm staying unless you ask me to go."

"I…I'm not sure. Can I have a minute alone with Noel?"

The D.A. nodded and left the room.

"Rachel?"

She immediately went into his arms. "Did you mean what you said before? That you loved me?"

He crushed her mouth to his. "Does that answer the question?"

Her breath rapid, she turned her cheek into his chest. "But what may come out here might change your feelings. Will you still love me after you've heard everything?"

"That couldn't happen. Nothing said here will make me stop loving you."

"Are you sure?"

"Rachel, we've been over this before. I know you went to have sex with the man, but that doesn't make what he did right."

"But he isn't the only one I've had sex with. What if they try to prove I'm promiscuous."

"You are not promiscuous. How many has there been? Six, seven?"

Rachel didn't answer. She kept her head down.

Noel shook his head. My God, what was he asking? The number didn't matter, did it? Did he care if it was six or twenty-six? Well, twenty-six would bother him. Surely, there wouldn't have been that many.

She was still looking at him, questioning.

Shit! He loved her. That's all that mattered. Whatever the number, it was in the past. He would help her get through this.

Noel took her hand again and looked into her eyes. "Look. I can't say I like the idea of you having had sex with anyone besides me. But that's just male ego and dominance talking, not reality. I'm not so stupid as to expect you to be a virgin. God knows, I'm not. We've both been married before. We've both been with other people since. That's all in the past."

He pulled her to him, holding her tight. "The most important thing right here and right now is that you were raped. This wasn't sex. This wasn't love. This was criminal rape."

She hugged him tighter, but at least she wasn't shaking anymore.

He put a finger beneath her chin and raised it so he could look straight into her eyes again. "Are we clear now? Do you want me to go? I'll go if it will make it easier for you."

"No, I want you to stay. I love you, Noel. I don't deserve you, but I love you." She tilted her head and parted her lips, her hand snaking up to his head. When he followed her lead she gave him the slowest, most truthful, soul filling kiss he'd had from her yet.

Afterward, all he could do was hold her tight, praying that this ordeal would be over soon and they could put it behind them and get on with building a life together. When the D.A. re-entered the room, they were still in a tight embrace and Noel did nothing to hurry out of it.

The attorney cleared his throat and took a chair. "I take it you're staying, Mr. Kershaw."

"That's right." Noel and Rachel said at the same time. She smiled and looked up at him, her eyes shining with thanks.

When she sat at the table again, her chin slightly tilted, her spine straight and determined, Noel's eyes misted with pride for her. He had never known a woman who had been raped, and he couldn't imagine what it must take to put herself up for examination like this. Tough, yet vulnerable. It had to hurt like hell.

She looked straight at the attorney, her voice strong and clear. "As I was saying, I had barely taken a sip of the beer when he started to pull my clothes off in a rough manner. He ripped the buttons from my blouse. I thought it was too quick and told him to slow down."

"But you didn't say no."

"The truth is I was depressed and I was willing to hurry it up if he wanted. It wasn't until he pushed me down on the bed and started tearing my clothes off that I started to get scared. When I tried to raise myself up to stop him, I realized I couldn't move my arms or legs—that I'd been drugged."

"You suddenly couldn't move your arms or legs? That seems unlikely, Ms. Cullen."

"I felt some tingling earlier, but I chocked it up to the fact I drank the glass of beer so fast. He was sweet-talking me at first when I sat on the bed. Then, yeah, it did seem like everything happened at once and I couldn't move any part of me."

"Did you still have your clothes on when you laid down on the bed?"

"Yes, but he was pretty quick about getting them removed."

"Had he touched you, sexually, in any way before you realized you were drugged?"

She hesitated. "I'm not sure. It all happened so fast. He may have touched my breasts…or put his mouth on them. I just remember thinking that whatever was going to happen was going to hurt. I wanted to slow him down."

"But not to stop him."

A silence that felt like a chasm filled the room. Noel held his breath.

"No, I still didn't want to stop him." Rachel's voice had dropped and the confidence she had shown earlier slipped.

"Did you ever try to stop him? To say no?"

"I remember wanting to. I remember trying to raise my arm to stop him but I couldn't. That was when I knew I was drugged. I was so shocked at the realization that I couldn't move and that I would have no control over the situation that it took me awhile to figure out what to do. By the time I could think of the words to say, he'd already undressed and had his…his…well you know…in my face."

"His penis?"

"Yes." She grabbed Noel's hand again and he squeezed back to reassure her he was still there.

"Then what happened?"

"I think I said something like 'You really don't want to do this.' Then he slapped me."

Shit! Noel sucked in a breath and clenched his teeth to stop himself from saying something. Though she had summarized the story for him earlier, and it was enough then to make him want to kill the son-of-a-bitch, this was even worse. Hearing the play-by-play made it like he was there, watching everything but unable to stop it.

"Then what happened."

"What do you think happened?" She pushed the chair back and stood, her face red with anger.

The D.A. sighed and took his glasses off, laying them on top of his legal pad. "Ms. Cullen, I know this is hard but you have to tell me in you're own words."

She took in a deep breath and let it out in resignation, but she remained standing.

"He told me to suck, and I did. Soon after that he stuck it inside me and went at it."

"You mean he penetrated you?"

"Yeah, that's what I mean. The only thing good about it was that he used a condom and he finished quickly."

"He used a condom? Did you ask him to?"

"By that point I wasn't asking anything. I was too afraid of what would happen. I was just doing as I was told and praying it would be over soon, that he would fall asleep and somehow the drug would wear off and I could sneak out of there."

"I see. So, when he was done…with you, what happened next?"

"Then he got off me and called in Drake."

"Now, this is important. At any time did you see Drake watching? During the sex act."

"It wasn't sex," Noel interrupted. "It was rape. Get used to saying it counselor. If you can't say it, the jury won't believe it either."

They stared at each other for a moment, jaws clenched. Noel wasn't going to back down. He may not be able to make it easier for Rachel, but he was going to be damn sure the D.A. was one hundred percent on her side.

Rachel sighed and pulled Noel back to his seat as she sat next to him again.

The attorney ducked his head and put his spectacles back on. "You have a point." He tapped his legal pad and then looked at Rachel. “At any time during the rape, did you notice Drake watching? Did he say anything that led you to believe it was a set up?”

“I didn’t see him until Flint…I mean Frances, Frank…was done and called him. Though I’m sure he heard everything.”

The D.A. wrote something on his yellow legal pad. “When Frank was done, did he say anything that led you to believe it was a set up?”

“Yes, he said ‘she’s all yours.’”

“She’s all yours? What did you think that meant.”

“Christ! What do you think?” Noel stood and leaned on the table, his face inches from the D.A.s

“Please sit down, Mr. Kershaw.” Rachel tapped his arm at the same time.

Reluctant, Noel lowered himself back to the chair. “Shit, I’m sorry. It’s just hard to hear. It’s hard to see her have to go through this.”

“Remember, we are trying to establish forcible rape here. Forcible rape means forcible compulsion which would get us beyond the concept of consent.” The D.A. tapped his pencil for a moment then continued. “Forcible compulsion is easier to prove when there is physical force that overcomes reasonable resistance, or a threat that makes the victim believe death may be imminent, like waving a gun or knife around or being held down while the woman is kicking and screaming and yelling for the person to stop. So far, Ms. Cullen's story suggests she was consenting up until the time she realized she was drugged. But she still didn't say no. The fact that she was slapped is not enough to prove force, as some people like to be slapped to bring on arousal."

Noel shuddered at the thought. He would never think of slapping a woman before or during sex, and he would refuse even if she asked. In fact, it would turn him off completely.

"What about the drugs? Doesn't the fact that she was drugged mean she couldn't consent? There is no woman alive who would ask for drugs that don't allow her to move. Even if Rachel wanted this, which it's obvious she did not at this point, she would never choose to be drugged and avoid any chance at pleasure."

The D.A. stood and paced. "I've tried a lot of rape cases, and they are never easy. Often, some surprise sneaks up to bite you in the ass. I need to establish force." He sat again and twirled his pen before continuing. "Forcible compulsion does include the use of a substance administered without a victim's knowledge or consent which renders the victim physically or mentally impaired so as to be incapable of making an informed consent to sexual intercourse."

The attorney made a couple more notes, drawing a circle around one section on the page. He tapped it and looked up again. "We have two problems with this prosecution." He looked directly at Rachel. "The fact that you obviously consented all the way up until you realized you were drugged leaves the door open enough for the defense to say it doesn't matter whether there were drugs because you were willing to go forward anyway. The defense may even say you wanted the drugs or brought them with you."

"That's ridiculous, what—"

The D.A. held up his hand before Noel could finish. "On top of that, though the hospital records prove you had drugs in your system, we can't prove the defendant knew they were in your drink. He could claim that his friend put them there."

Noel ground his teeth. He looked at Rachel. She was sitting perfectly still. If her eyes hadn't been open, he'd have wondered if she'd died on the spot. He put his arm around her and she let her head fall to his shoulder.

He turned his attention back to the D.A. "What about the fact that Drake was in the room. Isn't there something in the law that shows that this guy was next and the first guy knew it and now she was drugged and she couldn't possibly consent, that…hell I don't know, conspiracy, contributing to a crime, something is wrong here you can pin on the guy."

"Please, let me be the attorney, Mr. Kershaw."

Rachel sat up again and Noel put his hand over hers on the table, his thumb working small circles along her knuckles and back to her wrist.

"Ms. Cullen, back to the question. When Frank said 'she's all yours' did he then stay around to watch or say anything else that made you believe that someone else would be next? That it was a set up for this Drake guy?"

Rachel sighed. "He didn't say anything, but I knew I was in deep trouble."

"How's that?"

"After he said, 'she's all yours,' Drake was standing at the end of the bed laughing and Flint…I mean Frank…left the room."

"If he left the room, what makes you think he knew what was going to happen?"

"Because anyone who knows Drake, knows what he's like. He has… aberrant tastes."

Noel snapped his head toward Rachel and stood, knocking over the chair.

"Oh my God, you knew this guy?" His stomach revolted and threatened to come up into his throat. "You'd actually had sex with this guy before? Consensual sex? This guy who did …what he did to you?"

Rachel's eyes flashed and her chin shot up. "Yes, we had dated before. One of the reasons we stopped dating was because he was rough and he wanted to do things I didn't want to do."

He pressed his hands to his stomach and paced the room. He couldn't believe it. How could she actually date a monster like that? Pictures of his daughter crying in his arms about the men who had been with her mother flashed through his mind. It mixed with the time he had come to pick up Claire and move her to his house. He'd heard two men upstairs laughing with his wife—teasing, sexual teasing.

He shook his head. Was he that stupid? Had he made the same mistake again? Fallen for a woman who used sex to get what she wanted. Maybe he'd been all wrong about Rachel. Maybe his first instincts had been right. Maybe she was indiscriminate about her sexual encounters and it just happened that because he didn't like it rough or he didn't manhandle women, that she'd changed her desires for the time being.

"Mr. Kershaw, please sit down so we can finish this."

He stopped and looked at Rachel. Her eyes were on him, questioning him, reminding him of his promise to stand by her through this ordeal.

God he loved her. But was it enough? What other revelations would he have to endure? Could he really live up to that promise? She said Drake had aberrant tastes. Had she participated in whatever those things were while they dated? What was her line in the sand? Two men? Three? Did she allow him to watch while she did it with someone else? Maybe this whole rape scenario was a repeat of some sex game they'd played before.

He turned and looked at the window. Is it possible Drake could have actually thought she wanted this? His ex-wife flashed again before his eyes, all the men she'd had in their home.

She'd admitted there were other men. He assumed…. He shook himself. He assumed nothing. The truth was he didn't want to know. He'd made assumptions about those liaisons, but never included someone like Drake as part of them.

He took several deep breaths, trying to steady his racing pulse. He closed his eyes and talked himself down. It didn't matter that she dated Drake. Maybe he was different then, not quite as deviant, not quite as mean. Maybe he'd changed for the worst.

He shook himself and opened his eyes again. It didn't matter. What mattered was that she didn't deserve what he did to her. It was still a rape, whether she knew him or not. She didn't deserve the gun, the beatings, the knife cuts, the death she'd barely escaped. He could learn to accept this part of her past. It would take some time, but he could do it. Obviously she'd chosen to end the relationship; she'd recognized the monster for who he was and ended it.

Finally, he was able to sit again. She took his hand and he let her, but he held his breath afraid of what might come out next.

"I have to admit, Ms. Cullen, the fact you'd dated this Drake guy before doesn't help the prosecution. It opens up the door even wider to consent, not only with Frank but with Drake as well."

"I would never consent to having sex with Drake. He was awful. He frightened me. Even when we dated I was scared to be with him." She paused and captured Noel's eyes. "He forced me to do things I didn't want to do." He squeezed her hand and held her gaze as she continued talking to him instead of the D.A. "That was why I decided to end our relationship. It took me several months to leave him because he'd told me that if I ever did he would kill me, and I believed him."

She paused, her eyes still questioning Noel. Begging him for a response. He wanted to say something, but he couldn't find the words. His mind was too full of chaotic emotions.

Rachel continued, "When I saw him standing there at the end of the bed, I knew it would be only a matter of hours before I was dead."

"Did you file a restraining order? Do you have evidence of previous abuse?

She released Noel and looked back to the D.A., her shoulders sagged. "No."

"Did he abuse you? Do you have doctor visits, hospital visits? We could show a pattern, we could show this was pre-mediated."

"It was pre-meditated all right. As he was raping me and cutting me, he told me all about how he'd set it up and that he was going to kill me slowly, and how much he wanted me to hurt while he was doing it."

Noel shuddered and wrapped his arms around her. He wasn't sure if it was to warm himself or her. Whatever second thoughts he'd had warred with his desire to protect her from this monster. He couldn't begin to imagine how awful it would be to go through all that she'd endured, expecting to die in the end.

"Doctor's visits? Previous signs of abuse?" The D.A. was like a dog, worrying at a bone, single focused in his questioning.

"No, he was too clever for that." She pushed herself from Noel's arms. "The things he did weren't the kinds to leave bruises, they were fear and terror-based. I was torn up inside a couple times, but I figured as I agreed to the relationship there was nothing I could do about that."

She paused and looked to Noel for a few moments, then turned back.

"Look, I thought I could handle it. I thought it was over. I met him on the road and after we got together he followed me around for about a month. When I dropped him, we were moving to another gig a long way away; and when he didn't show up I figured it was over. I lived in a completely different state. I never gave him my address or anything, so I figured he'd never find me."

For once the D.A. looked like he had nothing to say. Noel let his breathing return to normal. Maybe this was it. Maybe they could go back to the hotel now, take a long hot shower together and put this behind them until the trial. No more revelations, no more surprises.

The attorney turned over a page in his yellow-lined tablet and sighed. "Ms. Cullen, it appears to me that you may have a pattern of casual sex. Would that be fair to say?"

"I'm not sure what you're asking."

"What I mean is: if you have a habit of picking up guys or letting them pick you up at gigs, then the defense is sure to bring it out. We are already really iffy on proving forcible rape with Frank, which means we may have to go only for sexual assault. And, in the absence of proof of consent, they will look to a pattern of indiscriminate sexual behavior, to show that you picked up men all the time and that you partied, used drugs, and liked it rough. So, you need to tell me now so we can plan for it." The D.A. leaned forward. "Is this a habit of yours? How many men have you seen in say. . . the last two years?"

Noel bolted out of his chair. "Wait a damn minute!" He wasn't sure if he wanted to hear the answer or not, but he wasn't going to make Rachel answer if she didn't want to. He grabbed her up and held her. "You don't have to answer that, Rachel. Don't answer."

"Mr. Kershaw." The D.A. was standing now, his voice echoing the tiredness Noel felt.

"I thought they couldn't bring up a woman's past in a rape trial," Noel said. "I thought every state had this law that a woman's past sexual experiences could not be admitted in court."

"Missouri does have a Rape Shield Law, however it's not as black and white as it sounds. As of 1994, evidence of the victim's sexual reputation is inadmissible. However, evidence of *specific* instances of the victim's prior sexual conduct *is* admissible, particularly if there was previous consensual sexual conduct with the offender that the defense can use to prove consent. Furthermore, the defense may plead, and the judge may grant, that the immediate surrounding circumstances of the alleged crime makes the evidence relevant.

"You may have heard of the recent rape case in Colorado involving a celebrity athlete. In that case, the judge allowed in three days of reported sexual activities that occurred prior to the alleged rape. These reports of sexual activity were used to show a pattern of consent. That could happen here if the defense can find witnesses to show that Rachel had a habit of picking up guys and having sex with them at each gig."

Rachel slumped against Noel. "It's true. I do…I mean I did have that pattern."

Noel pushed her shoulders away from him, his hands holding her at a distance as he looked in her eyes. Tears formed and trickled down her cheek.

Oh God, it was true. She was promiscuous. He couldn't gloss over it. How many? His mind did a quick calculation. She'd been divorced for three years or was it four? How many road trips? How many stops? His worst nightmare was coming true. Before he'd thought twenty-six was too many—never imagining it could be that high. Could it be fifty? More? Could she even remember their names?

No. This was one revelation he couldn't handle. He couldn't speak, couldn't react, he was numb. He guided her back to the table and sat beside her, his hand still in hers, but he was only going through the motions of support now. All of his rationalizations, all of his assumptions splattered like a broken egg yolk on a burning sidewalk. How stupid he had been to fall for someone like his ex-wife all over again. What was wrong with him?

He held back a groan as he sat stiffly at her side. His mind was in such chaos he could no long focus on the continuing conversation. He couldn't take anymore in. He just wanted this to be over with. He wanted to get her through this, but then he would have to let her go. He had a daughter to consider, and Claire's needs came first.

Shit, just last night they'd made love without a condom—twice. With her unable to have children, she said he didn't need it. She wanted to feel him instead of a rubber.

What diseases must she have after all those men? How stupid he'd been. After he found out about his wife, they never had sex without a condom again. He couldn't afford to be sick, or worse to die. What would happen to his daughter?

Poor Claire. She would be heartbroken that Rachel wouldn't be a part of their lives anymore. But what choice did he have?

CHAPTER SIXTEEN

Rachel felt Noel stiffen beside her, but he didn't let go of her hand, he didn't withdraw. She knew it must be difficult for him to hear about her past in such detail—particularly all the men. When he promised to stand by her, he didn't really know how many there had been. She prayed it didn't change anything.

It was the most horrific thing to happen to her, to be raped and left to die. But if she lost Noel over this, it would be like being raped all over again. It would be hard enough to go through the trial—but without him, or without knowing her life would be better when it was over, she wasn't sure she could make it.

"Ms. Cullen?"

She looked up at the D.A. Had she missed his last question?

"Ms. Cullen, this is going to be an uphill battle and it's likely to get very nasty. It's possible that whatever career you have will be ruined if everything about your previous sex life gets out. I need to make sure you will follow through to the end on this if I'm going to try it. I still want to go for the forcible rape conviction. But you have to know it's likely it will get knocked down to sexual assault, and the defendant may only get one or two years. The other possibility is that we'll end up making a deal with him in order to get him to turn over Drake, if we should ever find him."

The D.A. paused and peered over the top of his spectacles at Noel and back at her. "Are you absolutely sure you still want to go forward with this?"

Rachel searched Noel's eyes for clues, but they were dead-fish blank, as if he were looking right through her. He'd closed down.

"Yes," she whispered.

"You're sure?"

She took a deep breath and raised her voice. "I want the bastard to pay, and if you have to let him go free to get Drake I'll live with that. I don't want any other women to be hurt by Flint or Drake. Whatever I need to do to make that happen, I'll do."

Noel drove back to the hotel in silence, his eyes straight ahead, his spine ramrod straight. He held the steering wheel so tight Rachel thought it might break in two.

They ordered from room-service. They spoke, but not at all about what had happened with the D.A.

When they went to bed, he wore his briefs and immediately turned off the light, turning his back to her.

She reached over and let her fingers trail along his back and down his thigh. He didn't move. He didn't moan. He didn't turn toward her. She reached around to push her fingers down the front of his pants.

He stopped her hand with his and removed it from the waistband. "I'm really tired, Rachel. It's been a long, emotional day for both of us. Let's just go to sleep."

She turned away, her eyes misting. She'd lost him.

Her back to his, she let silent tears slide to the pillow.

* * * * *

During the plane ride home it seemed as if an anvil was pressed against her chest and it was getting heavier with each passing minute. Noel hid behind an opened book he'd purchased at the airport, his eyes on it at all times, even though he didn't seem to turn a page.

She searched for something to say—some way to end it and put them both out of their misery, but if she did that it relinquished all hope of salvaging the relationship. She wanted to rail at him, to accuse him of false promises. He had made her believe someone could truly love her in spite of her past. She should have known better. She should have run when she started falling for him.

She clenched her jaw and lifted her chin. Well, she was fine before she met him, and she would be fine again—except for the fact it seemed she was wearing a scarlet letter on her forehead now.

She turned to Noel and snatched the book from him, closing it with a resounding snap.

"What the hell?"

"You haven't turned a page in the last forty-five minutes. Stop pretending you're reading."

"I was reading. I was just resting my eyes for a moment."

"You're eyes were wide open."

"Look. I can't talk right now. If I do, I'll say something I'll regret. I don't want to hurt you."

"Well, it's too late for that."

"Rachel—"

"It *is* too late. It's written all over your face. You didn't turn toward me once last night. Before we saw the attorney, you couldn't keep your hands off me, then last night you're too tired? Give me a break. I get the picture…loud and clear."

"Rachel," he took her hand in his, but she withdrew. She needed to stay mad. She needed to hate him or she would die. He turned away. "I don't know what to say. I just wasn't prepared…"

"The truth is: it's better this way." She forced out a low laugh. "Look, it was great while it lasted.

You're the best lover I've ever had. I'm not ashamed to admit it. You also helped me get past the whole sex-after-rape thing. I'll always be grateful to you for that."

She paused and shrugged her shoulder, putting all the nonchalance she could into her posture. "But I've learned all I can from your technique and I need to move on. It's better that I move on while the memories are hot…not after I get bored."

He sat up, clenched his jaw. Then he relaxed again. "You don't mean that. You're just saying that to make me mad."

Was it possible he would be jealous if she saw someone else? Was it possible there was some small amount of love left in him?

"Would you be mad?" she asked, unable to keep the hope out of her voice.

"I'd hate to see you throwing yourself into casual sex just to get back at me."

"Dear God, what an ego you have. You think just because you said 'I love you' and you'd stand by me that I believed it? Don't flatter yourself. You used me. I used you. That's all it was. You know my pattern: pick 'em up and when I get bored throw them away. Well, I'm bored."

His eyes were needling through her, but she couldn't read them. She had no idea what he thought. No. Don't even think about finding out. Just get it over with. Don't let him in again. It will hurt even worse next time.

"Rachel, I want to be there for you, through the trial, to help you through this."

"No, you don't. You feel obligated and that's different."

Noel looked stunned. Was it because he hadn't really put it all together? Or was he surprised that she could read him so well?

"Besides, I don't need you. I'll have Michele and Sarah and Theresa there with me. Even Kat knows what I went through. They were there when all of this happened. They nursed me back to health. They stood by me without any moral judgment." She looked straight at him, accusing. He didn't flinch. "So, you're off the hook."

He let out an audible breath and then he looked straight ahead again. "If that's what you want."

The bastard! He was taking the easy way out. Well, that was why she offered it wasn't it? To get closure. Therapists always talked about it like it was a good thing. Well, it hurt liked hell when the closure caught your heart as it slammed shut.

She knew he would take the chance to get off the hook, just like most men. But she'd still hoped she was wrong. She'd hoped that he would fight for her, that he would overlook the past, that he would want to be with her no matter what—like he said he would when they started this trip. That would be true love. Damnit! She was acting like Kat, believing that true love even existed. She knew better.

Maybe she should have told him all the gory details up front, admitted to the men by the numbers, slapped him up side the head with it. Maybe if she'd done that he would have spurned her from the beginning and her heart wouldn't be breaking now.

She looked straight ahead, nurturing the anger. "Yeah, that's exactly what I want."

* * * * *

"But why, Daddy? Why can't I go to my fiddle lesson?"

"Ms. Cullen isn't able to teach you anymore. She's very busy right now. You have to remember that she travels with the band a lot…and stays up late…and she just doesn't have the time."

Right, and she was probably out screwing a new guy already. It shouldn't bother him, but it did. He felt like crap, the way he'd handled everything a week ago. If it weren't for Claire, maybe he could have forgiven her, but…

"Why didn't she tell me then? How come she hasn't called? What about next Saturday? I was supposed to play with them next Saturday, remember?"

Oh hell. The Meinig Park festival. He'd forgotten all about it.

Claire's lip trembled. "Did I do something wrong? Is she mad at me?"

He could tell she was trying not to cry. This was exactly why he should have never gotten involved with the woman. Fuck. What kind of a father was he?

He reached out and gave her a big hug. "No, honey, she's not mad at you, she's just busy."

"Then I can still play with her on Saturday?"

How could he deny her? It meant so much to her. But how could he stand to see Rachel again? If he saw her flirting with another man, he wasn't sure he could be held responsible for his actions.

"I'll call and check, okay?"

"And ask about practice too. When should I go to that nice lady's house and practice with the band?"

"Right." There must be some way he could work this all through Theresa or Michele and not have to talk to Rachel.

* * * * *

Rachel put her fiddle in the corner of her room and fell into bed. Somehow, she'd made it through four band practices and two gigs without falling apart.

She'd heard from the D.A. in Missouri only once, letting her know the trial date had been set for July—four months away.

Four more months to wait for closure. Four more months without Noel.

The phone rang and she lurched off the bed. Who would be calling at midnight on a Saturday?

"Hello?"

"Hey pretty lady, wanna get laid?"

The voice sounded slurred, as if he'd been drinking, but she didn't recognize it.

"Who is this? I'm calling the police."

"No…no, Rache, don't hang up. It's George." He drew out his name as if he wasn't sure.

"I don't know a George, and you're drunk."

"You've pierced my heart. Two years ago. You were looking for some fun. I was the young cowboy from East Texas. New to Portland. You were my Mrs. Robinson."

It all came back to her. She had seen her ex with his new wife and she couldn't take it, so she'd run to the nearest bar and picked up the youngest guy she could find. Dark hair, dark eyes, and lots of stamina. He'd been what, twenty-three? Twenty-four? It lasted all of two, maybe three months on weekends but it had made her feel sexy. Then he dumped her flat. Ended up he had a girlfriend, a virginal girlfriend who was becoming serious.

"Okay, I remember. You're drunk and whatever you want I'm not interested."

"Come on Rache, we were good together. I might not be good tonight, but when I wake up I could show you a great time."

"Still not interested."

"Come on, you're not mad at me are ya?"

"What happened to your girlfriend? You know, the one you were going to get serious with."

"Yeah, we broke up. Turns out she wanted to marry a virgin. Can you get that? Shit."

Rachel laughed loud and long. Served him right.

"So, like, I'm free, ya know. We can spend more than just a couple hours together this time. We can spend the whole fuckin' day if ya like. Fuckin'. Ha that's funny. Come on, for old time's sake."

"You're hard up, aren't you George? What happened? Did every other divorcee turn you down?"

"How did you know about…oops."

"Good night. Don't ever call me again." She slammed the phone down.

Whatever had possessed her to screw with a kid? Looking back on it, it wasn't nearly as good as she'd thought. They hadn't even cared about each other a little bit. They'd never had a conversation about anything except sex. She must have been really desperate.

Then there was Noel. He'd been the exception. He'd been the only one who really mattered. No one would ever be as good as Noel.

She shook herself. Now that was *not* the right attitude for getting over him. All right, so maybe there was something to be said about a caring, loving relationship and the sex with that. But that was over.

Maybe there was something in between. She just had to pick up someone closer to her age, someone she could at least have a conversation with.

She looked at the clock again. 12:15am. Saturday had just turned into Sunday. What would still be open? Where could she find a little older crowd? She tapped her fingers against her thigh.

Lucky's was open until 2:00. That should be enough time to snag someone. She hadn't been there since the first year after her divorce. She did remember the crowd was older, and the bar held up to its name. She chuckled. She did get lucky there two or three times.

She opened the closet. Should she go screaming sex with a micro-mini, or try the demure but irresistible lace mini with scalloped décolleté? No, neither one was right. She didn't want to look like she was begging.

She settled on the sapphire blue, tea-length gown with a handkerchief bottom and a slit on one side well up her thigh. A girl still needed a definite flirtation. She shimmied into the dress, loving the way the satin skimmed her form. The tank style bodice and v-necked cowl was just right to invite roving eyes without screaming "look at my boobs." She turned her back to the mirror and looked over her shoulder. If the front didn't draw them in, the low back scoop definitely would. It scooped all the way to her waist and underneath the only thing she was wearing was a matching blue thong.

She slipped on a strappy, ebony sandal with a short heel. She really didn't like the spiked heels that so many women favored—way too uncomfortable.

One last look in the mirror and she was satisfied she would find someone tonight. Preferably someone who wasn't already drunk and who would take some time to make her forget Noel.

She bounced into Lucky's to the beat of Cheryl Crow's *All I Wanna Do is Have Some Fun.* She let the music sweep over her and was immediately caught up in a dance with someone old enough to interest her. Within the next hour she danced with eight different guys. She ruled out most of them because they were too greedy, not even waiting until the half way point of the song before slipping their hand down to her butt. That was a definite sign they wouldn't meet her needs.

Then there was the virgin accountant. Well, maybe he wasn't a virgin but he sure acted like it. He didn't even make eye contact. Definitely a non-starter, or an early-finisher.

By one-thirty, most people had partnered with someone or the newly coupled were just finishing the negotiations. At this time of night, Luckys dimmed the lights and kept the music slow and bluesy until they closed at two. It was time to make her move or she'd be coming home alone.

Rachel had already made her choice. He was nothing like Noel—short blonde hair, brown eyes, a well-groomed beard, maybe five eleven. When they'd danced a couple of times, he had a way of looking at her that said he knew what he was doing and it was all for fun. Now it was time to make her move, to see if he was willing to go the distance.

She spotted him across the room with a beer in his hand, talking to another guy. She walked toward him, a definite sway in her hips. When she caught his eye, she smiled. He swallowed and stepped away from his friend. She sidled up to him, took his drink from his hand and sipped, then handed it back as her tongue moved slowly along the top of her lips.

"Craig, right?"

"Yep." He looked her up and down without shame.

She swayed her hips to the slow ballad the DJ had selected. "You're not too tired to dance a little more are you?"

"I imagine I can get up some energy."

She placed her hand on his shoulder. "Good. Can you do it slow? Real slow?"

He laughed and placed a firm arm around her waist, pulling her close as he turned her onto the dance floor with two steps. "Oh yeah, I can."

He dipped her low and followed her head with his, his mouth only a breath away from hers. "How slow do you want it?"

She threw her head back and laughed, arching in his arms as he rained kisses along her collarbone. Yes. She could do this and she would enjoy it. Within an hour Noel would be completely out of her mind.

When he brought her back up she put both arms around his neck and one leg between his legs, swaying with him as if they were one. She brushed lightly against him until she could feel him getting hard. Then she turned so her back was to him and he put his hand against her stomach as they continued to sway. He rubbed himself against her butt, and she accentuated the sensation by adding more rotation to her hips. When she turned back around, they swayed from side to side and he dipped to kiss her. She threw herself into the kiss, opening her mouth for a tongue dance to the fast Latin rhythm now playing.

Without pause he moved his hand up her side and his thumb caressed one nipple until it stood tall. Dammit! She wasn't feeling it. She'd just have to try harder.

"Mmmmm. That's good," she said. "Let's just keep it fun." She worked her leg along his length again.

"You're callin' my number, baby." He twirled her quickly several times as he held her to him. The momentary dizziness, mixed with the spicy aroma of his after shave was a bit scary. She took a deep breath and steadied herself. She could do this. She had to do this to prove Noel meant nothing.

When the song ended and the next one started there was no question of them separating. His hand stroked her bare back and then moved to her shoulders. He slipped her sleeve off the shoulder and dipped to kiss the indentation. It was a slow kiss filled with promise. Then he put the sleeve back in place.

Still nothing. What was wrong with her? This guy knew what he was doing. He was the right age, the right type, not scary, just sexy. She turned her face into his neck and kissed it up the side to nibble his ear. If she just kept playing, it would eventually excite her. Right?

"I like the all night kind of slow," she murmured into his neck.

He laughed and twirled her again, pulling her so close she thought his hardness would tear a hole in his pants as it strained toward her. "You do, huh? Personally, I like to mix it up. Slow dance at night." He rotated against her. "Fast dance in the morning." He took two more quick twirls, then turned her out and pulled her back in with her butt against his growing erection, his right hand splayed across her stomach, and his left draped over her shoulder fingers entwining hers. He held her still as he brushed against her. "And then a slow rockin' the rest of the day."

"I could use some slow 'rockin,'' she said, a catch in her throat.

He turned her back to face him, and she stiffened.

He stopped and looked into her eyes. "Hey, you okay?"

She nodded, but a stray tear said otherwise.

"Ah, shit." He wiped a finger along her cheek and moved her off the dance floor. "Just broke up with someone didn't you?"

"I'm sorry. I thought I wanted this, and I do…I mean I should. Really, you are exactly my type."

"Yeah, obviously."

"No really. If I'd met you say three months ago, this probably would have been a great thing. It's just that…"

"You love him, though, right?"

Her eyes misted. She swallowed and turned away from him. Yes, damn him. She loved him and now he'd ruined her forever. Now she couldn't have him and because there could be no one else, she couldn't even enjoy casual sex anymore.

She turned back and kissed Craig on the cheek. "Thanks for trying."

He stayed her hand. "He's one lucky son-of-a-bitch."

"I'm sorry. Really."

He shrugged and released her, walking her to the door. "Don't worry about it. If you change your mind, I have no problem helping you forget him next time."

"I wish it were that simple." She crossed the threshold and closed the tavern door quietly behind her.

CHAPTER SEVENTEEN

Noel drove up the mountain hoping he wouldn't have to see Rachel. It had been a rough two weeks, and the last thing he needed was to have his resolve tested. His plan was to drop off Claire without getting out of the car. He would watch as she knocked on the door. Kat or Theresa would answer and he'd ask her to call him when they were done. Then he would wave good-bye. He should be in and out without a problem.

"Daddy? Are you going to come listen to me play?"

"Not this time, honey. I have to go to the store and buy something for Grandma and Grandpa. But I'll come back and get you when you're done."

"But you might miss Rachel. After she hears me play, she might want to give me lessons again."

"Claire, we've already been through this. She's too busy."

"But maybe she's not busy anymore."

He sighed. Maybe he should tell her the truth. Maybe it was better this way. He didn't want Claire to think it was her fault.

He waited until they reached the Wildwood campground, then he pulled into the parking lot.

"Daddy, this isn't the right place."

He turned off the ignition and turned toward Claire.

"Honey, Daddy needs to tell you something. It's very important."

She turned and her eyes widened. "Is it a secret?"

"No. But I did something and I'm very sorry."

"Were you bad?"

"Yes. Daddy told a fib."

"Umm. But grownups never lie."

Oh, how he wished that were true. There were so many little lies he'd told his daughter. Lies about her mother so she wouldn't be too scared. Lies about what happened to things Clarissa had taken from the house and sold. Then there were all the lies Clarissa had told. He was even telling himself lies about Rachel. But a young child didn't need to know all those things. But this, she needed to understand. Somehow.

"I'm sorry, Claire. I didn't tell you the whole truth about Rachel being too busy to give you lessons."

"You didn't? Why? Don't you like the way I play?"

He ran a finger along her cheek. "I love the way you play, honey. You're the best fiddle player ever."

"No, I'm not. Rachel is the best. But if I keep practicing I can be just like her."

"Claire, Rachel and Daddy had a fight, and that's why you can't take fiddle lessons from her anymore along with her being very busy."

"A fight? Like the kind of fight I had with Jessie when she got mad at me and pulled my hair?"

"Not exactly, but we did get mad."

"But Daddy, when I got mad at Jessie you made us talk to each other until we made up, and now we're friends again. So you just have to talk to Rachel and then make up."

He sighed. "It's not that easy."

"Why? You're a grown up. You said if I made up with Jessie then I would be grown up too. Now you just talk to her and make up, just like me and Jessie. Then I can have my lessons again."

That was the problem. He really wasn't acting like a grown up. He had turned away from the woman he loved because he couldn't accept her past. He had equated her with Clarissa, when she was nothing like his ex. Rachel was a loving, caring person who had given Claire a new lease on life. More than that she'd showed him what love could feel like when someone gave all of herself to him. Then he'd shattered that love by running away. To be fair, he didn't exactly run away. But he didn't make any effort to stay either.

To be honest, it was as much about his ego as about his ex. The thought that she'd had more sexual partners than he did really bothered him. He knew that was a sexist way to think, but he couldn't help it. The truth was he could count on one hand the number of partners he'd had, including his ex-wife. But Rachel. Could she even remember half the names? The thought of being a forgotten name in Rachel's past bothered him even more than the number of men.

"Daddy? Are you thinking? Do you want me to tell Rachel you're sorry?"

In his haste to get Rachel out of his mind, he'd hurt Claire too. It's just that he knew if he saw Rachel every week, he couldn't trust himself not to want her again. And now it was too late. He'd completely broken her trust by not living up to his promises. How could he possibly explain all that to a child?

"Daddy!"

He looked up. Had she yelled his name a couple of times?

"Can we go now? I don't want to be late."

He glanced at the clock. They might still make it on time. He turned the ignition and pulled out of the parking lot and back onto highway twenty-six. Maybe he should let Claire continue the lessons with

Rachel. He wasn't afraid Rachel would hurt Claire. It was only himself he was protecting.

Ten minutes later, along with Claire's ongoing chatter about Rachel and playing the fiddle interspersed with her singing the *Froggie Went a Courtin',* he pulled into Theresa's driveway.

He took a deep breath and got out of the car, walked around to the passenger door and helped Claire out of her seat. He threw his shoulders back. He might as well face the music. Taking Claire's hand in his, they went up the two steps together and knocked on the front door.

The tension left his shoulders when Kat answered the door. One meeting avoided.

He waved to Claire and promised to be back soon. Maybe during the next two hours he'd find a way to convince himself he could talk to Rachel without his heart jumping from his chest and landing in her lap.

* * * * *

Claire ran into the practice room, her violin case bouncing against her leg. Rachel threw her arms around her and held tight, the case pinned between them. The rest of the band looked up from tuning and shouted their welcomes to Claire.

Rachel held on, as if letting go would lose Claire to her forever. After the blowup with Noel, she wasn't sure if he'd ban his daughter from playing with the band. Thank God he was being reasonable.

When Claire started to wiggle, Rachel let go and tousled the top of her head. "Ready to practice?"

"Yes!" Claire rushed to the table with all the instrument cases, unsnapped her violin case, carefully rosined the bow, and put the fiddle to her chin.

"Need help with the tuning?" Rachel asked.

"Let me try it first." Small fingers plucked each string, then moved to the tuning pins and turned them as needed. When Claire was satisfied she placed the bow to the strings, and played a few scales.

"Good job!" Rachel was still amazed at how quickly Claire learned. She saw more talent in this six-year-old than in other children she'd tutored for several years. Claire was destined to be a fiddler.

"Shall we do the pieces with Claire first, then move onto the rest of the set?" Theresa asked.

Claire beamed. "Yes!" She held her fiddle at the ready, and Theresa called the count. They launched into a couple of traditional reels, and then Claire led the group on her favorite song, "A froggie went a courtin'." They laughed when she threw in her own variation by adding "ribbit, ribbit."

After a couple more old standards, Rachel turned to Claire and said, "I have a surprise for you." Claire's eyes went wide. "I want you to play the song you composed, the one called 'Missy and Me.'"

"Really? The one I made up?" Claire bounced on her toes in anticipation.

"Yup. I want the rest of the band to hear it, so we can learn how to play it with you."

"Okay." Claire put her bow to the string and played a couple notes, then stopped. "Wait. That's wrong. Let me start again."

The second time she went straight through. The song referred to her dog, Missy, who was always bouncing around her knees and ready to dance whenever Claire needed. She'd fashioned a fiddle tune that, though rough around the edges was great for a six-year-old. It would be a hit in Newfoundland. It had that total New Breton sound.

Rachel looked at her bandmates, their mouths agape. They'd known Claire was good, but this was the first time they'd heard an original composition. By the end, all of them stood and clapped, rushing to give her hugs and congratulations.

"We'll have to put that on our next CD," Kat declared, and everyone agreed. Claire beamed.

"Can I play more now?"

Michele stepped up. "The rest of the set are tunes you haven't learned, but if you want to play skip beats on the side, that's fine."

Delight welled in Rachel's heart. Though Claire's talent was her own, she felt happy to be a small part of guiding her gifts and including her in the band. Her eyes misted. This must be what it's like to take pride in your child. Only a few weeks ago she'd dreamed of eventually being an even more integral part of Claire's life. Now she would have to be satisfied with always being on the outside. She squared her shoulders. It would just have to be enough.

At the end of the rehearsal, Claire tugged on Rachel's arm. "How come you're too busy to give me lessons anymore?"

"What?" Rachel pulled her aside, away from the others.

"Daddy said you were too busy now because of the tour and the gigs." Claire's lips quivered. "I don't want another teacher. I want you. Maybe I could come every other week instead. Then would you teach me? Please." She looked up to Rachel, her eyes glistening with tears ready to fall.

Rachel pulled her into her arms. "I'm sorry, honey. I want to teach you, it's just that…"

She was going to kill Noel with her bare hands. Just because he didn't want to see her was no reason to take Claire away from something she loved. Her stomach roiled. She gritted her teeth, so as not to start swearing profusely.

Claire slowly disentangled herself from Rachel's embrace. "Daddy also said you had a fight. I told him he had to makeup with you."

Rachel bent to Claire's level and looked her in the eye. "No matter what happens between your Daddy and me, I will always love you, Claire."

Claire looked down at her shoes. "That's what my mommy said, too. But I didn't believe her."

Rachel pulled her back into a hug. "I'm so sorry, honey. I'll talk to your, Daddy. We'll work something out."

* * * * *

The moment he saw her, his pulse raced ahead. Rachel was sitting on the front stairs with Claire. He could feel beads of sweat forming on his brow. He slowed and pulled up to the door. Neither Rachel nor Claire stood.

He turned off the ignition and sat in silence. They must have made a secret pact while he was gone. They were going to make him get out of the car and talk. He could see it in their eyes. Who knew a six-year-old could be so crafty?

He rounded the back of the car and stood a few feet away from the porch. This should be a safe distance for a brief chat.

"Ready to go, Claire?"

Rachel and Claire stood at the same time.

"Rachel needs to talk to you, Daddy. And she said I could have another cookie and lemonade with Kat and Theresa while she talked."

Shit. That was just great. Rachel had it all planned out. He didn't have any say in the matter.

Claire turned the door handle and opened the front door. She turned around to close it, but stepped back onto the porch. "Remember, Daddy, you have to make up now." Then she turned, stepped back inside and closed the door.

Noel forced his eyes away from the door and onto Rachel's face. The dimple he remembered wasn't there now. Her eyes were narrowed to slits. Her teeth were clenched. He watched as she took two slow, deep breaths. Yup. It was going to be bad.

"Why did you tell Claire I couldn't give her lessons anymore?" Her voice surprised him. He expected anger, not this soft, constrained tone.

He'd thought this through during the rehearsal, but whatever limited plan he'd made just went out the window. He could fight anger, but he couldn't find any words to counter the contempt he heard.

"Are you afraid I'll rub off on her? That I'll teach her to be a *lamhrag* and by the time she's a teen, she'll be just like me?"

"A what?"

"*Lamhrag.* A slut."

"I never called you that."

"No, you're too polite to say that. But you thought it, didn't you? Or maybe you wouldn't admit it. Maybe you would be a little more poetic and just call me a flirt-gill."

She was getting louder now, and he noticed that when her anger rose her brogue became more pronounced. Flirt-gill, Shakespeare's loose women. She was right; that is why he ran.

"You didn't seem to mind having a flirt-gill crawling all over you before." She stepped to within inches of his face. You didn't seem to mind my *lamhrag* mouth on you. You didn't stop me from straddling your—"

He crushed her mouth to his to stop what she was going to say. He remembered every picture from their time together, every move, every smell. He'd been dreaming of her every night for the past two weeks. This was why he couldn't be near her.

She ravished him as much as he ravished her, their tongues darting, exploring. His pulse raced. He ran his fingers through her short white hair, inhaled her scent, and pulled her closer still.

Then she pushed him away, hard.

His mind reeled from the dizzying sensations pulsing through him. He concentrated on slowing his breathing. Stupid. Stupid. Stupid. He'd fallen right into her trap.

"I'm fine for sex, but not good enough to be around Claire. Is that it?"

Dear God, she was so damn frustrating! How could she twist everything around so much?

"I'm sorry." He barely managed to get the words out between breaths.

"Sorry for what?" she shouted. "For having sex with me? For letting a *lamhrag* get you hard? Or for letting me around Claire?"

“Neither,” he shouted back, as if he could overpower her voice with his. She closed her mouth and her eyes widened.

He ran a hand through his hair, he didn’t know what to do with his legs. He wasn’t sure if he could keep standing and looking at her. But he knew he couldn’t look away. He raised his eyes and looked straight at her.

“I’m sorry for hurting you. Okay? I’m sorry.”

She fell silent. Her body so stiff and still, he was sure she’d turned to stone. Her eyes were open, but unfocused. He was afraid to move, afraid to touch her, afraid that if he spoke another word it would be his last.

Then he saw the pain, the confusion, the slight tremble as she stiffened even more. He raised his hand toward her face.

“Don’t touch me.” Her lips had barely moved, but the words were a command. “Don’t ever touch me again.”

He lowered his arm. He wanted to start over. How did it go so wrong when all he’d wanted was to make amends?

“I shouldn’t have tried to stop Claire from continuing her lessons. I was wrong. I was just unsure…uncomfortable…I guess I wanted to spare us the difficulty of seeing each other.”

“By taking her away from me? By making her think that I didn’t love her anymore?” She stepped forward and pressed her index finger into his chest, her voice so cold he could feel the ice cubes dropped one by one down his spine. “How dare you put words in my mouth and give them to Claire. *You* may be able to retract love at the drop of a hat, but I can’t. I would never hurt someone I love like that. I would never say I was too busy.”

He hunched his shoulders. His stomach felt like a knife was scraping it clean. He rubbed his finger from the bridge of his nose to the top of his forehead and closed his eyes for just a moment.

“You’re right. I was wrong. I shouldn’t have let my problems get in the way of Claire’s happiness.”

“Damn right, you self-righteous, selfish bastard.”

Good. She was getting angry again. He could deal with anger.

“So, here’s the deal. I want to continue working with Claire. She has a real talent for the fiddle and I think it’s important to her to have something she can call her own, some way to shine above the crowd.”

“I agree.”

“Good. We also can’t avoid each other every time you bring her over. I know you would prefer not to lay eyes on me, but I’d think you could put aside your feelings for Claire’s sake. I’m willing to keep our relationship professional if you are.”

Hell. He didn't want a professional relationship. He wanted her back in his life, in his home. He wanted her back in his bed. He wanted to wake up with her. But that wasn't going to happen now that he'd blown it big time.

"Can you put aside your feelings and at least pretend we're friends for Claire's sake."

"Yes, I can manage to keep our relationship professional." And no matter what her words said, they would always be more than friends. He may not ever get a chance again to act on it. But he could never be *just friends* with Rachel Cullen.

Rachel opened the door behind her and called into the hall. "Claire, time to go home now."

Claire came skipping down the hall, a chocolate smudge on her cheek. Rachel laughed and reached out with a finger to clean it off. "Looks like you had a chocolate chip cookie."

She smiled, wrapped her arms around Rachel's small hips. "Yup. And it was soooo good." She untangled herself and turned to Noel. "Did you make up, Daddy? Are you friends now?"

His eyes sought Rachel's but she was looking everywhere except at him. "Yes, honey. We made up."

"Yippee! Can Rachel come have dinner with us and play a game then?"

Rachel bent to Claire's level and gave her a hug.

"I'm not going to be coming to dinner for awhile. I've been ignoring all my other friends lately and spending all my time with you and your Daddy. So, I've decided that I have to be careful not to forget my other friends."

"Does this mean you won't ever come for dinner again?" Claire's bottom lip pooched out.

Noel held his breath, waiting for her answer. Would she ever consider starting over? Could she forgive him and let him do it right this time?

Rachel's lips lifted slightly, in the mysterious smile of the Mona Lisa. "Never say never, Claire girl. But for now, you and I can spend time together with lessons and the band, and maybe some other time we can do something special with just the two of us. Okay?"

Claire wrinkled her forehead. "But what about Daddy? When is he going to spend time with you?"

Rachel speared him with a look that said 'You're turn. You got us here, now you fix it.' At least that's what he deserved to hear from her.

"I get to spend time with Rachel whenever I take you to lessons and whenever you play with the band."

"But that means I get more time than you. That's not fair."

"That's okay, pumpkin. You can tell me all about your time together and then it will feel just like I was there too."

She wrinkled her forehead again. Then, her shoulders lowered and she smiled. She gave Rachel a quick hug and ran over and hugged Noel too. "Okay. Let's go now. "

"*Slán go fóill... a chuisle mo chroí...*"

"*Slán.*" Claire giggled. "She called me her little treasure, Daddy. Isn't that funny?" She waved to Rachel as she pulled on his hand, anxious now to get him into the car.

Noel hesitated. "We'll see you on Friday then for another rehearsal?"

"That's right. Bye, Noel." She turned and went inside, not looking back again.

Bye. Not the easy *slán* she shared with Claire, or the endearment she'd added on the end. Bye was too short. It sounded so final—even more final than when they'd been on the plane. This time there was no emotion attached to her words, no attempt at cover up, no sense of her pain. He'd even take anger right now. At least that would show she still cared.

But she showed nothing. She was professional now. Already, she had moved on. Now why couldn't he?

CHAPTER EIGHTEEN

April moved far too slowly for Rachel. Every glimpse of Noel pulled the scab off a wound that would never heal, but better this pain in her heart than giving up Claire. When the trial finally started, it was almost a relief. She wouldn't have to face Noel for several weeks.

In all the preparation for the trial, Rachel had become more comfortable with the D.A. She even called him by his first name now, Jack. He reminded her of one of her father's friends—brusque but compassionate An former military man, he was always on time and on task. He hadn't made it easy for her, but she felt well-prepared with her testimony. They'd practiced every possible question, every horrific scene until she could do it without falling apart.

Rachel unbuttoned her black woolen blazer, hoping she'd breathe better without the restriction. She'd debated for an hour this morning on what to wear. Jack had cautioned her to wear something conservative, businesslike, non-sexual. She'd vacillated between a basic black chemise and this pantsuit. April in Missouri was unpredictable, so she'd gone for warmth, pairing the black blazer and pants with an aqua sweater.

The courtroom was only half full. She turned to reassure herself that all the members of Sweetwater Canyon still sat in the front row. Kat gave her a thumbs up, and Theresa put a hand over her heart. Sarah and Michele smiled encouragement. Rachel's eyes misted as she put her hand to her mouth, then dropped it forward in the sign for 'Thank you'.

She hadn't asked them to come. In fact, taking on her usual martyr role, she'd insisted it would be better if she did this alone. Thank God, no one had listened. Michele had led the pack, saying she was showing up whether Rachel liked or not. And, it was Michele who popped into her hotel room last night and stayed with her while she worked through her testimony one more time.

The hardest part of her testimony would be guarding her emotions. She'd wanted to keep them under control. In fact, she'd been practicing how to respond to the most difficult questions and stay calm. If her emotions crept in, even a little, she'd end up curled in a fetal position on the floor and they'd drag her away to the funny farm.

When the Jack had prepped her the day before, he was disappointed with her detachment. She blanched when he asked if the rape even bothered her anymore. Of course it bothered her. Did he think she'd put herself through all of this for the fun of it? He liked that response. He'd urged her to react naturally and release her feelings. He'd said it was real emotions, whether they were anger or fear, tears or shaking, that the jury responded to. So, Rachel and Michele had stayed up late to see how Rachel could undo the control she'd so carefully constructed, yet keep some semblance of self-preservation.

Rachel pasted on a smile for her friends. She didn't have much hope for this trial, but she was determined to go through with it. Not only for herself, but for Kat. It seemed that Kat had bounced back from her ordeal on the mountain, but every once in a while Rachel noticed that haunted look in her eyes. She recognized the look. For Kat and for herself, she wanted to prove that she would no longer be held down by this one event. It was time for life to get back on track, permanently.

Her eyes caught a movement at the back of the courtroom. Her breath hitched as Noel stepped into the room. She couldn't move. She couldn't breathe. She couldn't believe her eyes. Why was he here?

Noel stood tall, his shoulders defined by the cut of his charcoal grey suit. He'd never looked so good. Rachel consciously closed her open mouth. He smiled at her. Her skin tingled and she could have sworn she heard bagpipes playing *Dòmhnall nan Dòmhnall* in the background, her warrior lover come to town.

"All rise! Court is in session. The honorable John Mosier presiding."

"Good morning, citizens. Please be seated." He turned to each table. "Good day, counsel."

"And to you, sir," each responded in turn.

Rachel's spine stiffened. This was it. This was when everything would be retold and questioned, and her life's ugliness and mistakes trotted out again to remind Noel exactly why they weren't together.

The rotund judge adjusted his glasses and peered at the case docket. "Is the prosecution ready?" he asked.

"Yes, your honor."

"And the defense?"

The defense counsel rose. "May I approach the bench with opposing counsel?"

The judge nodded and his pudgy right hand waived them forward. Rachel looked to Jack as he rose. Though she'd felt the prosecutor was fit and strong for an older man, in comparison to the judge his dark suit suddenly seemed to make him appear insubstantial.

The judge flipped a switch and the microphone in front of him went dead. He spoke quietly with the attorneys at the bench. Rachel couldn't hear what they said, but she saw Jack waving his arms in denial of some request, his stature growing before her. Then it appeared he relented but with a smirk. Finally, both attorneys returned to their tables.

The judge spoke in a low grumble, obvious derision lacing his tone. "As a plea agreement was filed prior to trial and declined by the defendant, but is now being requested to stand, and the prosecutor has provisionally agreed with the request based on a possible revision, we will have a two-hour recess so that the prosecutor and his client may discuss whether to continue with the trial or accept the plea."

Rachel's eyes widened. Did this mean she wouldn't have to testify? She wouldn't have to be cross-examined?

"All rise." They stood and the judge exited the room.

The court room buzzed as Rachel let Jack guide her from the court to an adjoining office, his hand strong upon her back..

She paced the room and pressed a hand to her face, unsure whether to be relieved or angry. "So what just happened in there? I thought he turned down your plea agreement."

"He did," the attorney agreed. "And the time to change his mind and accept the plea ran out yesterday at five. So, we don't have to renegotiate if we don't want. But hear me out." He pulled a chair from the table. "Would you like to sit? Can I get you something? Water? Coffee?"

Rachel placed a hand on the chair. She felt lightheaded, but she was afraid to sit—afraid she would lose what little control she had left. "No. I need to keep moving or I'll collapse."

"Okay. Here's the deal. Overnight either Hunter's attorney convinced him of the strength of our case, or he thought about it on his own. In any case, I think he realizes if he goes to trial he will probably lose. Worse than losing he could easily receive two life sentences, one for the forcible rape and one for attempted murder."

Rachel's head reeled and she sat in the chair after all. Her head sagged onto the table.

A hand softly touched her shoulder. "Are you all right?" Jack asked.

"Just give me a minute. Maybe I'll take that water."

Footsteps retreated toward the door and she heard it open and close. She took in a deep breath and let it out, her head now pounding.

It was too much to take in. She'd realized that if she prevailed Hunter could get a life sentence, but she'd never really hoped for it until now. She'd expected Hunter to take the first plea, twenty years in exchange for information on Drake. When he didn't take it, she'd been so angry she had to go through with the trial that she was determined he'd get the full boat. Now it was all topsy turvy again. *Chac!*

The door opened and soon a glass of water appeared in front of her. A chair scraped next to her and she raised her head slowly. Jack sat back in his chair, waiting, as if he had all the time in the world. She lifted the glass to her lips. Just start with a sip, she told herself. Then another.

"Need something for the headache?" Jack asked, his voice sympathetic.

She squinted, the light bothering her. "Got something? And could we keep the lights off for a while?"

He rose and flipped the switch by the door, then stuck a hand into the bottom of his briefcase. He extracted a small plastic bottle of ibuprofen, flicked the cap off with his thumb and shook out two pills. "Two enough?"

She nodded, then regretted her head movement as spikes of lights danced in her eyes. A migraine was playing around the edges. He placed the medicine into her open hand, and she popped both in her mouth and took a longer drink. Twenty-minutes. In just twenty-minutes she'd feel better. "Thanks."

"Take your time, I'm not going anywhere."

The next time she raised her head, it seemed Jack hadn't moved. But the headache was now a dull pain in her forehead instead of the raging pressure in her eyes that it had been.

“Feel well enough to talk now?”

“Yeah, thanks.” She sat up and smoothed her hands along the leg of her pants. Another half hour and she might actually be able to walk out of here under her own power instead of collapsing at the first sight of her friends. “So, what’s the deal now?”

“Because the time was up, I said I was adding ten years on to the sentencing recommendation, and I still wanted Drake.”

“And?” Rachel held her breath.

“His attorney said he’d agree.”

“He knows where Drake is?” Her pulse accelerated. Was it possible they’d actually catch him? Was it possible she’d have to go through the trial preparation again, and worse, face Drake in court?

“I don’t know if he can actually lead us directly to him, but his attorney says he will give us all of Drake’s hangouts, friends, and any plans he shared with Hunter over the past six months. In other words, whatever Hunter does know we’ll know. I think then it will just be a matter of time before the police catch up with him.”

Rachel’s breathing shallowed. Nausea rolled through her gut. “Excuse me a minute. I’ll be right back.” She stood and rushed out the door and down the hall to the restroom.

She locked herself in a stall, fully expecting to throw up but nothing came except tears. She let them flow and her stomach settled. Is it possible she was nearing the end of her ordeal? Maybe not today or tomorrow, but maybe in the next year it could finally be over. When she felt steady again, she stood at the sink and splashed cold water on her face.

She ran a comb through her unruly hair, pushed back her shoulders and lifted her chin. She'd made it this far, she was ready to finish it—however long it took. She'd go back and tell the prosecutor to take the plea, and let him know she'd go through this again if Drake was stupid enough to ask for a trial. No one was going to have control over her life anymore. No one except herself.

The next day they were all back in the courtroom, the plea documents filed and signed, and the judge ready for final sentencing.

"Will the defendant please stand," the judge said.

Frank Hunter stood with his defense attorney. His pasty skin looked worse than the day before. He rubbed his thumb against his fingers in nervous circles at his side. Rachel sat up taller.

"Do you understand the charges in this case, that you will plead guilty to forcible rape and be sentenced to thirty years in prison without opportunity for parole?" the judge asked.

"I do, your honor." His voice caught on the I do.

"Do you then waive your right to trial?"

"I do, your honor." He looked straight ahead.

"Then how do you plead to the charge of forcible rape?"

"Guilty." It was almost a whisper.

"Speak up," the judge demanded.

"Quilty," he raised his voice almost to a shout.

Rachel closed her eyes and sent out a brief prayer of thanks. Even though she knew his guilty plea was part of the bargain, it still surprised her to actually hear it and know it was recorded.

"As part of this plea agreement you need to tell the court, in your own words, what happened."

Rachel held her breath. How would he represent her participation? Because he was admitting forcible rape he couldn't say she agreed or anything was consensual as he alleged previously, but how far would he go in condemning himself?

Hunter looked directly at the judge as he spoke, his southern drawl more pronounced with each sentence.

"Well, I knew Drake from old times. He was in town and we met up at a strip joint we both know. This was, like, about a week before I was to help him with the girl. He had a copy of this band's tour schedule from the web, and he said he wanted to get back at the bitch with the gold hair." His lip quirked up in a smirk.

Rachel clenched her fists. So, it *was* planned far in advance. How long had he been waiting for her, storing up his anger?

"Go ahead," the judge waved toward Hunter.

Hunter looked up, his attitude growing more cocky as he continued. "Anyway, Drake laid it out—I mean, he had the whole thing planned—and well, I figured I get a pretty good piece of tail out of it." He chuckled, then sobered. "Of course there was also some big bucks so I wasn't complainin'. You know what I mean?" When the judge didn't respond he looked directly at Rachel and smiled. "He gave me a sweet picture of you naked, just in case I needed to think on it. Of course, that was enough for me." He licked his lips and grinned. Rachel wanted to smack the grin off his face.

"You will face me during your statement," the judge reprimanded Hunter.

"Yes, your honor." He paused again and then raised his chin. "My job was to sweet talk her before they played their gig, then followup with gettin' her to my room later that night. He wasn't so sure she'd go for comin' up to my room, so he said if she didn't wanna come, I was to slip her somethin'—you know, in a drink, to make her more accommodatin' like."

Rachel's eyes widened and her mouth dropped open. It wouldn't have mattered whether she'd agreed to go to his room or not. The rape still would have happened. They had a plan from the beginning. She'd made it easier by being in his room, but it wasn't her fault. Thank God, she could finally let go her guilt.

"Maybe I wouldn' hafta give her anything even after we got there," Hunter continued. "But I wasn't sure and Drake only gave me, like, fifteen minutes to fuck her. 'Cause he said he wanted the rest of the night to do his thing.

So I didn't wanna have any problems with her fightin' me or anything. So soon as we got in my room, I plugged her beer. She didn't know what hit her. Man that stuff works real fast. It wasn't even five minutes and she couldn't move. When she finally figured it out and begged me to stop it was too late. The bitch couldn't move and boy, that was one of the sweetest fifteen minute fucks I've ever had." He looked at Rachel and smiled as he pumped his hips forward, then quickly looked back at the judge again.

Even though the bile in her stomach threatened to choke her, Rachel stared straight back at him. She would not give him the satisfaction of hurting her anymore.

The rest of the allocution was difficult, but she'd been through the telling of it in therapy so many times that she was able to sit, stoic, and listen to the entire tale once again. She tried to hear it as if it had happened to someone else.

Rachel shuddered at Hunter's obvious lack of remorse. He told the tale as if it was something he did every day and never thought twice about his actions. He said that Drake had not only watched the whole thing, but recorded it on video. He then set up the camera to record on its own saying he wanted to have it as a souvenier for when he was done with her.

Rachel closed her eyes and bit the inside of her cheek. She'd forgotten about the camera—even in therapy she must have blocked it out. The thought of Drake still having a tape was too frightening to think about.

Hunter said he didn't know that Drake planned to kill her, but then he wouldn't have put it past him either. He said Drake was one scary dude, and if the cops did find him he was going to insist they weren't in the same prison.

When the allocution was over, the judge said, "What I've just heard today is so disgusting, I wish I could sentence you to life without parole. That is what you deserve for what you did to this young woman. I'm also sorry that the attempted murder charge was dropped in your plea agreement, because it is clear to me that legally you should face that charge as well. However, pursuant to the sentencing recommendation in the plea agreement, I sentence you to thirty years in prison. Be assured those thirty years are to be served without any possibility of early parole." He paused and looked directly into Hunter's eyes. "And, if I hear that you did not cooperate fully with the prosecution by giving all the information you can about Drake, or if any information turns out to be false, I guarantee you will be back in my courtroom and not facing such leniency."

The judge pounded the gavel. Everyone in the court rose as he left the room.

Rachel sagged in her chair as her friends gathered around her. They hugged and touched her arm. Michele laced her fingers with Rachel's and Sarah rubbed her arm. Kat stroked Rachel's hair and Theresa massaged her shoulders. They surrounded her, protected her, covered her.

Out of the corner of her eye she saw Noel standing, watching. It seemed their eyes connected—his sad, hers questioning. But he said nothing. Then he turned and left the court.

CHAPTER NINETEEN

Noel crumpled the paper and threw it on the floor. The clock in the corner of the desk read 1:23. He stood and stepped away from his desk. He had to stop this late night writing. He was getting to his morning classes half asleep. This morning—actually yesterday morning—even his students had noticed he wasn't his usual self.

It had been two weeks since the trial and everything he'd heard still haunted him. He'd wanted to simultaneously hold Rachel against him and protect her from having to even look at Hunter, while at the same time pummeling Hunter into the ground until his body was sucked into hell itself. Instead, Noel had been spending his late nights writing poetry, trying to work through the darkness of his guilt and how he'd handled everything in their relationship.

Relationship. What a joke—they had no relationship anymore. Outside of brief glimpses of Rachel at the door when he dropped off Claire, there was nothing between them. But he ached for her—not just the sexual ache but the ache in his heart. Dammit. He was even more in love with her now, knowing how strong she was—knowing how much he had thrown away by letting his past prejudice their time together.

He picked up the crumbled paper and unraveled it, stroking the edges until it would lie flat. Perhaps the poem was done for now. Like him, perhaps it needed more time to be finished. The middle two verses in Rachel's Walk begged for resolution, but it would take both of them—and he wasn't sure Rachel would ever reach for him again.

I fought to part thick curtains of shadow,
only to be startled by the moon's stained innocence,
and my soul was blinded with fear.
The hardness and brightness and far-reaching singleness
of that wide stare unfurled the solar wind.
Your spirit opened in splinters and shards,
and I tripped as the earth trembled with heartache.

Then I fell like a stone in the abyss—
pleading for your touch, an oblation, your kiss,
an absolution.
Only shrouded silence marked my landing.
I stood where I was—
within the indecisive walls of my patio of words,
the stone ramparts raised by memory.

Yet, the numinous sword of the morning sun
pierced me and planted a seed inward,
putting forth roots.
Delirious branches unraveled,
reaching to the new moon.

Resigned, he turned off the light and headed to his room. Only four hours and Claire would be struggling with the toaster while he made breakfast and she would chatter about another day at school and her next fiddle lesson on Saturday. His love for Claire kept him putting one foot in front of the other, forcing him to sleep, and to wake, and to face another day. As he shucked his robe and crawled into bed, his dreams began with a white-haired fairy, soft curls about her face, one leg dangling from a tree branch, her wings still in motion as she smiled at the new moon and Noel watched from the bushes.

* * *

"Daddy, are you gonna stay this time?"

Noel looked at the small studio on Mississippi Avenue on the north side of Portland. He had successfully avoided seeing Rachel for a month of rehearsals now, and his feelings of guilt and loneliness had not abated. He knew it was his responsibility to make an apology if there was any chance at all of renewing their relationship. He also knew that if he apologized and she still didn't want him the pain would be unbearable.

"Daddy? Are you listening to me?"

"Yes, honey, I'm coming in with you."

He released Claire's seat belt and opened his door. Two deep breaths and moved out of the car. Determined to muster his confidence, he slammed his door closed. Claire stared up at him, eyes wide. Stiff-lipped he took her hand and thumbed the lock. The double beep marked their step over the threshold and into the theater.

Claire ran forward, her fiddle case in hand, and bounded past the stage and into a side door. Noel followed more slowly, peering through glass and into the studio. Already, Kat and Michelle were warming up and embraced Claire like a little sister. But no Rachel.

Unsure, where to sit or stand, he remained outside the studio enclosure. Then a solid wooden door opened bumping him on the back.

"Oh, I'm sor…"

He whipped to the voice that cut off so abruptly, and found Rachel standing perfectly still, her eyes wide.

"Noel?"

His voice escaped him. What should he say? How should he make the first step toward reconciliation?

"Rachel."

She made no move forward or backward. After what seemed like several minutes, she notched her brow. “Are you staying?”

“I thought I might.”

She dropped her eyes and her shoulders raised as she took a deep breath. “I see.”

“Rachel, I …”

She held up a hand. “Don’t.”

“But….”

“I don’t want to hear apologies. I don’t want promises you can’t keep.”

He reached for her, but she side-stepped and he found his arm hanging in mid air.

He stepped back to face her. “Rachel.”

Her eyes raised to his.

“I was wrong.”

She shook her head. “Stop. No.” She tried to move past him, but he trapped her exit. “Let me pass.”

“We can’t keep avoiding each other. We need to talk.”

“I haven’t been the one doing the avoiding, Noel.”

“You’re right.” He moved closer.

She placed a hand on his chest to stop him. “I can’t do this now. I need to get ready. I need to concentrate.”

His hand covered hers and he inhaled her scent. The citrus shampoo she used in her hair, a slight saltiness from her skin. He wanted to kiss her. He wanted to forego any discussion and convince her that she still loved him. But her eyes held a hurt he couldn't touch right now—a hurt he knew he caused.

"I'll wait," he said. "We can talk afterward."

She swallowed, then slowly withdrew her hand from his chest. "Don't press me."

"Will it disturb you if I stay?" He hoped it would disturb the hell out of her. At least that way they'd be on equal footing.

She took a deep breath. "You can wait in the sound booth for Claire, if you want. But don't expect anything more."

He moved to the side to let her pass, but as she reached for the studio door he came behind her and stayed her hand. Her spine stiffened, and she refused to turn.

"It's not too late, Rachel," he said to her back. "Not for me. I'm not giving up."

She turned the knob on the glass door and he let go. She walked into the studio without looking back, letting the door close on its own.

He watched her go straight to her fiddle case, unpack it, rosin the bow, and begin tuning—all with her back to him. Everyone else was in the room now, but they must have sensed her mood. No one moved to talk to her.

Claire looked over and waved, then she played something on her fiddle while doing a little dance at the same time. He couldn't hear it through the soundproofing, but he smiled and gave her a thumbs up anyway. He wasn't the only one who wanted Rachel back in their lives. And that gave him even more reason to keep trying.

He moved to the sound booth, greeted the engineer and was pointed to a seat away from the mixing board. Now he could hear everyone tuning, as they prepared for the first recording.

There were some starts and stops in the beginning, as the band began their work together and wanted to be sure that their mix and the harmonies worked well. But then they settled in to cutting each track.

The first track featured Sarah and the guitar with an original piece she'd written about her childhood in the Midwest. Then the next one had everyone involved, including Claire as the two fiddles played off each other—Claire with the traditional jigs and Rachel offering some ornamentation with deft devices like trilling grace notes, pitch-sliding accents and double-stop drones. Rhythm pulsed through her playing, which often fluttered around an authoritative downbeat. Once again he acknowledged her strength.

Later in the day, Claire joined him in the booth and Rachel worked through a solo piece—one that employed a more flowing shape-shifting piece in a minor mode. Her tone was dark and spacious, especially in the lower register, where she maintained a tonal baseline with one meditative drone.

Claire rejoined the band for a medley of dancing jigs, and Sarah added a hornpipe that she whipped up with Theresa on the guitar. The end of the medley switched from jigs to the waltz-like polkas of pre-modern Sweden with Claire continuing to play her part without a problem. He'd known Claire was talented, but he hadn't realized how far she'd come with her playing and how quickly. He burned once again with thankfulness that Rachel had taken her on as a student and given her something special—something all her own.

When the band stopped for a break, the engineer left the booth and went down to talk to them about bookends for the CD—two songs with a similar theme to open and end it. After some discussion, Rachel's choices prevailed. Claire rejoined him in the booth and was soon asleep on his lap as the band practiced and retuned for the last two songs they would cut today

The opening song was *My Lagan Love*. With Rachel on the fiddle, he sat forward and listened. The stunning technique, the overwhelming power of the group together left him speechless. Then Kat sang the words which hit home his dilemma. For a moment he wondered if Rachel had chosen this to make a point with him.

He wasn't sure of all the Gaelic, but he knew it was about *leannán sí*—faery lover, or perhaps ghost or spirit lover. This type of Faery Lover was known for taking a person's love and then returning to his kind in a mystical land, leaving the human pining for her lost love. In the tales of *leannán sí* the poor mortals often died of sorrow.

The last song was also on the theme of love, again a Gaelic tune, this time by Mairéid Sullivan called *Anam Chara*—soul friend. The lyrics spoke of the imperceptible curtain between dreams and reality when two people communicate so meaningfully they become one soul. The song ended with "Digging in the earth of pain and shaping love. Fragile, delicate, beautiful love, enduring love, eternal love, perfect love passionate love, devoted love, yearning love, true love, young love, enchanting love, precious love, sweet love, endearing love, compassionate love, unconditional love, beloved love, my beloved love."

He smiled and hugged Claire close as the last notes died. Maybe there was hope after all.

* * *

Rachel slowly packed her fiddle. She was in no hurry to face Noel again. She no longer believed they could have anything close to a normal conversation. For the last three months, he'd always dropped Claire off without getting out of the car and he picked her up with little more than a wave of acknowledgement. Of course, Rachel hadn't gone out of her way to talk to him either, and she tended to make herself scarce the moment his car turned into the drive.

When he'd trapped her against the sound room door, she was afraid he'd kiss her. She thought she saw the passion in his eyes and she knew if he followed through, she'd be lost in him in a matter of a seconds. No matter how much she hurt and how much she promised herself she wouldn't get close again, she still loved him and couldn't resist his touch. That was why she had chosen Anam Chara as the last song on this CD. She truly believed they were soul mates—but soul mates destined to never be together.

She looked around the empty studio. Everyone had left without her. She snapped the fiddle case close and stepped to the door. She wasn't sure what to make of him staying to watch them play this time.

Nothing. That's what. Don't even consider getting your hopes up.

She reached for the light and Kat opened the door. Her eyes danced from side to side as if looking for an escape. She smiled at Rachel and then dropped her gaze to the floor.

"Now don't get mad," Kat said.

"About what?"

If Kat wasn't looking at her, she knew it was a doozie.

"We took a vote."

“About what?” Now she *was* getting mad.

Kat looked up, her eyes wide and took a deep breath. “We decided it was the best thing to do, even if you didn’t like it, because we love you, so Theresa and I are taking Claire home and putting her to bed, so you can talk to Noel. And don’t bother to fight with me, because I can’t change it. Gotta go.” She turned and raced around the corner.

Rachel took off after her. “Wait a damn minute, don’t I get…” But Kat was already out the door, and filling the only exit to the street was Noel.

Damn ! Damn! Double Damn!

“We’ve been set up,” he said, his voice a low sultry whisper. “I can’t say I’m sorry about that though.”

“How dare they think they can tell us what to do with our lives.” She stomped toward the door, but he didn’t move to let her pass. “I can’t believe you agreed to this. I can’t believe you agreed to let Claire go with Kat. That’s playing dirty, even for you.”

He grinned. “Yup.” He took her face in both hands “And so’s this.”

His lips brushed hers with a feather touch. He rained kisses across her closed eyes, then returned to her lips and very slowly worked her mouth until she willingly opened, invited him in. What else could she do? She melted.

“I love you, Rachel. You’re my *Anam Chara*—my...”

She closed off his words with her mouth, this time with passion, with desire, with forgiveness, with all the love she could no longer hold alon . No more words were needed. His being here was enough. Since he'd quietly appeared at the trial in Branson, she'd dreamed of him coming back to her—of him loving her, wanting her, needing her. She no longer wanted to dwell on the past—only the present. The here and now and how to move forward.

"My place," Noel managed between breaths.

"Yes."

Hours later, they laid wrapped in each other in Noel's living room. They'd barely made it into the house. Clothes were strewn around them, neither spoke. They reveled in the silence except for the breath of life.

The shrill ring of a cell phone broke their mutual reverie. Noel groaned as he rolled away from her. "It's mine." He crawled toward his jacket and pulled out the phone. He frowned. "It's Kat."

"Hello."

"Ohmigod, you've got to get her quick. Some lady is arguing with Mom about Claire. She says she's Claire's mom and she's going to take her. I've called the police and Mom is holding her off, but I don't know what's going to happen. Hurry! Hurry!"

CHAPTER TWENTY

Noel sprayed rocks under the tires as he slammed on the breaks at the top of the hill to his house. The police car parked in the drive had its door open, and he saw the backside of a woman with short reddish-blonde hair being pressed into the back seat. It was definitely his ex. Noel jumped out of his car and raced forward.

"Claire? Where's Claire? Is she okay?"

The screen door slammed and Claire sprinted out of the house. "Daddy! Daddy!" He turned and caught her up as she jumped into his arms, wrapping her legs around his waist and her arms around his neck, pressing her face into his chest. She sobbed loudly and tears streamed to his collar. "Mommy," she choked out between the sobs, "tried to take me to jail." She shuddered in his arms. "I don't want to go, Daddy. I don't want to go."

He stroked her hair and her back. "No one is taking you to jail, honey. It's okay. I'm here now.

You're not going anywhere. You're staying right here with me."

How could it be that no one told him Clarissa was being released? Her sentence had at least another six months to go. He'd been marking it on his calendar so he could prepare Claire for seeing her again.

He stood in the drive, swaying back and forth, holding Claire tight until her choking sobs finally stopped. He hadn't even talked to his attorney about a visitation plan yet. When his ex went to prison, it was all he could do to deal with Claire's nightmares and questions.

Rachel still stood a few feet away. He released the hand holding Claire's head to him and stretched toward her. She immediately stepped forward and embraced both of them. No words, just action. There was no doubt they were a family.

Was it only moments ago they had laid together, forgiving each other their pasts, reaching for the future? What would happen now? It was one thing to have Rachel a part of their lives when Clarissa was nowhere around. It was entirely different to incorporate her into the mess of his family. This was not the best way to renew their relationship.

"Honey," Noel shifted Claire in his arms and Rachel stepped back. He nudged his daughter's face to look up at him. "Daddy has to talk to Mommy for a little bit. Can you go inside with Rachel until I'm done?"

"You won't let her take me?" Claire's voice was a whisper, tears threatening to start again.

"No, sweetheart, no one is going to take you anywhere."

"Okay."

Rachel held out her arms and Noel shifted Claire to her. Claire's head immediately tucked into Rachel's neck. He mouthed a thank you, and Rachel turned slowly and moved into the house. He watched until the door closed behind them and he saw Rachel move to the sofa and settle Claire in her lap. It looked like she might be singing her a lullaby. Claire seemed calm.

"Mr. Kershaw?" The policeman approached with a clipboard. "I've called in Mrs. Kershaw's information. I see she was released just yesterday. If you want to file a complaint, I can take her in."

Noel stood, unable to put voice to his thoughts. The easy solution would be to have her thrown back in jail. Certainly, there were some rules about contact in the divorce papers. He just couldn't think of them right now. On the other hand, he didn't want Claire's only memory of her mother being that of a jailbird.

He cleared his throat. "Is she on drugs?"

"I don't think so," the officer said. "She seems coherent. Her eyes aren't dilated. Except for showing up without warning, she seems pretty normal. Of course, without a drug screen I can't say for sure. She's supposed to be screened regularly over the next year as part of her early parole."

Noel swallowed and looked back toward his house. Rachel was still sitting with Claire on her lap. Theresa and Kat sat across from her. They were talking, but Claire wasn't participating. He hoped that meant she'd fallen asleep.

He turned back to the officer. "Can I talk to her?"

"Sure. But I suggest you talk through the window. She was pretty upset about not being able to see her daughter."

Noel nodded and moved toward the car.

The officer stood near the trunk. "I'll be right here if you need me."

Noel opened the door and sucked in his breath as Clarissa turned toward him, a tentative smile on her lips—just enough to form the dimple in her left cheek he'd always loved. It was as if he was seeing a ghost. The ghost of the woman he'd fallen in love with and married ten years ago, instead of the woman he'd seen strung out and in prison.

She was beautiful, even though her hair was cut short in a style similar to Mia Farrow. Her hair was again shiny and clean. Her face was clear of the under-eye bags and acne he remembered when she had been using. Her makeup was perfect, as perfect as it had been all through college. And her smile. She must have had dental work in prison, because the meth had already begun destroying her teeth when they'd gotten divorced. She was wearing jeans that formed to her tall curves, and a fashionable tee that barely reached her waist—lifting with each breath she took to expose a little skin. A memory niggled in the back of his mind. He'd thought he'd hit the jackpot when they first began to date in college. A tall, model-slim woman had been his fantasy through high school and college. In the playboy magazines he'd regularly perused, it was always the tall blondes that were part of his dreams. Then he'd met Clarissa, and within days after graduation they'd married. He'd been the envy of all his friends.

He swallowed. "You're uh…looking good, Clarissa."

"Hi Noel." She said his name in the intimate manner she'd used when they were dating long ago. "Sorry for all the ruckus." Her hand fluttered in front of her. "I just had to see Claire. It's been so long. I didn't think it was a big deal."

Noel sighed. Even with her renewed beauty, there was no love left—just a few fond memories.

"You know the divorce agreement was to arrange visitation after you got out."

"I know." She leaned back into the seat, a finger resting on her lips, her gaze at the floor. "I guess I just didn't expect you'd be anywhere without

Claire on a weekend. I guess I kind of expected you were still waiting for me." She rolled her neck toward him, her eyes widening in invitation.

He clenched his jaw and looked her straight in the eye. "You guessed wrong. You killed anything between us when you put Claire in danger."

She looked away. "That woman you came home with…the one with the platinum hair. Please tell me she's just a plaything. She's so not your type."

"Her name is Rachel, and I love her. And Claire loves her. And I'm not going to let you change that."

She smirked. "Love? I thought you told me I'd ruined love for you. That you'd never be able to love anyone again? I guess that was all a lie. Just like the lie in our wedding vows, you remember, the one that you'd stand beside me through sickness and health. I was sick, Noel, and where were you? "

Noel ground his teeth. "I stood by you, Clarissa. I stood by you through three rehabs. I stood by you even when I knew you were out at night prostituting yourself for drugs. But when you started bringing those men to our home, during the day, while I was at work and Claire was there…" He breathed deep, consciously unclenching the fist that wanted to raise and smack the self-righteous words back into her mouth. "That was the end. Don't you dare throw our vows back in my face without looking in your own black mirror first."

He took more deep breaths, tamping his anger back into a corner of his mind.

Clarissa stiffened in the seat. "You have a point."

After what seemed like an interminable standoff, she threw her shoulder back, flipped her hair behind her, and laughed. "Okay, so I was a mess. I admit it. I can see that there's no chance us getting back together."

"None!"

"Well then, I guess it's lawyers at dawn." She laughed again, but this time it was restrained.

She looked away for a moment and he watched her shoulders sag, then straighten again as each vertebrae lined up like soldiers ready to spring. She turned back to him and speared him with her best I'll-get-what-I-want-and-you-can't-stop-me look.

"I'm going to be part of Claire's life, Noel. And that means I'm part of your life too, whether you like It or not. I've worked hard to clean up my act. I'm off drugs forever and I'm starting my life again. I hope you won't try to stop me."

"I have no interest in keeping Claire from you, as long as you stay clean and sober." He didn't trust her. How could he? He knew the statistics on relapse. She'd been a prime example. It was so easy for her to say she'd stay clean, when she'd been out of prison all of one day. But he wasn't going to say those things. He did want her to stay clean. No matter what she had done, the best thing for Claire would be to have a mother who didn't cause her nightmares.

"I want you to succeed," he said softly. "I don't want Claire's only memories of you to be as a strung out meth and coke addict. I want the nightmares she has about you to stop."

Clarissa turned away. "Nightmares?"

"That's right. Nightmares about the men you brought home—the ones who frightened her."

Clarissa sucked in a sharp breath. "Oh God, they didn't…"

Noel sighed. "No. Thank God. At least we don't think so. I've had her in counseling for two years. And the counselor believes she wasn't molested, but she feared for her safety and evidently at least one man made overtures that scared her terribly.

Tears strained Clarissa's cheeks as she looked back at him. "I…never knew. I thought…Oh, God, I'm so sorry."

Noel looked away. He'd been waiting to hear some true regret from her for so long. It wasn't enough to make up for everything. But it was a start.

"Look," he turned back. "As long as you're clean you can have visitation. But I'm not letting you keep her without me there and you can't have her overnight, until you've proven you can stay clean and you can take care of her. And don't even think about custody. Even if I believed you were completely reformed, Claire couldn't handle it right now. We have to take it slow. We have to give it time."

Clarissa nodded. "Okay. I understand."

"Good."

"How about next weekend? Can I come up next weekend? With you here, of course."

Noel paused. How had everything been turned on its head so quickly? Next weekend was a local concert at Timberline Lodge, and Claire would be playing with the band again. He wanted, needed, several weekends with Rachel—weekends where they could reconnect, firmly establish their relationship. He wanted Claire and Rachel and him together, like family.

He sighed. Might as well let Rachel know now what the rest of their lives together would probably be like if Clarissa was able to hold it together.

"Claire has taken up the violin—actually the fiddle," he said. "She plays with the Sweetwater Canyon band on weekends if the gigs are close by."

"Sweetwater Canyon? I don't think I know them. Is it kids her age?"

He swallowed. "It's the band Rachel is in. Rachel plays the fiddle. She's been teaching Claire."

"Oh. I see. So things are…rather involved, are they?"

She didn't know the half of it and he wasn't going to tell her.

"If you want to see Claire play, they'll be at Timberline Lodge from noon to two. Then we'll be coming back here for an early dinner." He took a deep breath. "You can join us…if you want."

"Yes. I would like that very much." Clarissa took his hand in hers. "Thank you, Noel. Thank you."

"Yeah."

He hoped he wasn't making a mistake. He hoped he wasn't screwing up the best thing that had happened to him and Claire in the last four years.

CHAPTER TWENTY-ONE

Rachel stepped up to the front door at Noel's house, her stomach turning somersaults. Voices echoed from the back of the house—probably near the kitchen. What was that? A woman's voice, and then Claire's laugh? She inhaled and counted to five, then exhaled. She understood why Clarissa needed to be part of Claire's life. She even agreed with it. But she was scared to death this meant the end to any chance at the family life she'd pictured with Claire and Noel. One amazing love-making reunion broken up by the ex was not an auspicious beginning to a life-long relationship. She pasted on a smile, turned the knob, and walked toward the voices with her head held high.

Claire stirred something in a big pot on the stove. When Rachel entered the kitchen the sweet child looked up and grinned. Noel paused with his cook's knife over the carrot he'd been chopping. Clarissa shuttled between the two of them, winking at

Noel, sharing a giggle with Claire. They looked like a family Rockwell might have painted in the fifties—only the clothing was updated, especially the form-fitting scoop-necked tee shirt Clarissa wore. When she caught Noel staring down at those pushed up boobs, Rachel stepped in.

"Careful with that knife," she said, covering his hand and brushing his mouth with a kiss.

He smiled. "Good to see you. Thanks for coming." Then he went back to his cutting.

"Hi Rachel," Claire squealed with glee. "I can't hug you right now, 'cause Mommy's teaching me to cook."

"That's what mommies do," Clarissa said, hugging Claire to her side. "Should we make Daddy keep cutting? Or do you think we have enough."

"More!" Claire glanced behind her. "More, Daddy, more."

Noel dramatically wiped his brow. "Am I your slave now?"

Claire giggled, "Yup, you and Mommy are my slaves."

Rachel bumped Noel playfully. "I can be a slave too. How 'bout you take a break and I'll do some cutting."

"No!" Claire pronounced. "You're my friend. Friends can't be slaves, only mommies and daddies."

Clarissa looked over her daughter's head directly at Rachel and smiled.

Was that a smile of happiness? Or a warning? Rachel swallowed. So, that's how life would be from now on. She'd hoped this could all be somewhat civil, no competition. Now, she wasn't so sure. Clarissa wanted the whole family thing just as much as Rachel did.

When dinner was served, Noel pulled out a chair for Rachel. She sat to his left and Claire to his right. Clarissa squeezed between Claire and Rachel.

"So," Clairissa began. "How long have you and Noel been together?"

Chac!

Noel and Rachel spoke at the same time.

"About six months," she said.

"About a week," he said.

Rachel whipped her head toward Noel. He blanched.

Clarissa raised a brow.

"It's complicated," Noel and Rachel said together.

"I'll bet." Clarissa barely controlled a giggle as she sipped another spoonful of soup.

"They had a fight," Claire offered, and Rachel sagged. "But the band decided they had to make up last week, so we forced them to be alone and it worked!"

Clarissa smiled. "I see." She drew out the word see like she knew way too much already. "How nice for you two."

Yeah, nice. Rachel fidgeted under the table. How long was this dinner going to last?

The rest of the meal seemed only slightly less tense. By the time Noel served his signature dessert, even the smell of toasting pecans and carmalized sugar of the delicious pie wasn't enough to keep Rachel from her natural flight response. She needed something to do or she'd burst.

She stood. "I'll do the dishes." She hoped Noel might join her and they could get a little time alone in the kitchen. She wanted to know where all this was going. It felt like Noel was at least as confused as she was about this new foursome. Or had he already figured it out and not told her where she fit in the family now.

Noel clasped her hand. "We can leave the dishes until later," he said.

"No, I need something to do. I'm antsy." She picked up each plate and stacked them at the end of the table.

"I'll help," Clarissa said, quickly grabbing glasses and bread plates.

Noel cleared his throat. "Well…uh…I guess this slave will have the evening off then."

"Yea!" Claire tugged at his hand. "I challenge you to Jenga."

"I've been practicing, you know." Noel pretended reluctance as Claire giggled and pulled him from the room."

"You'll never beat me, Daddy. Your hands are too big. You always knock over the tower."

"Not this time, I have a plan. I'll…"

Their voices faded as Rachel joined Clarissa at the sink. This wasn't the way she'd wanted the evening to work out. She'd fantasized about coming to dinner, getting to feel comfortable with Clarissa, followed by some declaration that Clarissa was so happy Noel had found someone and that their daughter was happy. Then, Rachel had taken the fantasy a step further with her and Noel married, Claire living with them full time and increasing visitations with her mother. Now it seemed that fantasy bubble would burst from the tension, and Rachel wasn't sure if she'd still be included when all the pieces were put back together.

Clarissa rinsed the dishes and stacked them to the right of the sink. Rachel slid each one into the dishwasher racks. What could she say to this woman who'd borne the child they both wanted, who'd married the man she loved? Her hands worked fast and steady. The sooner they finished the job, the sooner she could be back in the room with Claire and Noel.

"I have a favor to ask," Clarissa said.

"Okay." Rachel turned slowly to face her head on, a handful of forks throttled in her hand and begging to be put in the silverware holder.

"I'm sure Noel's told you about my past."

"Some," Rachel hedged, her eyes darting away.

"Well, it isn't something I'm proud of, but now I'm back and I'm fine." She handed Rachel a glass. "I'm just starting to get to know Claire again. I need her to know I'm not that awful person I was before."

Rachel turned and dropped the forks into the holder, then opened the top of the dishwasher for the glass. Keep breathing.

"It seems you've made a good start," Rachel said quietly.

"Yes, I have, but it's not enough." She handed her the stack of bread plates.

"What do you mean?"

"The problem is you."

Rachel bristled, a plate in her hand. "Wait a minute now. I've been nothing but loving and caring to Claire. There is no problem with me."

"I'm sorry, I said that badly. What I meant was with you always around, it may be confusing to Claire."

"Claire didn't seem confused tonight," she said.

"Of course not. This is the first night we're all together. She's still reeling with the knowledge that I'm back and in her life and not some crazed murdering jailbird. But it will become more confusing as each week goes by."

Rachel's heart accelerated. "So, what are you suggesting?"

Clarissa paused and pursed her lips. "Do you love Claire?"

"Yes," Rachel whispered. "I love her as if she were my own daughter."

"I thought so." She took the plate from Rachel and laid it on the counter. "Then you'll understand what I'm asking." She took Rachel's hands in hers. "I'm not asking you to give up Noel or Claire. I'm just asking you to give me a fighting chance to regain Claire's trust. A chance to be a mother to my daughter."

Rachel's head spun with fear. "She knows you're her mother. I don't see how my being a part of Claire's life is stopping you."

"Oh, but you are. When you're with Claire and Noel, she looks at you as her mother."

"No, but I …"

Clarissa raised a hand to Rachel's cheek. "Yes. I can see the longing in your eyes. It's the same longing I feel."

Rachel shook her head to deny it, but she knew it was true. She didn't really want to share anyone with Clarissa—not Noel, not even Claire.

"All I'm asking for is one month. Just one month to get to know my daughter again and to spend time being her mother without you doing the same. Is that too much ask?"

Yes! Yes it was too much! But Rachel didn't say that. She wouldn't admit how afraid she was to anyone—afraid that the love she and Noel had rediscovered last week wasn't real.

Clarissa's eyes widened. "It's not really Claire you're worried about, is it? It's Noel."

"I'm not worried about either of them." Rachel lifted her chin a little higher. "I'm just not sure this is the right answer. I'm sure Noel would understand me being gone for a month, but I don't know if Claire would."

"Of course, Claire would still go to her lessons and play with the band," Clarissa offered. "I wouldn't stop her from that. She loves music, and she's obviously very talented. I owe you for bringing that talent out in her."

Rachel released the breath she was holding.

"I just ask that you limit your contact with Claire to only those times she's in lessons or rehearsals. No family dinners, no little family outings with the three of you together. That's what's confusing."

"And what are your intentions?" Rachel asked. "Are you trying to insert yourself back into this family?"

Clarissa held up a hand and fluttered it to her heart. "No. No, of course not. I'm just trying to prove to Noel that I can handle the responsibilities of motherhood without drugs. I need to prove that I'm capable of being a good mother again, so eventually he'll allow me unsupervised visits." She paused and turned the water back on to finish the dishes. "Really, you should be happy that's my intention. After a month or so, he'll be more willing to share custody with me and then you'll have Noel all to yourself…alone. I'm sure that's appealing."

"And Claire? What are your intentions with her?"

"Shared custody." She handed the last glass to Rachel. "I'm willing to share her with you and Noel once everyone feels comfortable with me again."

Something wasn't right, but Rachel couldn't put her finger on it. It seemed reasonable. She could understand Clarissa's need to prove herself. She certainly seemed genuinely changed. But Rachel wasn't sure she should trust her. Or was that just jealousy and fear rearing its ugly head.

Noel walked into the kitchen. "Hey, what's going on in here? Please tell me you two aren't plotting together to gang up on me."

Clarissa giggled and swatted him with a towel. "Absolutely. That's exactly what we're doing." She shot a glance back to Rachel. "Do we have a deal?"

Rachel nodded. Now, how would she tell Noel and Claire? Worse, how would she survive the next month?

* * *

Noel tucked Claire into bed and kissed her cheek, his other arm around Rachel keeping her close.

Rachel stepped forward and brushed the hair from Claire's eyes as she bent to place a tender kiss on her forehead. A tear welled as she thought of all that was at stake, all she might lose. She stood quickly, squeezing Noel's hand with all her might.

"*Slán go fóill... a chuisle mo chroí,*" she whispered.

"*Slán,*" Claire echoed. "See you next weekend." She closed her eyes and within seconds fell asleep.

Noel tugged Rachel through the door. "Are you sure about this, Rachel? You don't have to do this. It may just be some crazy plan of Clarissa's to separate us."

"I trust you," she said, her mouth opening in invitation. "I trust our love is strong enough to weather this month. I'm doing this for Claire. Not for us…for Claire."

His mouth pressed hers with a slow, searching kiss that quickly deepened to the ravishing she remembered from last weekend. She drank him in, memorizing the feel of him, the taste of him and prayed he was doing the same.

His tongue rimmed the outline of her mouth and then thrust inside, dancing with her lips and her tongue, searching, caressing. She moaned, and pressed further into him. Over and over he devoured her mouth as if he'd never get a chance again. In one sweeping motion, he lifted her into his arms and carried her to his bed, his lush lips never once leaving hers. Easing her onto the coverlet, he rose above her, his fingers working down the buttons of her shirt.

"No," she pushed him back. "I can't, being with you—knowing we won't see each other for a month, and not knowing—" She couldn't finish the sentence, she couldn't admit to her fear that he wouldn't come back to her. "It's too hard. It's too . . . "

He growled. "Yes, you can. I need this. I'm already missing you and the month is barely started."

He opened her shirt wide and released the front catch on her bra, then dove between her breasts, his mouth and fingers pleasuring one and then the other. She inhaled the citrus scent of shampoo from his hair and raised her hips to his fingers as he unzipped her pants and slid them down and off her legs. His fingers worked down her stomach and delved to her center, quickly driving her up but not letting her go over the edge. Their naked arms and legs wove so tight together that she wasn't sure where one started and the other ended. He entered her in silence and together they set a tempo for a sorrowful doloroso, rising and falling together—remembering, reliving, regretting, reviving and then coda. She closed her eyes and moved her hips tortuously slow, tucking every sensation—the silken rub of skin, the deep salt smell of his lust, the warm desire in his soul-deep eyes—and hugging them to her memory. He kept her on the edge of release, both of them holding back, not wanting their joining to end.

She wasn't sure how long they continued, but it felt like hours. Her body throbbed with need. "Please, Noel. Finish it."

Her center clenched stronger and tighter with each deep slow pulse of him. Tears streamed from her eyes, rolling down her cheeks. His eyes darkened. His thrusts slowed even more. He bent to kiss away her tears, soft lips brushing her skin in time with each new pulse inside her.

"I love you, Rachel." He captured her lips again in a sharing of heat and sorrow so deep it drew even more tears from her. "I need to bury myself so deep inside you that you will never doubt I'm with you."

He lifted her hips, tucking a flatish pillow in the small of her back. He draped her legs over his shoulders and raised himself upright on his knees. Noel's each exquisite push and pull went deeper——so deep she was sure he touched her soul and knocked on the door to her heart.

Colors exploded all around her until she spun, on the verge of passing out, but their song wasn't ready to end. Noel increased his pace to a moderato, bringing her back and finally taking her over the edge again and again—as if all the releases she had saved up over the past hours could wait no longer. She clutched him, her nails digging into his shoulders, her hips pushing him harder and harder—deeper and deeper, her body calling out for speed and the oblivion of the *bohdran* beating faster and faster..

His arms vibrated above her as the tempo increased to *vivacissimo*, and it was all she could do just to breathe. The tendons in his neck stretched and he arched like a bow, the arrow in the quiver taut and true. He called out her name as his release filled her with all the colors of the rainbow at once. She reached for him and tried to hang on one last time, grasping first at green, then blue, then purple. But she could sustain no longer. Her rhythm faltered, fully spent she stepped over the edge for the last time.

CHAPTER TWENTY-TWO

Rachel marked an X over the last day in August on her calendar. Four long weeks ago she'd last laid in Noel's arms. She still saw him every time he dropped off or picked up Claire. He always brushed a quick kiss along her lips, but nothing more. They'd agreed that sneaking around Claire would be too hard, especially since Clarissa planned some kind of family outing every weekend. Claire came to her fiddle lessons with stories of all the trips she and Daddy and Mommy had taken together. Hiking in the gorge, boating on the Willamette, even camping at the beach with grandma and grandpa.

Rachel sighed. Each day and week that went by drew her dreams farther away. Was Noel staying faithful or had Clarissa won him back? Now that their isolation was finally over, she would see if she'd made the right decision. She only hoped it wasn't too late.

She shrugged out of her sweats and pulled on a pair of white shorts and a light pink tee, then headed to her car and the Fred Meyers store. The super store was the largest shop in Sandy. Rachel had a list of groceries to pick up for the week, and she'd also planned to find a back-to-school gift for Claire. With fall term only two days away, she knew she'd soon be competing with school schedules as well as Clarissa's plans for weekends to try to make sure Claire still continued her fiddle lessons.

Rachel moved directly to the stationary aisle and searched through journals, art supplies, pens and pencils, looking for special paper. Claire had mentioned she wanted some staff paper for her fiddle tunes. In the past month, Rachel had taught her how to write down her own compositions. Some of the tunes Claire composed were amazingly complex for a seven-year-old. Rachel found a clerk who pointed her toward the music section. As she reached for the one and only book left, a slim hand sporting a good-sized diamond reached at the same time.

"Oh, excuse me, I wanted that," Rachel said as the hand reached right over her and took the last staff book. She turned to protest and her shoulders dropped immediately as she recognized the tall reddish-blond pixie cut hair. She wore a demure white coat dress that buttoned from neck to hem, though the top buttons from the collar were undone just enough to show a peek of creamy breast. The look screamed of sexy sophistication—but much toned down from the last time they'd met.

"Clarissa?"

"Oh, Rachel, I didn't know that was you from the back. I'm getting staff paper for Claire as a back-to-school gift. She's been asking for some."

Rachel frowned. "Yeah, I know. That was my thought, too."

Clarissa giggled. "I guess we think alike."

Rachel sighed. Would they always be in competition?

"You know, I'm actually glad I ran into you," Clarissa said. "I've been meaning to have a little chat."

A spike of fear worked its way down her spine, causing an involuntary shiver.

"About what?"

"Well, I know the month is over and you probably haven't had time to think about what you were planning next, but…seeing as you're here I might as well tell you." She tapped her mouth with the hand that sported what appeared to be a large diamond engagement ring on her left hand. "The most wonderful thing is happening. Noel and I are getting married again."

Air rushed out of Rachel's lungs and the store seemed to spin as her world darkened around her. She leaned on the shelf next to her. "When?" she whispered.

"Oh, well we haven't picked a date yet, and it's not quite official. But it will be. Soon. We're just waiting for the right time to tell Claire. I'm thinking Christmas. That's such a romantic time. Don't you think? You'll be invited of course."

"I…I…"

Her cell phone rang and jarred her away from the fear threatening to engulf her, though her accelerated heart continued to skip beats at random. "Hello." She clutched the phone like a lifeline, hoping it was someone telling her to wake up—this was all a bad dream.

"Michele's having her baby!" Kat said. "David just called and said her water broke and he just got her to Providence Hospital, and something about dilated that I don't remember, but it sounded like the baby would be there soon. Anyhoo, I told him I'd call everyone so he could go be with Michele. Mom and I are in the car now, coming down from the mountain. I'll see you at the hospital, Rache. Hurry!"

Then the phone went dead.

Rachel looked back to Clarissa holding the staff book to her chest and smiling. "Problem?" Clarissa asked.

"No. Happy occasion." Rachel clicked her cell phone shut. "Michele is having her baby. Gotta run."

She moved as fast as she could without running out of the store. What could she do about Noel and Clarissa? Is it possible Clarissa was stretching the truth? Noel loved her. She knew it deep inside. Well, whatever the situation Rachel wasn't going down without a fight. But right now she'd get to greet a new little life. The baby of her best friend was coming into this world and that was all that mattered at this moment. That she could deal with. That was enough for now.

* * *

Kat, Theresa, and Sarah stood at the window with Rachel. Each cooing and waving as David proudly held up his new daughter to the glass. The bassinet next to him had the name Tamara Rachel Blackstone written on its little pink card. She couldn't believe it. After all the grief she'd given Michele during the past year, she'd still given her daughter Rachel's name. This was proof that the bonds of love weren't easily broken, even when she screwed up royally.

She wiped tears from her eyes as she grinned so wide her cheeks hurt. Certainly, this was the most beautiful child ever born. How was it possible that a baby that small could be complete with fingers and toes, and even nails? David pointed to the card and mouthed Tamara Rachel. She nodded and crossed her arms over her chest in a thank-you gesture as tears flowed again.

Michele had stuck with her through thick and thin. She'd been there through Rachel's divorce, and then through all of her gallivanting with men while she tried to prove herself worthy. She'd stood by her after the rape, and made sure Rachel went to counseling every week in those first couple of months when all she'd wanted to do was curl up and sleep for days on end. Even when Rachel had treated her poorly, Michele forgave her. Somehow she always knew what was really in Rachel's heart.

A white-starched, middle-aged midwife came to David in the window and pointed down the hall. He waved good-bye to all of them. Time for him to leave. Time to go back to Michele, and bask in the love of their beautiful new family. She blew kisses then joined in a hug with her band mates, her best friends. No matter what happened, they'd always been there for her.

* * *

Noel stood next to the car and watched Clarissa bend to straighten the barrette holding Claire's hair out of her face. "You'll be the prettiest and the smartest one in school," she said brushing a kiss to her forehead.

He looked from Clarissa to Claire, his heart contracting on the bittersweet moment. They seemed like a family—but not. Nothing would ever be like it was before. He still loved Rachel, but Clarissa had been pushing him to get back together for their daughter's sake.

Claire kissed her mother and gave her a big hug. "I'm so glad you're here," she squealed.

Noel handed the rock star lunch bag to Claire. "I'll be here to pick you up after school, okay?"

"Okay."

He bent to kiss her cheek, and she pulled him toward her as if she had a secret. She cupped her hand near his ear. "Don't tell mommy, but I miss Rachel. I love Mommy, but I love Rachel, too. Before mommy came back, Rachel said she would go to school with me and you."

"Well, she couldn't be here today."

"Did you tell her today was the first day of school?"

"Well, no. I…"

"Do you still love her, Daddy?"

Noel sighed. God he loved her, but over the past month he wasn't sure what was best for Claire.

"Do you, Daddy?"

"Yes, honey, I do. Very much."

"Good. Then I can have two mommies, like my friend Jessica. You make sure, okay?"

Noel grinned. If children ran the world, relationships would never become so complicated. Love was pure and enduring for Claire. He shouldn't have questioned his intuition.

"I'll see what I can do," he promised. "Now hurry. You don't want to be late for your first day back to school."

She brushed his cheek with a kiss, hugged him tight and then ran toward the school door. She turned and waved to both of them with a big smile then disappeared inside the large steel door.

Clarissa took his hand and smiled at him, her eyes dancing with need. “I’ve been thinking,” she said. “Everything is going so well, that maybe I should move back in with you and Claire.”

Noel extricated his hand. “Clarissa.”

“Please, just hear me out. I know you don’t love me right now. I hurt you deeply. But you did love me once, and I know I could make you love me again.”

“It’s too late. I’m in love with someone else.”

“But it’s been a month, and you haven’t been with each other. I know, I’ve watched.”

“And I have counted every minute and every day of this past month, waiting for your experiment to end. Now it’s over.”

“But…”

“You have what you want, Clarissa. Claire loves you. With the pure love of a child, she has forgiven everything you did—every hurt, every fear. She is even offering her trust. I hope you won’t break that trust ever again.”

“And what about you, Noel? Have you forgiven me? Is that why you won’t consider trying again?”

“I’ve given my heart to someone else.”

Clarissa looked down and whispered, "Do you love her more? More than you loved me when we married?"

Noel looked into his heart. Yes, he did love Rachel more. His love for Rachel was a mature love, a deeper love born out of experience and a passion that embraced each others faults and still flamed bright. His love wasn't built on adolescent fantasies, nor on ideas of perfection.

He took Clarissa's hands in his. "I hope that one day you find someone who can love you, knowing your past, yet seeing your bright future. But that person isn't me, and it never will be again."

She rose to her toes and kissed his cheek. "Rachel is a lucky woman." She turned to her own car and opened the door, then turned back to him. "Thank you for this month with Claire. It means more than you'll ever know. I'll have my attorney draw up a proposal for weekends and holidays." She slid into her car, closed the door, and drove away without another word.

Noel pulled out his cell phone and dialed.

"Theresa? I need your help with a little surprise."

* * *

Rachel stood on the porch to Theresa's house, fiddle case in hand, and stared at the metallic blue Honda in the drive. She'd know Noel's car anywhere. What was he doing here? It had been a week since their forced isolation had ended and she still hadn't seen him. Had he come to finally tell her about his plans to remarry Clarissa? No, he wouldn't do that in front of the entire band. He must know how she'd feel.

Oh God, maybe something's wrong with Claire. She raced inside calling his name. "Noel? Noel?"

He stood in the doorway of the practice room. She stopped suddenly in front of him. Unsure what to say or do. He looked amazing. She remembered the last time they were together. Heat from her center moved through her core and up to her face.

She scanned his fingers. No ring. She looked up again.

"Claire? Is something wrong with Claire?"

"No, everything's fine." He took her hand and twined his fingers with hers. "Come in, I have something to tell you."

She looked around the room. Where was everyone? It seemed they had abandoned the house. Maybe this was a dream. The music of Dunoon swelled behind her. It was a ballad about seeing things through someone else's eyes, experiencing the world anew even if the place was familiar. A ballad about coming home.

Then Kat, Theresa, Sarah, and Michele entered singing—in Gaelic even—and Claire played

Rachel's part on her small fiddle. Noel clutched Rachel closer.

"I love you," he said. He fumbled with a piece of paper, then shook it open.

"I'm not a singer, but I do have a type of song for you." He turned her to face him. She fell into the deep brown pools of his eyes. "I've finished Rachel's Walk, and I need to see if it still speaks to you."

Was it possible? Could it be that her dreams were still alive?

The band moved into an instrumental rendition of the ballad, soft in the background and Noel began to read. She remembered the first two verses of the poem. The ones he'd written when she first fell in love with him. Verses that spoke of the difficult journey she still had to undertake, and his inability to take the burden for her. The second two verses she'd never seen. As he read them she hurt for the man who'd struggled with his own demons and still tried to deal with hers. She buried her head in his chest and hugged him close. They'd both needed to heal in their own way. They'd both needed to close their past before they could move forward.

She held her breath as the music stopped and Noel read the final verse.

As the moon wanes,
wedge-shadowed gardens lie in wait.
The last stars look at me with your eyes,
and the wind sings your name.
Wake from your dream
and transform the garden with me.
Enter my eyes with your sun-filled skies.
Spread out through my blood
with a wide sustaining river.
Together we will fill an urn with celestial ashes
and fling it to the keening pulse of love.

He bent and claimed her lips with his. His kiss at first a request, then a demand that she open fully and join with him. Her soul answered in kind, accepting him and demanding her own promises. "*Anam Chara*," she murmured.

Claire ran forward and flung her arms around them both. "Now we can get married and be a family, right?"

Noel laughed and lifted Claire between them. "What do you say, Rachel?"

She hugged both of them tight and answered with confidence. "Yes."

HEALING NOTES

ABOUT THE AUTHOR

Maggie Jaimeson writes romantic women's fiction and romantic suspense with a near future twist. She describes herself as a wife, a step-mother, a sister, a daughter, a teacher and an IT administrator. By day she is "geek girl" – helping colleges to keep up with 21st century technology and provide distance learning options for students in rural areas. By night Maggie turns her thoughts to worlds she can control – worlds where bad guys get their comeuppance, women triumph over tragedy, and love can conquer all.

The next book in the Sweetwater Canyon Series, TWO VOICES, will be available in late 2013. The four book series follows the members of an all female bluegrass and Americana band as they navigate careers in music, overcome heartache, and find love.

If you haven't read Book 1 of the Sweetwater Canyon Series, UNDERTONES, check it out today.

Other Maggie Jamieson Books available at Windtree Press

ETERNITY
UNDERTONES
HEALING NOTES
SHIFTING WATERS

Windtree Press
www.windtreepress.com